i

c

o

p

e

D0921140

THE ACCOMPLICES:
A Civil Coping Mechanisms Book
🐱 🐱 🐱

For more information, find CCM at:
http://copingmechanisms.net

COLDWATER CANYON

ANNE-MARIE KINNEY

For Abe and Dee Dee

PART ONE

1

Shep wondered if he would like being a fisherman. He couldn't recall ever having gone fishing, but the occasional windswept morning in the valley made the idea of life on the water seem, momentarily, both appealing and possible. He hadn't expected it to be so cold when he stepped outside, only wearing a flannel shirt with holes at the elbows that he'd closed up with safety pins. His overgrown mustache itched his nostrils. He scratched with his left hand, gripping Lionel's leash tightly in his right, because the little dog had gnawed off the loop some days before, leaving a ragged wet nub in its place. The dog pulled, requiring him to pull back every few feet as they walked to the end of the block, the wind whipping Shep's hair into his eyes.

Parkdale's wasn't open yet, so the two waited at the door. Shep tied Lionel up to the bike rack in front of the store and paced back and forth, stopping at the telephone pole at the corner, where a swath of flimsy notebook pages had been stapled from a foot off the ground up to Shep's chest level. Though the older ones had faded considerably since he'd first noticed them weeks earlier, he could still make out the faces drawn in a child's hand, some with wild scratches of hair, some stone bald, some filling the page, some just fist-sized, floating near the middle, all of them with big round jaws, tiny ears and pointed teeth, and skinny little necks protruding from the bottom. He counted thirteen missing persons. When he crouched down, he saw that there was a new one with floppy arms beneath the little neck, hanging slack, with dots drawn for buttons at the wrists.

Lionel started barking, and Shep straightened up from his crouch as the lights inside the store flickered on. Hung appeared at the door and flipped the closed sign to open.

"Don't move," he said to Lionel, who was still barking plaintively, his muzzle pointed up at the cloud-covered sun. "I'm gonna be right back. I'll be back so soon you're gonna feel foolish."

Hung was already at his stool behind the counter, staring down at the word jumble, drinking a cup of soda with ice. It used to be Hung's dad who always opened the store, but he'd been retired since a stroke left him unable to move the left side of his body. Now he spent his days watching game shows in the apartment upstairs, scowling lopsidedly at the TV, the volume turned up so loud you could hear the studio applause from the street below.

Shep went to the fridge at the back of the store and pulled out a Miller tallboy. When he got to the counter, without looking up from the paper, Hung handed him a cup, which Shep filled to the brim, tucking the can on a shelf by the cash register. He pulled a package of beef jerky off a hook and ripped it open with his teeth. He tore off several pieces of jerky and threw them outside, at the dog's feet. Lionel gobbled them one by one.

"T-I-G-A-N-E-R," Hung called out as Shep took his own seat behind the counter. "Last one. What the fuck does that spell?"

"Don't ask me. I'm no good at puzzles. Sounds like tiger something."

Hung pushed the paper aside in disgust. "Man, I don't know my right from my left this morning. I had this crazy dream last night—like, I went to put on contact lenses, but I opened the case and inside were these big floppy things, like the size of pancakes, but still contact lenses, you know, all drippin' liquid. Then I get to my job— I'm working in some kind of office— I sit down at my desk, 'bout to turn on my computer, when I see that instead of a keyboard, I got a big yellow sponge, like, in the shape of a keyboard. I was like, 'What am I supposed to do with this shit?' Then I woke up.

And I don't even wear contact lenses!"

"That's fucked up," Shep nodded, and topped off his beer.

"You ever have dreams like that?"

"Nah. I don't dream so much."

"They say you're dreaming the whole time you're asleep, it's just you don't remember it."

"Then I don't remember."

An old black man entered the store, wearing a khaki suit with a sweater vest underneath and walking with a shiny wooden cane. He had a small Styrofoam bowl secured over his left ear with medical tape. The man shuffled slowly down the aisle, picked up a bottle of Tabasco sauce and carried it to the counter.

"Give me a scratcher, Hung," he said, tapping the counter with two fingers.

Hung rang up the Tabasco sauce and pulled the ticket out from a locked drawer beneath the register.

"Six twenty-five," he said, dropping the sauce into a noisy plastic bag.

The man paid, then pulled a nickel out of his pocket and scratched the three silver boxes on the ticket one by one, brushing their ash-like debris onto the floor. He looked down, looked up at Hung, then quickly tucked the ticket into his right breast pocket.

"Thank you, son," he said, then took his bag and walked out, patting the right side of his chest.

"You see his ticket? Think he won something?"

"Nah, man," Hung said, "he always does that. If he had a winning ticket every time he squirreled it away like some damn priceless jewel, he wouldn't be here. He'd be living on a yacht or some shit. He probably stores them all in boxes filling up his house like on that show about hoarders, all sleeping in the hallway 'cause their bedroom's full of thirty-year-old magazines and spelling bee trophies from the fourth grade."

Shep drank the last swallow of beer and tossed the can

in the trash. "I'll be back."

He rose from his stool and nodded to Hung as he grabbed an airplane bottle of tequila from behind the counter on his way out. As he approached the door, he could see Lionel wagging his tail and shuffling back and forth on his paws. The sun was pushing its way through the clouds now.

"Ingrate," Shep said.

"What?" Hung squinted at him.

"The jumble. That's what those letters spell." He'd finally hit on it after trying out countless configurations in his head.

"Ha!" Hung said, and shook his pencil in the air.

Shep untied Lionel and turned the corner toward home. The Cowboy had arrived, and was sitting in his usual seat, a nook carved into the side of the building that served no purpose but for sitting. He was a thin man, and old, his lined face like tanned leather. He always wore the same thing: a thin, almost translucent button-down shirt, brown polyester slacks, and a ten-gallon hat pushed back on his head to reveal an inscrutable, unwavering gaze. His left hand was perched on the handle of the shopping cart that held all his belongings, loose silver and turquoise rings threatening to slide down his bony fingers. Shep didn't know where the Cowboy went at night, but most days he spent hours in that nook, alternating between reorganizing his things—several stiff wool blankets, an old transistor radio, a plastic shopping bag of unknown contents—and sitting still, staring out, speaking to no one. Hung periodically tried to offer him a cup of water or something to eat, but he always declined with a raised palm. Shep stopped for a moment. He nodded, as he always did, but the Cowboy didn't nod back.

It was early yet, but he didn't feel like going back home just to wait around, so he took the alley back to the carport shared by the four apartments that constituted his building and climbed into his fifteen-year-old Ford, lifting Lionel up onto the passenger seat. He'd intended on saving the tequila for later, but when he sat down, the little bottle began to bother him, digging into the meat of his thigh. He pulled it out, tossed its contents down his throat and popped the empty bottle into the glove compartment, where it rattled into the others as he slammed the compartment shut. Lionel gave him a look.

"Who're you to judge me, huh? I don't begrudge you your vices."

Lionel turned three times, curled up in his seat and let out a little sigh as he closed his eyes.

"You're just full of ideas, aren't you?"

Shep leaned his seat back and settled down to a nap, though he never sank fully into sleep, instead hovering at the lowest level of consciousness, aware only of his breath and Lionel's, and the intermittent *coo coo-woo* of a mourning dove.

Some time later the sun shifted and the car grew toasty. Shep opened his eyes and smacked his lips, feeling clammy all over, his mouth hot and parched. Specks of lint floated through the sunbeams that cut through the windows. He looked at his watch—it was nearly eleven.

"Lionel, wake up." He patted the dog's back. Lionel grumbled and rolled over onto his other side.

"Do what you want."

Shep put his seat back up and plugged the key into the ignition. To start the car, he had to first let it run for a minute or two, then rev the engine once or twice before he could pull it out of the carport, the engine, he imagined, made of hardened dust that could loosen and crumble at any time but that somehow hung together through the sheer force of his will, or the grace of God, or just somehow.

As he pulled onto the freeway, his thoughts returned to the Cowboy. It was confounding to him that the man could sit in one place for so long, day after day, looking at nothing, and yet people did it all the time, behind counters, at toll booths, front desks, everybody just sitting. He'd managed to dodge such a fate for the most part. He'd spent eight months driving a truck in Desert Storm, but that wasn't quite the same thing; the constant threat of calamity and alien landscape had offered more than enough excitement. Most civilian jobs he'd held had kept him outdoors, from his first job detasseling corn as a twelve-year-old to his last, landscaping in Kearney—the only city within forty miles of his hometown of Harner, NE—until he couldn't do that anymore either. Now, he could fill his days as he pleased.

There was a traffic jam at the mouth of the valley, where the 101 skirted the hills. Shep turned the radio dial looking for a good song. In the summer corn fields, among all the other twelve- and thirteen-year-olds, he would tune himself in to a world of his own creation, blasting the songs he'd copied off the radio on his portable tape deck as he moved down the line, yanking the tassels off one by one, wearing thick work gloves that would be worn through by week's end. He came to associate his favorite songs, the ones he'd fast forward to get to—"Dream On," "Brandy (You're a Fine Girl)," "Love Hurts," songs that had been his mother's favorites, the records he'd found amongst her things in Gran's attic—with the feeling of the sun boring through the top of his head, the smell of fresh corn, the mosquitoes buzzing, the cramps in his fingers as the days wore on, and the simple solitude of work. Every time he heard those songs, he was transported to days when he didn't have any past. He took certain songs as talismans to hold onto throughout the day, not promising success or good fortune, but reminding him, at least, that the passage of time allowed for some small threads of continuity. No luck this time, as all the stations seemed to be on a synchronized commercial break. His back ached. His knees were pulsing and restless. Lionel snoozed on the seat beside him.

After several minutes at a slow creep down the freeway, Shep came to the source of the delay. A jeep was pulled off to the side of the road with flames and black smoke climbing up from its hood, the driver on a cell phone, pacing through the wiry brush on the other side of the guardrail. A lone firefighter climbed out of the rig that had pulled up behind the jeep, shrugging his coat on, taking his time, because the fire wasn't going anywhere. In their cars, everybody turned their heads to watch, windows rolled up and AC blasting, while the black smoke floated in clouds along the overpass.

Shep exited the freeway at Sunset and parked with a clear view into the front window of a café somewhere on the hazy barrier between Hollywood and West Hollywood. He checked his watch and scratched Lionel's neck, his coarse brown fur warmed by the sun, like Shep's own hair when he would board the school bus that would take all the kids home those corn field summers, the metal of his headset burning his neck, the tops of his ears screaming red. Once seated, he would stare drowsily out the window at the ocean of land, at one with the bumping rhythm of the dirt road.

This too gave him some measure of relief: the constancy of the sun, and the fact that it was the same sun, here as there, then as now. He checked his watch again. She was late.

A young couple on the café's patio caught his attention. They were drinking lemonade from tall, sweating glasses and chattering over each other, gesturing dramatically, laughing like kids. When the server brought their food out, they bugged their eyes out, making approving *oh boy, oh boy* faces at their plates. He wondered how they got and stayed so pleased.

Finally, she appeared on the sidewalk in the wake of a wheezing orange-and-white bus. She ran toward the front doors with her apron gripped in one hand, strings flying, her dark blonde hair tied up in a messy bun on top of her head as she hurried inside and behind the counter. The manager followed her, speaking calmly but pointedly. Shep's jaw tightened. She shook her head in apology as she tied the apron around her waist and smoothed the loose strands of hair around her face.

He should go have lunch, he thought. He could have lunch here. He could sit at the table beside the young couple, ask to hear about the specials, choose thoughtfully, tip generously. He could pull the manager aside and tell him what a fine waitress she'd been, smooth things over, help her out. She'd been late a few times lately, and he didn't want her to lose her job over it. There was nothing on earth stopping him from getting out of the car, crossing the street and pulling up a chair. He wasn't hungry yet, though. And who was to say they allowed dogs on the patio—a lot of places didn't, and it had gotten too warm out to leave him in the car.

"We're living in a dog-phobic society," he said. He paused, watching her make the rounds of the place with a pitcher of ice water.

"Who needs 'em."

No, he wasn't hungry. And he didn't like that kind of food anyway, those artfully arranged little salads and baguettes full of tooth-cracking seeds, all of it described on the menu as "artisanal" and served on rectangular slabs instead of plates, so food would probably fall off the edge and you'd get down on the ground to pick up whatever you'd dropped, then hit your head on the underside of the table with everybody looking. *No thanks*, he thought, watching the girl through the window, barely remembering to blink.

When her shift ended a few hours later, he watched her take her hair down and slip on a pair of giant tortoiseshell sunglasses. She dragged herself to the bus stop and sat down beside an old woman who was reading a paperback with a magnifying glass. The girl tucked her knees up under her chin and wrapped her arms around her ankles, looking like a little kid waiting to be picked up after school. Shep started the car. The engine sputtered for a minute before settling into a hum.

2

It was near dark, but the Cowboy hadn't left yet. Shep stopped by the man's cart and scooped Lionel up under his arm.

"Nice day today," he said, "I mean, not too hot, not too cold."

The Cowboy adjusted his grip on the cart's handle.

"I bet you like days like that, being out here."

The Cowboy swallowed, blinked. Shep noticed he was just barely tapping his cracked leather boot in a steady rhythm on the sidewalk.

"Hey, can I ask you something?" He pointed toward the telephone pole with the flyers, the missing persons. "Have you ever seen who puts those up? Those drawings? I keep seeing new ones, but I don't know where they come from. Thought maybe you would've seen."

The Cowboy stood up slowly and reached into his cart. He pulled out a small blanket, unfolded and refolded it, and laid it back in the bottom, then nestled the plastic bag more compactly into the corner of the cart.

"You have a good night," Shep said.

He tied Lionel to the bike rack and swung the front door open. Hung descended upon him immediately.

"Jesus, dude, I been waiting on you!"

"How'd you know when I'd come by?"

Hung snorted.

"Other people notice when you got habits. What you do every day ain't some secret between you and your diary."

"Don't mean it's set in stone."

"Just wait here. I gotta go get the pizzas."

Hung, his baggy jeans hanging so low it was unclear how they stayed up, jogged to the back room, where a staircase led directly into the apartment he shared with his parents. Shep grabbed a beer and settled in behind the counter, where he poured it into a Styrofoam cup. Hung's puzzles were spread out all over the counter, his word jumbles, crosswords and Sudoku, all filled in. He hoped there wouldn't be any customers while Hung was away. Hung had shown him how to work the register, but he didn't like to touch it, convinced he'd press a wrong button or give somebody the wrong change.

Hung returned with a stack of thin white boxes piled high in his arms. He jogged to the vacant pizza counter and threw several uncooked pies into the big industrial oven, then arranged a few slices of a finished one into the heated display case on the counter and returned to where Shep was seated.

"Fuck, man, I don't know how much longer I can do this. It was one thing when Mom ran the pizza counter. Now she's afraid Dad'll spontaneously combust or something if she ever leaves the apartment. She doesn't even come down to do the books anymore. She took all that shit upstairs. All she does anymore is hover over him like a damn hummingbird." Hung dramatized this by fluttering his hands with a dazed look in his eyes.

Shep shrugged. "If it makes her feel like she's helping…"

"I'm the one gives him his meds, cooks his breakfast, helps him get dressed on his bad days. She just stands around looking terrified, hands all balled up at her sides." He demonstrated this too, with the same hunched shoulders and slack-jawed stare, his fists squeezed tight. After a few seconds Hung resumed his normal posture. He slumped onto his stool and began shuffling the newspaper pages into a pile.

"She still makes the pizzas though, right?"

"She *assembles* them. I'm the one runnin'."

Shep sipped on his beer.

The bells chimed and a middle-aged biker came in. He wore a black T-shirt with the sleeves torn off and sported a deeply layered sunburn under his mosaic of tattoos. Hung had the man's carton of Marlboro Reds out before he'd reached the counter, and they proceeded with a wordless transaction.

Moments later, the motorcycle's engine roared outside, with Lionel's indignant barking immediately following.

"Knock it off!" Shep yelled. He got up from his stool. "You mind?"

Hung waved his hand, and Shep helped himself to a hot slice of pepperoni from the pizza counter. He'd forgotten to eat anything yet that day, and the salty cheese was just what he wanted. Though Hung fretted every night about the "dinner rush," it was mostly the two of them who ate the pizza, plus a few stoned youngsters and bachelors on their way home from work. The extras got thrown in the fridge, to be heated up the next day. It wasn't good pizza.

"You want any?"

"Nah," Hung said, wrinkling his nose. "I'm sick of that shit." He shuffled the newspapers some more and shoved them exasperatedly into the drawer under the counter.

"Don't usually stop you," Shep said. He leaned out the glass doors and tossed some rubbery pepperoni out onto the sidewalk for Lionel.

"Where're your folks at?" Hung asked, then looked up and tilted his head as though to mitigate the question's bluntness.

Shep scratched the back of his neck. He'd known Hung for some two years now, but had yet to share much of anything about his past, just tales of drinking mostly, a couple of his most trivial war stories.

He shook his head. "No folks."

"Sorry," Hung said, "I was just curious. Mom's been getting on my case all day, callin' down, asking me to do shit. Got me wondering."

"No kids, right?" Hung asked a minute later.

"Just me and Lionel." Shep sat down on his stool again, licked grease from his fingers and took a long swig of beer. He coughed and tasted the beer again, coming up just to the top of his throat.

"Mom's asking me when I'm gonna give her some grandkids. I'm like, bitch, I'm busy running your store. When am I supposed to date, huh? I didn't call her a bitch. I'm just sayin'."

Shep was about to respond when loud house music came pumping out from the other side of the strip mall that housed Parkdale's, a cyclical beat backed by some electronic instrumental.

Hung launched himself out from behind the counter and pushed one of the doors open. He craned his neck and stared out for a moment, scowling, then backed away and shook his head.

"It's that goddamn water store. What the fuck is a *water* store? I'm telling you, I've never seen one customer—it's just dudes in their track suits playing cards, smoking cigarettes, polishing their Bentleys. I mean, for real, what the fuck is a water store?"

"Some people buy water," Shep shrugged.

"You ever *see* anybody buying water over there? I know I haven't." Hung raised his eyebrows at Shep in what seemed intended as a meaningful look.

Shep leaned his elbows on the counter. The bright lights buzzed overhead. It wasn't as though Parkdale's was swarming with customers either. He wondered how they stayed afloat. He'd never run a business, never even thought of such a thing.

Hung marched to the back of the store and began straightening shelves, shifting boxes of cereal into precise rows, pushing bottles of condiments to the front, a tic he indulged whenever he was agitated. The music across the way grew louder, and Hung snorted and shook his head as he readjusted the revolving rack of sunglasses, repositioning pairs that people had tried on and lazily discarded, smudging the lenses while they were at it.

"I think I'm gonna get going," Shep said.

"Yeah, yeah," Hung said, "save yourself."

Shep untied Lionel and picked him up. At the other end of the lot, several luxury cars were double-parked in haphazard clusters: Escalades, Benzes, at least one Bentley. Inside, the water store was dark. He couldn't tell where the music was coming from, some back room, he supposed. Though the store had been there as far back as he could remember, a dingy "Grand Opening" sign still hung from the awning. Next to the water store—called Water Store, according to their neon sign—was the barber shop, A Cut Above, which Shep had never entered since he was in the habit of cutting his own hair in the bathroom mirror. There was the twenty-four-hour donut shop, inside which somebody was always asleep at a booth and there never seemed to be anybody behind the counter. There was some kind of baby clothes store, with a sign in both English and an Asian language he couldn't determine, which also rarely appeared to be open. The rest of the neighborhood was residential mostly, pastel-colored apartment buildings and small stucco houses with bars on the windows. He gave Lionel a squeeze and set him back down on the pavement.

"Come on," he said. "I bet you're ready to turn in."

The Cowboy had gone for the night. The music faded into the background as Shep and Lionel made their way home, casting their two shadows under the streetlamps.

3

Shep filled the dog's bowls with kibble and water. His apartment was nothing special—a one-bedroom with the most utilitarian of kitchens, which he used sparingly, eating most of his meals from cans or from Parkdale's. He knew it could be cleaner. He would have to fix it up if he were ever going to have anybody over, he knew that, but it was just a thought that passed with some frequency, nothing that led him toward any particular course of action. A fly buzzed over the pile of dishes in the sink and Shep winced. He knew what it looked like. A pit, a bachelor purgatory. It was what he could afford with his disability checks and what remained from the sale of his grandmother's house. It was temporary, like everything else.

Shep began undressing, throwing his shirt onto a rocking chair with a floral embroidered design on the back that had been his mother's, the only piece of furniture he'd kept. He brushed his teeth, looking into the spotted mirror on the bathroom door, assessing his body. He'd been in impeccable shape in his military days, able to run a six-minute mile and do a hundred push-ups, no problem. He could scarcely remember what that kind of fitness felt like. Now his chest sagged hollow. He didn't have a pot belly exactly, but his midsection jiggled when he poked it with his index finger. His hair was still enviable at least, a lustrous, sandy-blond mane that showed no sign of thinning, just a little gray at the temples. His eyes were still a cosmic blue, eyes he'd been told more than once were *piercing*. When he stood up straight and remembered to wear clean clothes, he could even be considered handsome. He spat into the sink and set his frayed toothbrush on the counter beside his comb and gummy, rusted razor.

Every night, as soon as Shep lay down, his body cycled through its litany of aches and pains, his ankles first, then his shins, his knees, his wrists, followed by a feeling of pressure on his chest, as though someone were sitting directly on his rib cage. The feeling used to scare him, would sometimes send him spiraling into a panic attack, he was told it was called, that feeling that death was imminent. But after all these years, he'd grown used to it, had trained his memory to remind him that it would pass. It took some time for his body to relax enough to fall asleep. He waited for it like a bus that ran late, but it always came.

***

It was dusk, and he and Lorene lay in the field behind his grandmother's house, with the fireflies fading in and out as they fluttered amid the tall grass. A storm was coming; the late summer sky was gnarled into a bruise, and the air was thick with anticipation, or maybe it was just him, drunk on whiskey, and the smell of her hair, like how he imagined tropical fruit might smell, against his cheek.

"You don't know how long I've wanted you," he whispered into her neck. "You have no idea."

Lorene let out a quiet laugh. She rolled over onto her back and pulled her underwear back up under her red and white striped cheerleading skirt, then rolled onto her belly and fished around in her purse. "I'd say I've got some idea," she said as she pulled out her flask and a single cigarette from a squished pack. She took a swig from the flask before passing it to him. He tipped it back into his mouth, and the few remaining drops left a warm sting on his lips.

"You should be careful," she said. "You know you're technically a criminal."

"Only if your mom presses charges."

"I wouldn't put it past her."

"She'd change her mind if she knew I was planning on marrying you."

Lorene laughed. "Get a grip."

"I mean it."

"I'm gonna go ahead and finish high school if that's alright with you."

"'Course you will. And I'm gonna pick out a specialty—a good, stable one—or maybe I'll go to college after all. Or something, anyway…"

She shut him up with a clumsy kiss, her teeth clacking lightly against his. Her breath was smoky and sour, and mingled with the smell of her hair, the effect was dizzying, like floating at a high altitude. She punctuated the kiss by biting his bottom lip.

"You're cute," she said. She sat up and began gathering her things.

"Stay with me, just a little longer?"

"I've gotta be home for dinner. Mom's not gonna believe practice ran late again as it is."

"Right."

"And I thought you had to be someplace."

John looked at his watch. He had an hour to grab a bite to eat before heading to his weekend drill.

"What if I don't go? What if I come to your house for dinner?"

Lorene didn't answer, but rolled her eyes and stood up, brushing grass off herself.

"Well?"

She reached a hand down and ruffled his hair with her chipped French-manicured fingernails. He sat up and watched her walk down the road, past the water tower and west toward her house, the McAllisters' beagle crossing her path as she continued alongside the old railroad tracks, which remained, years after the trains stopped coming through.

"I'm gonna call you when I get back Sunday night. I'm gonna take you to a late movie in town, Lorene," he called after her. He loved to say her name.

He noted the grass stains on her white canvas tennis shoes before she turned the corner, watching in hopes that she would look back, but she never did, though he knew she'd heard him. She was sixteen, but carried herself like a woman much older. Her confidence was frightening. John sat alone in the grass and watched the fireflies, their light intensifying and weakening in a staggered harmony with each other, embroiled in their own mating rituals. The sky rumbled, turning a deeper purple, as drops began to fall on his shoulders. Without warning, the rain let loose, pummeling the field.

He leaned back and let it wash over him for a moment, overtaken by the smell of the warm rain as it hit the grass. There were so many scents in the world, so many textures and weights, he could scarcely focus on just one feeling at a time. He closed his eyes, imagining himself glowing like the fireflies did, pulsing and releasing. His body hummed.

When he decided he'd better get up and head back to the house, he found he couldn't move. He struggled to lift his arms, his head, but it was as though his will was divorced from his actions, his power sapped. Mud pooled around him, and the wind picked up, sending water flying down his throat and up his nostrils. He coughed and jerked, but his limbs were bolted to the ground. He began to sink into the mud, still struggling with all his might to get up. In his peripheral vision, he saw lightning flash, walling him in on all sides.

"Help!" he yelled. "Help! Somebody please!"

***

In his bed on Coldwater Canyon, with the trickle of the L.A. river snaking silently nearby, Shep tossed and muttered. He was back in his body, the dream forgotten, but still he struggled to move, awake but not awake, desperate and alone. Though he couldn't open his eyes, he could feel shadows looming, figures towering over him, crowding the room, and hear skittering across the floor—rats, ghosts, it didn't matter. Everything was closing in. He would cry for help if only he could move his mouth or control his vocal cords. All he could manage was a series of grunts from deep in his belly.

In the darkness, Lionel hopped onto the bed, crawled up onto Shep's chest and began licking first his ear, then his cheek. He nudged Shep's throat insistently with his cold nose, and suddenly Shep was freed. His darting eyes opened and he lurched up to a sitting position.

"You're a good friend," he gasped, his hand shaking as he stroked the dog's head.

He held Lionel up to face him, and looked into his wet brown eyes in the moonlight. The dog finally squirmed out of his hands, and Shep let him down. He sat for a few minutes, letting his breath settle while the sweat on his back dried, before getting up and going to the kitchen. He poured a shot of whiskey into a coffee mug and sipped it gently, like medicine, in the dark.

Then he lay back down to let the cycle begin again, the ache in his ankles spreading like falling dominoes through his legs, up through his hips and groin, until the crushing weight settled onto his chest, but that would pass too.

4

September 1990

Dear Lorene,

I know you may be surprised to be hearing from me. I didn't get a chance to say a proper goodbye to you, and I've been regretting it every day since. They gave us a couple days' leave before we had to ship out. I went looking for you, but I couldn't find you anyplace. I didn't have much time. It wasn't because I didn't care, Lorene, I just couldn't find you when I needed to. Where were you? I'm sorry.

I've had nothing but time to think about you. About your face, your beautiful eyes. Your mouth. To tell you the truth, I was afraid to write to you until now, afraid of what I'd say. Lorene, I'm going crazy.

Since we got here we've done nothing but wait. We transported all the cargo, set up the FOB, and now we play cards. We watch E.T. over and over because it's the only video we have. We write letters. We clean our already clean weapons, and we listen for any rumor of a command. I'm with my new unit. I was gonna train to be a medic, but it all happened so fast, I don't know what I'm supposed to be doing. Some people are saying there won't even be a ground war after all, that we're waiting here for nothing. I've stopped listening. I do what they tell me.

I don't think you know my grandmother so well, do you? You've seen her around and all, but you probably haven't met or anything. She's mostly kept to herself, I guess. It's been just me and her since before I can even remember, you know. I never knew my dad, and my mom died when I was little. It's just been the two of us.

I don't know if I've been good to her, Lorene. How do you know if you're good? She's getting older. I try to write her letters. I try to tell her about my days. But I can never get past "Dear Grandmother." I write the date at the top of the page, I sign the bottom, and then I stare at the big white middle. Sometimes I get a sentence down, something like "It's been real, real hot" or "I haven't been sleeping," and then I just feel like I'm complaining to her and she doesn't want to hear that. I thought writing would be easier than talking in person, but it feels just the same.

I've put her through a lot of hassle, you know. She doesn't need me hanging around.

Has she given up on me now, or did she give up a long time ago? Did I disappoint her that much? It's hard to know what you're doing when you're doing it. A moment's gone before you even get your bearings, before you can even think to ask yourself.

I guess I'm telling you all this because I'm worried about her. And she doesn't really have a lot of friends in town. She's alone, and I guess she wants it that way, but… I know it's asking a lot, and hell, I was shocked and tickled to death that you even noticed me this summer, but I feel like I can trust you now, Lorene, more than anybody else I know, more than Marty even, or any of the guys here.

So, would you say hello if you see her at the store? Would you make a little stop when you pass by her house? Not every time, just…if it's not too much?

I wish I would've seen you, Lorene. I would've told you that when I come back, I'm gonna make you the happiest woman in the world. That's a promise. I don't believe I've ever made a promise to anyone before, but I'm promising you.

All my best,
John Shepherd

Unstamped and unsent, the letter sat for years at the bottom of Shep's rucksack, with all the others. It was probably, definitely, still there, the pack shoved into a corner of the top shelf of his bedroom closet, next to a broken, dust-choked electric fan. The paper would be brittle and yellow by now. He couldn't explain why he hadn't had the nerve to send any letters all those years ago, though he had some ideas, ones he quashed when the heat built up in his throat, the memory of his willful passivity.

Maybe everything would be different if he had managed to reach out, he mused from time to time, standing before the closet in his holey briefs with Lionel whining for his breakfast. Or maybe nothing would. Maybe he'd know one way or the other if he'd ever unpacked the things he'd brought with him, or any of the things he'd brought back.

5

Fourteen. Shep counted them up again, the number of faces on the telephone pole. The new one was an army man, with little pen marks made to resemble a buzz cut and clumsily rendered camouflage colored in at the shoulders. He looked around, thinking he might see the young artist watching from some hiding place nearby. He too had busily filled up notebooks with drawings of tanks and soldiers as a boy. He'd drawn gruesome battle scenes, complete with decapitated bodies and great fireballs in the sky, overpowering the round yellow sun with its squiggly rays.

Shep fingered the edge of the paper and was startled when it came off in his hand. The scotch tape on the back fell to the ground. He tried to stick it back up, but the tape had picked up too much dirt. Parkdale's wasn't open yet. He held the drawing carefully and looked again for the culprit, but there wasn't a body in sight, and when he looked up at the lightening sky with the moon still visible even as the sun rose up behind the mountains, he was transported.

You have just experienced the most powerful conventional bomb dropped in the war.

The words drifted back from so many years earlier, word for word, the English translation just below the Arabic:

It has more explosive power than twenty Scud missiles. You will be bombed again soon. Flee south and you will be treated fairly. You cannot hide. Flee and live, or stay and die.

He'd found the propaganda leaflet in the sand, and though he knew it was one of thousands that had been air dropped days earlier for the Iraqis and not for him, it chilled him all the same—*Flee and live or stay and die*—triggering a desire in him to run until he hit water. He remembered it too often still, though he'd dropped it like a hot rock and had watched it skitter across the sand on the desert breeze as soon as he'd read it. That very night at base camp the words had returned—*Flee and live or stay and die*—keeping him awake most of the night.

He held the drawing to his chest and looked around helplessly until he remembered the donut shop, always open. Lionel followed along behind him.

"Hello?" he called. He rang the bell on the counter and

breathed in the cloyingly sweet air for a minute until a white-haired man in shirtsleeves emerged from the back.

"No dogs," the man said.

"Oh, uh, hey, do you have any tape, or a staple gun or something I could borrow?"

"No dogs, no dogs," he repeated, making an ixnay motion with his hands.

"Okay, okay," Shep said, backing out of the store. The swinging door jingled behind them.

He lifted his wrist to look at his watch, but found he'd neglected to put it on. In fact, he realized with some disquiet, he could remember neither the walk here, nor getting up in the first place.

He and Lionel stood alone in the parking lot, Shep growing increasingly annoyed with his unwanted possession of the drawing. He couldn't just throw it away. He looked around again, and the corner was eerily still, not a car, not a person, not even a sound. He knitted his brow and rubbed the paper between his thumb and index finger.

He felt a presence then, a shift in gravity, and looked up to see an old man sticking his head out the window above Parkdale's. It took him a moment to realize it was Hung's father. Shep hadn't actually seen him since his stroke. The man blinked, his waxen face set in a grimace, but Shep couldn't tell if the old man saw him down in the parking lot.

"Mr. Phan?" he tried. The man didn't look down, but continued staring out grimly in the direction of the power lines that swooped low alongside the treetops.

"Hello, Mr. Phan?

Suddenly two hands grasped the man's arms and gently guided him away from the window. Hung appeared in his place.

"Shep? What the fuck—you can't wait ten minutes? Ain't no special hours for your ass."

"Sorry!"

"Just chill there for a minute, a'ight?" He shut the

window and drew the faded yellow curtains.

Shep sat on the curb, and Lionel leaned into his hip. The wind picked up and he held the sheet of paper down against his thigh. From where he sat, he could see that the other sheets of paper were fluttering precariously against the telephone pole. He imagined them all coming loose at once, flying off down the street, and him running after them in a doomed attempt at rescue. He watched the pages flap, their ragged spiral notebook edges dancing like dandelion florets.

Time passed in silence, how much time he couldn't begin to guess, but as the minutes ticked on, he began to worry that Hung would never come, that he'd in fact imagined their earlier conversation, and the encounter at the donut shop too, since, of course, there was no one behind the counter now. There were no cars on the road, no people, no one waiting at the nearby bus stop, no one, no one. He contemplated calling out a great echoing *Hellllooooooo*, but was hunkered down too deeply in his thoughts to turn any single one into an action.

You will be bombed again soon.

Now that the words had come back to him, they kept repeating, slipping in between other thoughts.

You cannot hide. Flee and live or stay and die.

And he remembered—even more than the smell—the sound of burning oilfields, like a storm raging on and on without end.

"Hey!"

Shep's shoulders jerked up.

"Hey," Hung said again, "you hypnotized? You deaf? That dog of yours been barking like crazy."

"Oh, oh," he muttered, disoriented still, but soothed by Hung's arrival, an indication that he had not in fact fallen into a crevice in time.

He looked down at the paper still pressed under his palm.

"Hung, you got any tape?"

"Yeah I got tape. Now get up off the curb, man, you're

blocking the handicapped spot."

Shep rose with some difficulty just as the Cowboy approached the side of the building, the wheels of his shopping cart cutting the silence, whooshing softly against the dusty pavement.

6

She'd be coming out the east side of the building. Shep knew because he'd been here before, because *she'd* been here before. He had followed her on two buses, from her stop on Colfax—just a couple of miles from his home—all the way to the casting office on Ventura. He'd watched her crouch in the parking garage's stairwell to check her makeup, her headshots and resumes tucked in a manila envelope under her arm, watched her make ethereal faces into her compact, practicing her poignant stare.

While he waited, he tried to imagine what those offices looked like inside. Were they Hollywood-slick, with real plants and glass tabletops, or was she sitting under buzzing fluorescent lights, the walls stuffed with asbestos, brushing the balls of her feet rhythmically against stained Berber carpet? He liked to imagine Lila in these quiet moments, daydreaming her surroundings, wondering at her thoughts. His gaze floated up to a billboard with a male model holding a bottle of Tanqueray, his hair slicked back and skinny tie flying three-dimensionally beyond the billboard's edge.

"I know you're bored, Lionel. I never promised you excitement." The dog lay on his side on the passenger seat, his tongue lolling slightly out the side of his mouth. Shep scratched Lionel's belly, and the dog kicked his leg in a jerky, circular motion. While he waited, Shep tried to ignore a drilling ache in his own belly, one he'd woken with that morning. He rested his hand on the spot as though holding the pain back from spreading through the rest of his body.

When she emerged a half hour later, it took him a moment to notice that she was in some kind of distress. She looked wan, with a new pallor, her jaw quavering. Her hands were trembling as she opened and closed her mouth, seemingly making a deliberate effort to breathe. The manila envelope slipped from her fingers onto the pavement, and she quickly crouched down to scoop it up before it blew into a puddle on the sidewalk. She clutched the envelope to her chest and took a few more deep breaths, then rose slowly, carefully, on her too-high platform heels.

Shep started the car and waited until she was half a block ahead of him before pulling out to follow. From behind, she looked so much like Lorene, though her gait was quick, her steps clipped and narrow, not like Lorene's at all come to think of it. Lorene always walked like she knew people were watching, like she was performing a walk. He remembered the first time he'd seen her outside Wilcox High. He was a senior, ditching last period with Marty Cumberland, who would be killed not two years after graduation, flipping his dad's tractor off the side of Highway 136 while Shep lay in a bunk in Saudi.

It was just a few weeks into the school year. They were smoking under the bleachers during a free period, he hanging lackadaisically with his hands gripping the aluminum bars while Marty repacked the bowl, when the double doors at the back of the gym opened, cutting the afternoon's lulling prairie stillness. He signaled to Marty to hide the pipe under his backpack. Then she appeared in gym clothes, cotton shorts and Wilcox Wildcats T-shirt tied in a knot at her hip. Even in tennis shoes she walked with purpose, her hips in a controlled swing, her backpack hanging from one shoulder, blond bangs swept low over her right eye. She pulled a tube of lip gloss from her bag and gently dabbed at her lips without consulting a mirror.

Marty pulled the pipe back out and flicked his lighter, satisfied that no teacher was coming, but Shep just stared. She must be a freshman, he thought, because he was certain he'd never seen her before. A black Chevy pulled up at the curb and the girl waved. She leaned into the window to greet the unseen driver before crossing over to the passenger side and climbing in. The truck pulled out of the parking lot, and Shep watched it all the way until it passed the water tower to the north, where it faded out into the dusty horizon.

"You see that?" he said to Marty.

Marty shook his Bic lighter and flicked it again, trying to get a flame. "Yeah, nice tits," he nodded.

Shep shook his head and resumed swinging from the aluminum bars.

The similarity must be in his head, he reasoned now. Lila didn't seem to be quite so aware of her beauty, not as blazingly confident. He hesitated to take note of her backside in the filmy sundress she was wearing, which threatened to fly up with every gust of wind. She kept her fingertips grazing its short hemline, clamping down with her palm every time the breeze picked up. She didn't usually dress like that. When she wasn't dressed in her work uniform, he usually saw her in jeans and T-shirts. He wondered if some fat cigar-chomping agent or casting director had told her she had to be sexier, and fumed a little on her behalf. Still, she was more beautiful than Lorene had ever been, if such a thing were possible. She'd taken her long, dirty blond hair down, and it blew about her tanned shoulders as she walked with her head down.

Suddenly, Lila stopped as though stricken. She ducked to her right and disappeared into an alley. Shep pulled over and, without thinking, stopped the car, Lionel barking in protest at being left behind as his master got out and approached on foot, thinking she must be sick or hurt or worse, not thinking of what he would say or do when he caught up to her.

He peered into the alley to find her crouched down on her haunches, her back to the wall, sobbing. Her eyes were squeezed shut as her shoulders heaved.

Shep froze, realizing that there was nothing he could do here. She wouldn't recognize him, surely, and he couldn't risk revealing himself. Besides which, he had no way of consoling her. He knew what this, what *he*, looked like. Even if he came to her saying "shhh, shhh, it's alright," as he would to a child, even if he said her name, good god, especially if.

Her crying tapered off, and she breathed roughly for a minute, wiping her face with a disintegrating tissue she'd fished out of her purse. Shep knew he should leave, that she would scream if she saw him there, snooping down the alley at her private despair. Was it the audition? Had they been cruel to her, or was it something deeper, a longstanding torment of which he knew nothing and could never hope to understand?

On a count of three, he turned away from her, resting his face on the white-painted brick for a moment before returning to the car. He heaved himself into the driver's seat as Lionel climbed all over him, lapping at every inch of his neck and chin. Shep set the dog back down on the passenger seat. He started the car up again and sat with his hands on the wheel, waiting for the engine to stop coughing. A minute later, she emerged from the alley, her face freshened as though nothing had happened, and continued on her way. He pulled out of the spot and followed, painfully aware now that the time he'd invested into following her was giving him an idea of her habits but no insight into her soul. There was no coming back from it, no way to replace the years.

They came to a red light. Shep stopped at the intersection, and Lila stopped just a few feet to his right on the sidewalk. What was he doing to her? Even taking her obliviousness as a given, this had to be a violation. But who was he hurting?

The light stayed red, and Shep's thoughts drifted to his

return from the Gulf in '91. No one had come to meet him at the airfield. He'd looked for his grandmother among all the crying, clutching families, knowing somehow that she wouldn't be there, surprised by his lack of surprise. He caught a bus to Harner, his pack stuffed between his knees and the seat in front of him. He leaned his temple against the window as the sun melted into the fields.

When he got to town, he found the streets empty. It was dinnertime. He pictured all the families inside at kitchen tables, sharing their days, with the windows closed and curtains drawn to hold in the warmth they generated together. He walked slowly, his thoughts scattered and ungraspable, as though his mind were a deck of cards with every card accounted for, somewhere, but strewn about the floor in disarray. The air was crisp, but there was no snow left on the ground, and he understood what had him so disoriented: he'd missed winter.

He walked right past his grandmother's house and found himself instead on Lorene's front stoop. He was sure she'd forgotten him, probably moved on to some boy in her class. But he had to see her. He had to ask her if he still had a chance. Did the time matter so much, if he could find the words to explain how thoughts of her had kept him alive when it felt as though the loneliness would drown him in his cot, how just closing his eyes and calling up her scent had blocked out the fear of death? He cringed at some of the words he felt brimming at the top of his throat, all the promises and revelations he felt buzzing within. He was sweating with the effort of containing it all.

Before he got a chance to knock, the door opened, and he was met with Lorene's mother's pinched face.

"What are you doing standing here like a statue?"

"I'm sorry, Ma'am, I was just about to—is Lorene home? I just wanted to see her."

Her face softened for just a moment as she noticed his

pack and the fatigues he was still wearing. But she steeled herself again just as quickly.

"She's not here."

"Oh…is there a game tonight? Is she at school?"

"No, she's not at…just go on home."

"Oh." Shep nodded, slightly dazed. "Well, do you know where I might find her?" It was dark now, and the moon was just a sliver short of fullness. He had a mind to wander back to the high school anyway, just in case.

"I'm sorry," she murmured, and shut the door.

Shep stumbled as he stepped down from the porch and looked up toward Lorene's bedroom window. He thought for just a second that he saw the white lace curtain lifted by a finger, but when he looked again, it seemed as though he hadn't seen anything after all.

Hangdog and heart-bruised, he made his way back to his grandmother's house. He was wary in a way he couldn't quite articulate. He'd always felt vaguely like a long-term boarder, benefiting from home-cooked meals but realistic enough not to expect too much in the way of familial affection from the woman he'd been foisted upon as a kindergartener. He'd often wondered why she kept him, why she hadn't surrendered him to some other family member, though he couldn't name any natural candidates. Now that he'd been gone so long, he half-wondered if he was still welcome. Maybe she'd taken in a renter by now, packed up his things and plunked them in the attic alongside his mother's boxes, relegated to the sealed-off past.

As he climbed the front steps, he was struck by a coughing fit. His throat convulsed as tears trickled from the corners of his eyes. Finally, the coughing subsided, and he spat thick black liquid into the soil beneath his grandmother's hedges. He kicked dirt over the puddle, wiped hot saliva from his mouth and caught his breath.

The windows were darkened, but he found the door unlocked.

"Hello? Gran?"

There was no answer, and Shep set his pack down softly in the entryway and removed his boots. He turned on the living room lamp and was startled at the mess. Piles of laundry sat unfolded on the sofa, spilling over onto the carpet. Filthy plates, cloudy glasses and sticky utensils were scattered on the coffee table, and a fine layer of dust covered every surface. He picked up a coffee cup and found a sticky ring underneath, swarming with ants. He sniffed the air. Something, somewhere in the house, was rotting.

"Gran, are you here?" he called louder now.

He found her upstairs, sitting on the edge of her bed. She was in her nightgown, slouched with her hands clasped in her lap, staring at the wall.

Shep lowered himself to his knees in front of her and tried to catch her eye.

"Gran? It's me. I'm back."

She didn't look at him.

"You...okay?"

Something struck him about the way she was holding her hands, and he reached out and gently tried to separate them from each other. Maybe he could help her up, take her down to the kitchen, maybe make her a cup of tea if she had any in the pantry. But the fingers were stuck in their position, gnarled around each other. Her thumb spasmed, and Shep clamped his palm down over it.

Her head rolled downward slowly toward him. Her eyes were glassy, bloodshot.

"Gran, can you hear me?"

She was facing him, looking into his eyes, but he could tell that she wasn't seeing him, or at least didn't fully recognize who she was looking at. He held onto her hands. He wanted to cry, felt that this was the time to do it, finally, if ever there was a time, but he didn't have any tears in him. He stared at the carpet. He breathed in the rot.

A horn honked behind him and Shep flinched. He drove ahead and scanned the sidewalk, finding Lila a block ahead of him already. What was he doing? Whatever it was, he was at an impasse, unable to stop himself but unable to get any closer either.

The girl made a right turn, and Shep signaled to follow her, but when he reached the intersection, he turned off the signal and kept on going straight. He squeezed the steering wheel tight, his nails digging grooves into the meat of his palms.

7

When Shep got to Parkdale's, Hung was in the middle of the parking lot, embroiled in an argument with someone he recognized as one of the fixtures at the water store across the way.

"Come on, that one's yours, that's his," Hung said, pointing at the huddle of cars that seemed to be expanding by the day, pushing out toward the low concrete walls that surrounded the lot: the tan Bentley, the onyx Beamer, the white Escalade with opaque black windows and others, all of them parked in a jigsaw arrangement they'd sort out at the end of each day, laughing and yelling to each other in a foreign language. "That one's new, but I know it's one of y'alls. You see what I'm getting at?" Hung's jaw trembled.

The man shook his head and tossed his cigarette butt onto the pavement. He was at least a head taller than Hung, and handsome in a languid, sun- and smoke-cured way, a thick gold watch on his wrist glittering in the afternoon sun. "It's not a good day for this discussion," he said, "you must agree?"

Shep noticed the flags on all the cars' antennae, red, orange and blue, hanging limp in the windless air. The same flag was displayed prominently in the water store's window, with *1915* written across it in black letters.

Hung sighed and sputtered, with no ready response.

"What is it you want me to do?" the man said calmly, which seemed to infuriate Hung all the more. Shep hung back and watched with Lionel cradled under his arm, thinking he ought to be ready to step in if he was needed.

"I got my eye on you," Hung said.

The other man smiled. "You must learn to share," he called over his shoulder as he returned to his friends, who were sitting at a plastic card table just outside the water store's entrance.

Hung didn't see Shep, and stomped back into the store with his head down. The Cowboy was sitting in his nook.

"You know what all that was about?" he asked, knowing that the Cowboy wouldn't answer. He paused a moment, while the Cowboy worried the handle of his shopping cart.

Shep gave the Cowboy a nod and followed Hung into the store, stopping first to tie Lionel to the bike rack. He found Hung sweeping the area in front of the counter in tight little swipes, a single vein in his left forearm bulging.

"Everything okay?"

Hung kept sweeping while Shep fetched his beer from the fridge. While he was making his selection, Hung stormed past him and flung the broom into the supply closet with a clatter.

"Where are my fucking customers s'posed to park if all Eugene's people are fillin' up the lot, huh? Ain't no street parking around here, all we got's fucking hydrants every ten feet, red curbs and wide-ass driveways, and if there's no place to stop the damn car then guess what?"

His diatribe didn't seem to be aimed at Shep exactly. He was reviewing his anger, situating himself inside it. Shep took his seat behind the counter

"And what the fuck response do I get when I ask nice,

like a gentleman, like a fellow businessman, if maybe the party could move to a different location, if they could maybe free up a couple more spots for the rest of us? All his dumbass friends smirking like they just owned my ass when they didn't even fucking do nothing. *Nothing*, fucking parasites."

Hung's outburst was interrupted by a customer at the door. He breathed heavily, quietly, behind the counter while a woman holding the hand of a little girl picked up a mini carton of milk and a box of animal crackers. He rang them up while Shep ran his finger along the cold side of the beer can he'd tucked under the counter.

When they left, Hung let out a giant breath as though he'd been holding it.

"And of course it's all on me,'cause everybody else on this damn strip is asleep standing up," Hung said. "Fuck, dude."

"Want me to talk to him?"

Hung shook his head down at the counter, tapping his pencil against its rounded edge.

"No offense, man, but you realize you don't work here, right?"

"So?"

"What, are you my security guard now?"

Shep shrugged. "I been in a couple of fights..."

Hung laughed.

"That was in Saint Cornfield, USA, or wherever the fuck it is you come from. These motherfuckers ain't good ol' boys at the honky tonk you can take down with a kick to the nutsack."

"I don't know, they don't seem as tough as all that."

"Do I have to spell it out for you? How long you lived around here, like two years? And you don't know what it means when a pack of dudes fuckin'...*hold court* all day in their empty-ass businesses? Restaurants only open three hours a day in the middle of the afternoon? Cafes that say they got free wi-fi but they give you a dirty look if you try to sit down at one of their wobbly-ass tables? Fucking *water stores* with just some plastic jugs and hookahs in the front window, like three bottles of Vitamin Water and a Yoohoo in the fridge? Come on."

Shep glanced out the window behind him, at the men huddled around the card table where they spent nearly every weekday.

"I know what I see," Hung said. "You don't wanna know how many times I've seen this shit, and it always ends the same way."

Shep paused, unsure what Hung was getting at. The beer wasn't settling his stomach like it usually did. A hollow ache permeated through his solar plexus.

"You know, honky tonks are a Texas thing," Shep said. "Not a Midwest thing."

"Sorry the nuance is lost on me," Hung snorted.

He could tell Hung's pulse was still racing, the way he kept picking up his pencil and putting it down, fussing with rolls of receipt paper, his fingers twitching and grasping.

Two years earlier, Shep came into the store for a six pack and found Mr. Phan on the floor in front of the ice machine, curled up on his side, his knees to his chest, his eyes and mouth wide open.

Shep called out, "Help!" as he tried to shake him by the shoulders. He heard a rumbling on the stairs, and a second later Hung, the son he'd scarcely ever spoken to, burst out from the back door.

"Shit," he said, down on his knees, grasping his father's head by each ear, looking into the black caverns of his eyes.

"You got a car?" he said.

Within minutes they were barreling toward Kaiser, Hung navigating in the front seat while Mrs. Phan keened in the back, her body thrown over her husband's as though she were shielding him from gunfire, Lionel cowering in Shep's lap.

Shep leaned his forearms against the counter. He sipped his beer slowly, rolling it in his mouth. He'd barely slept the night before, had only gotten up because Lionel was whining for breakfast, had stayed up because there wasn't any point in returning to a sleepless bed.

Hung flipped through the paper until he found the comics page, then folded it into a compact little rectangle.

"Okay, I got one for you," he said, tapping his pencil in a clipped rat-a-tat. "V-T-J-Y-I-I-L-O-A. Any idea what that spells?"

"Never." Shep shook his head. "I'm never gonna guess it."

"It's not about guessing. You gotta visualize the letters. Close your eyes and let them float in your mind's eye, where you can rearrange them any which way."

Shep closed his eyes, but couldn't conjure up any letters. He'd already forgotten what they were.

"I got it," Hung said. "You got it?"

"Not today."

"Joviality," Hung said. "Ain't that sweet?" He gave a weak laugh and pushed the paper aside.

"Aren't you gonna do the rest of 'em?" Shep asked.

"Not now. Gotta make 'em last." Hung stood up from his stool and walked toward the back of the store.

"You can handle things for a bit, right?" he called back to Shep.

"I guess so."

The back door swung behind Hung as he climbed the stairs up to the apartment.

Shep sat up straighter and looked around the store. Hung had been leaving him in charge more often of late, sometimes for five minutes, sometimes close to an hour. He had no way of knowing which this was going to be.

The night he'd driven Mr. Phan to the emergency room, Shep waited in the car with Lionel for hours, taking occasional walks among the grass enclosures surrounding the parking lot. He watched people being carried through the sliding glass doors by their loved ones, limp, maimed, blanched in the face, unloaded from ambulances, and pushed in wheelchairs. He watched, cataloguing the particularities of each new arrival. With the windows rolled up, the only sound he heard was the occasional siren.

He thought about the last time he'd spent any significant time in a hospital, when he'd taken his grandmother in for what would turn out to be the last time. He'd grown so accustomed to taking care of her that it never quite occurred to him that it would come to an end. When he returned to the house after the doctor told him she was gone but before the meaning of the words had penetrated, he sat at the kitchen table for a long time, with no idea what to do, no understanding of the time of day or what was expected of him. He stared at his hands, spread palms up under the kitchen lamp, with the ceiling fan whirring, shadows flashing across the ceiling.

Hung knocked on the window and Shep jerked his head back. Lionel barked. He unlocked the doors.

"You waited." Hung guided his mother into the back seat before climbing into the front.

Shep shrugged.

"You didn't have to."

There was a long silence as Shep pulled out of the hospital's driveway.

"I didn't mean to," he finally said, "didn't mean not to."

The sun was rising, a pink glow radiating from behind the hills.

Hung let out a weary laugh.

"I guess I don't have to thank you then."

In the backseat, Mrs. Phan began to weep quietly, shaking a little with each exhalation. Hung closed his eyes, leaned back against the headrest and rubbed a spot between his eyebrows.

8

Shep sat in the carport with the engine running. It was Wednesday, which meant Lila's shift would be starting at eight. He knew it was Wednesday, because the day before was Tuesday, because Hung had gotten his Budweiser delivery. The day before that was Monday, because it was a holiday— no mail. When he tried to go back further, he had to close his eyes. The sun was too bright, the air too thin. He tried to breathe slowly, deeply, the way the physical therapist at the VA hospital in Lincoln had taught him, driving the air all the way down to his diaphragm.

Breathe slowly, feel your lungs expanding, and focus, she'd said. *Visualize the tide as it comes in and slowly recedes.* He could tell she was just out of school by her practiced tone, the way everything she said to him could have just as easily been said into a mirror, or to the walls of an empty room. He'd stood before her, concentrating on pushing all the air out and refilling his lungs at the ocean's pace, though he was only guessing at it, having never seen the ocean in person. He thought he must be doing it wrong, because he was feeling lightheaded, and his hands began to shake again. *Open your eyes, Mr. Shepherd,* she'd said, holding his forearm, her eyes sweetly pitying. She signed a form and sent him on his way.

Shep held his hands on the steering wheel but made no move to pull out. Lionel wagged his tail and shuffled back and forth on the seat.

What am I doing?

He said these words in his head, over and over, stopping and starting: *What am I, what, what am I, what am I, what am I doing…*

…a mental stutter, but also a real question to which he had no satisfying answer. He stared down at his lap and let his arms go slack. Muscle memory sent him flashing back in time for a second, looking down at his lap in the passenger seat of his grandmother's Buick while she sat in silence behind the wheel, tapping her index finger in exasperation at a red light, which time, any time, with him shrinking beside her, picking at his hangnails, and then he was back—saying, *what am I, what am I, what am I doing?*—and still not moving the car.

Finally, he reached into the glove compartment and pulled out a mini bottle of vodka. At room temperature it was disgusting, but he swallowed it down, gagged, and ran his tongue around in his mouth to hold nausea at bay. He felt both better and worse.

Eight o'clock shift. That's what he was doing. He looked at his watch, but found he'd forgotten to put it on again. She may have started work already. Then she'd be inaccessible behind glass, or even more inaccessible than she already was. When he followed her from her home, he felt that there was at least a sense of possibility as they traveled in parallel, a chance for her to feel him beside her in the open air. He imagined he could make her feel safe. She wouldn't know what to call it, or what was causing it. She would only feel a caring energy that would boost her up above the world's sorrows and disappointments.

He sometimes fantasized that she knew everything. In his daydreams, she would approach his car. Climb into the passenger seat and let Lionel curl up in her lap.

Dad? she'd say. *I'm so glad you're here. I'd be all alone here without you.*

Take me home, she'd say. *I'm so tired. Aren't you tired?*

Shep sank into the fantasy as into a warm bath, letting the years fall away like grime he could just wash off, his fingertips wrinkles in time. In a past rewritten, there he was with little Lila on his shoulders and Lorene by his side at a county fair, the three of them sharing a great cloud of cotton candy that vanished like magic on each of their tongues, Lila's sticky hands wrapped around his jaw, Lorene leaning her body into his, their hands clasped, with the lights from the Ferris wheel twinkling, black powder in shells waiting for their fuses to be lit, to explode into fireworks and compete with the stars that were so close Lila could touch one if she just reached up. It was an image he'd invented at some point, continually adding details—the smell of caramel corn, the distant strains of Van Halen coming from the Gravitron, the smoky orange of the setting sun—because it warmed him from the inside out.

The whir of the road, the sun a white flash in his eyes, and the next thing he knew he was on the freeway, but, he noticed too late, he was going north, not south. His palms and underarms were moist, and he could feel a trickle of sweat rolling down the center of his back.

He wasn't even on the right freeway. When traffic slowed, he ran his hands back through his hair. He knew he had memory lapses from time to time, like anybody, but more sizable pieces of his days had been going missing. He found a sign and saw that he was on the 14, past Lancaster and approaching the Mojave. That was a good half hour stricken from the record.

He squeezed the steering wheel tightly, feeling that this would keep him tethered, would prevent the car from floating up and away. He turned up the volume on the radio to a Neil Young song muddled by static, the nasal vocals shot through with the hush of snow. Lionel perched his front paws up on the passenger side armrest and licked the window.

Before long the traffic dwindled and the wind picked up, kicking up dust in every direction. The land was so flat and vacant there was nothing to catch the sun, which had grown a yellow skin like butter left out. His AC was busted, so he could feel the sun baking through the car. He rolled down the window and the wind rattled the frame and deafened him to the radio, which had given way entirely to the static.

In the distance he saw snow-capped mountains, so far away it had never occurred to him he could ever go there. He wondered for a brief moment how much gas it would take to get him to their base, and to the top. Could he drive it in one tank? Would the air be thin up there, would it make him light-headed and dumb? He exited at the next opportunity, intent on getting his bearings. His tires ground into dusty road lined with wiry bushes, with snake holes hidden in each one.

He saw something then, much closer, up ahead. Just visible behind the sun's expansive glare was a massive lot behind tall, forbidding fencing topped with loops of barbed wire.

Unsure of what he was seeing, he veered to the right to get closer to it. The wind quieted as he followed the skinny road approaching the fence, behind which rows of airplanes sat under the sun, gleaming white and silver. He pulled over just outside the lot and took Lionel with him right up to it, clutching the chain link. There must have been hundreds of them, some commercial jets with peeling logos, some private aircraft that looked ready for takeoff. There was a helicopter, all white primer and unfinished edges, and beside it a jet engine with no jet.

Shep wandered around the perimeter and stopped at a junkyard of sorts, piles and piles of plane parts that looked, all together, like the aftermath of a cataclysmic crash.

"Where are we?" he said to Lionel.

A sudden breeze blew dust into his mouth. He looked back at the rows of airplanes, the detached helicopter blades and broken wings, and wondered about the planes that flew above him in the desert, the planes that alerted him to the fact that fighting had begun, that the war was real, just when he'd come to accept the monotony of transporting equipment to and fro, day after day, with no end in sight. He could call up the smell of his truck's interior at will, the mix of body odor and gasoline, and the sand that ground its way into the upholstery just as it settled in the folds of his clothes, in his hair, in his mouth. And his truck, where was it now? He supposed it was scrap too, melted down maybe, or in pieces, baking under the same sun, someplace far from here.

A wave of fatigue ran like warm water through his blood. He slumped forward and blinked down at the cracked, ancient earth.

What was Lila doing right now? Maybe her shift was already over. Maybe she was back in her apartment, watching TV with her roommate on a secondhand futon, eating microwave popcorn.

He let Lionel down to pee in the weeds that grew up under the fence, and the two got back in the car. He wished he could shut the sun out, curl up in the backseat and sleep like the dead. There were times back in the Gulf when it had been so easy to lose sight of the difference between day and night. After air attacks had set the oil fields ablaze, when the Iraqis set more fires to confuse the Allied forces, the smoke traveled far enough, and thick enough, to blacken the desert so you couldn't see ten feet in front of your vehicle. Other times, traveling by night, when illumination rounds were fired for better visibility, the night was turned, instantly, into day. It was easy to get disoriented. He wasn't the only one.

Lionel whined.

"What's the matter? You thirsty?"

Shep pulled a bottle of water out from under the passenger seat and poured it into a paper cup, which Lionel lapped up with gusto. He threw the cup on the floor and took a mini bottle of rum out of the glove compartment, drank it in one pull and put the emptied bottle back.

He looked down at the dog, who was now burying his nose deep in a crevice of the passenger seat. "We need a rest. That'll sort us out."

9

Shep found a cheap motel not far from the airplane graveyard and snuck Lionel in to avoid the added pet fee. He pulled the heavy motel drapes, shutting the day down hours before nightfall, then undressed and slid himself into the creaky, tight-sheeted bed. Lionel snored on the bathroom floor.

He dreamt himself back to Nebraska, as he so often did, not because he longed for the place but because, even after these two years, his new life hadn't yet settled into his unconscious. He'd followed Lila to California on a whim, because he realized in a fit of optimism that nobody would stop him, but it was as though not all of him had made the trip. His dreamlife hovered above the tall grass with the fireflies, when it wasn't buried with the chiggers in the soil.

***

He was five years old, and stood on tiptoes to rest his chin on the top of the fence at the hog farm of some half-step-uncle twice removed, where his mom had dropped him off with a wet kiss. He was a strange babysitter, certainly, the man in coveralls with one lazy eye, but she'd told him to follow "Uncle Chet" wherever he went, and Chet nodded as he hosed down the pens so they stayed muddy. John, still Johnny then, made eye contact with a sow inside the fence, her snout caked in mud, her eyes fierce black marbles.

There were new piglets who rolled in the mud, their cloven hooves kicking the air while their fat mother looked on with disinterest, and Chet stopped his watering. Curled beside the mother was a pale parcel, a slimy bundle, barely recognizable for what it was.

"The runt's dead," said Chet.

Johnny watched him climb gingerly over the fence to remove the body, narrating as he did it: *You know what they do,*

Johnny, when a runt dies? You gotta get it out of there fast, or the next thing you know she'll have pale little hooves dangling from her teeth, did you know that Johnny? Awful, hateful animals...

Johnny felt something tickling his neck. From his collar, he pulled a long, curled hair, shed by his mom, that flashed golden in the sunlight. He unclasped his fingers and let it float out on the breeze.

With his gloved hands Chet reached for the runt, stepping lightly so the sow wouldn't hear. He cradled it, just palm-sized, flat between his two hands. Just as he was climbing out again, one mud-caked boot hooked onto the wooden fence, without warning, the sow heaved up onto her feet and charged, a glint in her black eyes as she drove her snout into the backs of Chet's thighs, sending the dead piglet flying back into the mud.

She reared back and was on him again, tearing at his clothes with her teeth.

"Johnny!" Chet called. "Get the pipe!"

Leaning against the barn was a length of metal pipe, rusted at one end, its other end dug into the mud that covered every inch of the farm. He grabbed hold of the pipe as he was told, but it was too heavy for him to pick up. With considerable effort he found he was able to drag it through the muck, his hands barely wrapping around its circumference.

"Hit her! Hit her!" Chet screamed, kicking his legs at the sow's face to no avail. She kept punting and thrashing, holding him against the fence with her front hooves. His good eye squeezed shut while his bad eye stayed open, dilated as black as the sow's.

Johnny tried to lift the pipe but didn't have the strength. Tears ran down his reddened face as he moaned unintelligibly. The pipe grew slippery in his sweating hands.

Chet screamed again. The sow had drawn blood, which now soaked through his coveralls.

Chet's fifteen-year-old son heard the commotion and came flying out from the house, grabbed the pipe from Johnny's hands and began beating furiously at the pig's head until she let go and ran to the other side of the pen, snorting and bucking the whole way. He pulled Chet out and laid him down on the ground panting and whimpering. He was okay, his son said: *You're okay, roughed up a little, but you're okay.*

Johnny just watched, still crying softly. The little piglets all huddled together in one corner of the pen while the sow lay in another, snorting still, scratching her hooves through the mud. He wanted his mother. He was pretty sure he knew which direction she'd driven off in. If he followed the road, he was almost certain he could catch up to her. He started running in the direction of the road, but after a few steps, it became clear that he wasn't making any progress. He was just running in place, his feet sliding in the mud, carving a deepening groove into the earth. He kept running, though, running, running, thinking he would break off and make tracks any moment, but no: he was sinking. Soon he was buried up to his ankles, black mud soaking through his pants. He looked behind him, but Chet and his son were gone. He looked to his right, and the sow looked right back at him, flicking her tongue against her filthy snout.

His feet swished back and forth, digging a trench inch by inch into which he sank lower and lower, his heart contracting like a wilting flower in his chest.

The sun set, the moon emerged, and in an instant the sun rose again; round and round like a rotary dial the days and nights turned. He was knee-deep in the mud now and could no longer move his feet, but merely pumped his arms, crying all the while, days and nights, nights and days. Finally he dropped, landing backwards with a splatter into the mud. He let his hands sink down at his sides, the wet and coolness calming his overheated blood.

Two hands gripped him by the underarms. It was

nighttime, and he was so sleepy. The hands pulled him up and in, and his chin clamped instinctively onto a shoulder.

Mommy, he whispered.

The body carried him a ways, the rhythm of the walk lulling him into a drowsy sort of trance.

No, not Mommy, the body's voice said. *Not Mommy.*

In the distance a siren whined in shrill rhythm with the footsteps that carried him to his grandmother's Buick, red lights like molten sunset glowing from the interstate.

In the motel room, the air conditioner sputtered, its blasting cold air drying out Shep's mouth, hanging open against the thin cotton pillowcase.

Sleep, the voice said, *just go to sleep now.*

But the sirens perturbed the boy. He tried to lift his head from its shoulder perch, but it was so heavy, as though his skull had been replaced with solid lead.

Jesus Christ. The voice grew stern. *Keep your eyes closed. Don't look up, you hear me?*

He didn't listen, pulling with all his might to lift his head, to squirm free from his grandmother's grip, but he was stuck, overwhelmed now by the scent of her lavender perfume and unable to turn his face away from her neck. He struggled and wailed, but couldn't get free.

***

Lionel was already at Shep's side. He'd heard his moaning and the creak of the bedsprings as he jerked left and right. He licked his master's forehead, then his ear. Shep's breath was shallow and quick. His eyes remained shut, his eyeballs visibly rocketing back and forth beneath the thin skin of his eyelids.

Lionel let out a piercing series of barks directly into Shep's ear. Shep's eyes flashed open as he flopped involuntarily over onto his belly and propped himself up on his elbows. The sheets, the dark room, the dog's breath—his body was grown now, no longer trapped.

Lionel crawled into the opening between his elbow and armpit and pushed his wet nose into the hollow of Shep's chest.

"Settle down," he sighed, catching his breath. "You make too much of things, Lionel. You act like every night's the end of the world."

Shep lay down again. He rolled over onto his back and blinked into the cool dark.

10

Shep settled up at the motel's front desk shortly after sunrise with a basset hound-faced clerk who responded to his "Thanks, have a good one" with a wheeze and an impatient nod.

He'd taken a quick shower, forgetting that he didn't have any clean clothes to change into, and now his wet hair was dripping down the collar of his ripe, wrinkled shirt. "Come on," he said to Lionel as he started the car. "We've got ground to make up."

Upon exiting the freeway, he spied a landscaping crew digging out the flowery, hillocked entryway to a housing development that bore effusive banners: *Beautiful Townhomes! If you lived here you'd be home by now!* He watched the men who were digging, sweating already in the faint early sun. It would only get worse as the hours rolled on.

The first civilian job he'd managed to hold onto after returning from the war was on a crew replacing the sprinkler system at the old Kearney mall. He'd needed the money then, after months spent holed up in his grandmother's house, watching her watch television.

He'd been digging a trench one Tuesday while his boss, Todd, assembled the new hoses, stiff and plasticky smelling, fresh from the hardware store. It was nine a.m., just when the Indian summer sun was ripening, causing Shep to squint down at his own canvas-gloved hands digging himself sweaty. He stopped to catch his breath and grab a drink of water. Todd was taking a break too, smoking a cigarette in the front seat of his pickup with his legs hanging out the open door, his drive-time radio crackling from the speakers.

Shep leaned his head back, taking a big gulp from a jug of water, and when he opened his eyes, there stood Lorene on the other side of the driveway. At first he thought she was a shadow, a sun spot, any kind of illusion sunlight could conjure. It was the rhythm of her walk that convinced him she was no hallucination, the careful sway that still looped through his subconscious on lonely nights. Shep hadn't seen her in almost a year. He stood gawking, taking in the hang of her blonde hair over one eye, the sun glowing against the top of her head so she seemed surrounded by a pale mist, a warmth that entirely encompassed her perimeter. He was gripped by the memory of her skin, her hip bones in his hands, the humidity of her sour breath in his ear.

It wasn't until she began walking up the driveway, just ten yards from where he crouched, grass-stained knees dug into the hillside, that he noticed the cotton sling attached to Lorene's chest, out of which a chubby arm reached up and traced her chin. Shep stared openly, but she didn't notice him. She whispered *shhhh*, and squeezed her hand around the baby's trawling little fingers.

"Lorene!" he called out, startling himself. The impulse had overtaken him unbidden. His voice sounded hollow, tinny and little-used.

Lorene stopped, hesitating a moment before turning slightly toward him. He rose to his feet, dropping his shovel into the half-dug trench.

For just a second, too quickly to register or mean much of anything, her neutral gaze met his hopeful one. He tried to latch onto her stare, but it was as though she were looking past him, at some point on a far-off horizon. Then Lorene clutched the baby closer to her before turning back the way she was going, toward the entrance of the department store that anchored the mall.

Shep followed her a few paces but stopped short. Already he was doing math in his head.

It was a problem he revisited constantly, estimating the girl's age that day versus the time that had passed since he and Lorene were together. If only he could have held the child, seen her face, then he would know beyond a shadow of a doubt…but he did know. Something like that doesn't nag at a person for no reason. It was destiny pulling him— and something was pulling him. He felt it as sure as his sleeplessness, his headaches and weakened stomach, the magnetic reach of blood.

Shep pulled into the lot at Parkdale's with Lionel sitting upright in his lap, eye-level with the steering wheel. He hoped that Hung might've gotten donuts. He cracked the window for the dog, whispering, *come on now, come on, I'll be right back, you know*, as the dog whimpered and clucked like a sad little chicken.

He didn't know what time it was, since the clock on his dashboard had quit working some years earlier. The door swung open with a jingle, but there was nobody behind the counter.

"Hung?" he said. He glanced toward the pizza counter, then toward the back room. "Hello?"

He made his way toward the fridge to get his morning beer but stopped short at the canned goods aisle. Hung's dad was facing the corn, stooped like a hunchback.

"Mr. Phan?" Shep said.

Hung's dad slowly bent his neck down and to the left to look back at Shep. The back of his hand was shaking against the metal shelf. His mouth was shut tight, but his eyes shined like they were encased in cellophane, and he looked twenty pounds skinnier than he'd been the last time Shep had seen him in the store.

Suddenly Mr. Phan emitted a high-pitched whine like a tea kettle.

"Hey, hey hey," Shep said, placing a hand on his shoulder, "it's okay, it's okay…"

Mr. Phan's eyes darted back and forth in a panic, as though he didn't know the sound was coming from his own throat, then settled on Shep's face, the two men staring at each other, neither with any idea of what was happening.

The rattling of Mr. Phan's knuckles escalated to the point that a can toppled down to the floor. He was still making the sound, but it had quieted to a less urgent register. Shep let go of his shoulder and backed up. He craned his neck to search the corners for any sign of Hung.

Then he heard the flush of the back office's toilet. A second later Hung strolled out.

"Hung, you better come here," Shep called out.

"Shit," Hung sighed.

He came to them and grabbed his father's hand, whispering something unintelligible. His father didn't look at him, but grew quiet.

"Hang out for a minute," Hung said. Shep nodded, and watched as Hung gingerly led his father to the back of the store and up the stairs to their apartment, holding on patiently as Mr. Phan navigated the way up, dragging his barely-working left leg up after he'd climbed each one with his right.

Shep took his beer and a package of cheese crackers behind the counter, his heart still racing. Mr. Phan's stricken face called his grandmother to mind, the same confusion, the same implacable fear, a face burned into his memory. How many times had he guided her through such episodes—in the kitchen, in her bedroom, in every room of that quiet, festering house—and yet each time always felt like the unfolding of a brand new nightmare. Mr. Phan's particular malady wasn't Shep's burden to bear, but he was around, wasn't he? He was *here*, witnessing the widening gulf between the practical and the incomprehensible, and the points at which they converged.

A few minutes later Hung jogged back down the stairs. Shep got up from Hung's stool behind the register and took his own seat.

"He okay?"

Hung shook his head distractedly.

"No?"

"There's gotta be some new kind of question," Hung said, still shaking his head at nothing. He pulled out his half-done crossword and tapped his pencil's eraser against the counter.

"Can't watch a person twenty-four seven, everybody knows that…" Shep heard his own guilt talking.

Hung ran his tongue up and down along his inner cheek.

Shep backed off and tore into his crackers. For a few minutes he ate and drank in silence while Hung hunkered down with the crossword. The crackers had a stale, chemical taste to them as he chewed in bovine fashion, gnawing out an orangey paste between his teeth. He could now, if he wanted to, tell Hung how his grandmother's episodes had gotten easier to deal with as he adjusted his expectations of normalcy. If he thought it would help, he could tell Hung that he'd better start receding into his head now, already, before it was too late to disengage. But when he tried to formulate an opening, it caved in under the pressure of the past and his fear of calling it up here. Parkdale's was an oasis, outside time and lacking in place, where the white noise of refrigeration and fluorescence filled in for conversation, where customers broke up the hours into easy compartments, as tidy and symmetrical as the store's aisles. Shep sensed that details of his past would rope Parkdale's into his troubled orbit. He wanted to spare Hung from that, he thought, meaning he wanted to spare himself.

"I can pay my tab on the first of the month, when my check comes in," he finally said, offering the only tangible help he could think of.

"We go over this every month, dude. Learn to accept gratitude. Makes life easier."

Shep scratched the back of his neck. The deal had been struck the morning after Mr. Phan's stroke, when Shep dropped them off at home. When Shep got out of the car to open her door, Hung's mother launched herself into his chest. She threw her arms around him and spoke in impassioned Vietnamese.

"She says everything's free for you. She says our store is your store," Hung translated, gently tugging on his mother's fingers to loosen her grip on Shep's shirt. "She's…emotional."

"*Tab*," Hung teased now. "What is this, *Cheers*? Ain't nobody keeping track of any tab."

Shep kept a handwritten list in his car of everything he took from the store, with the approximate price of each item in a second column. He wanted to be prepared when the family's gratitude ran out, as everything eventually did.

Shep finished off his beer and crackers, his stomach settled, placid at last. He realized Lionel must be hungry too, and rose from his seat to browse the dog food shelf. He selected a bag that featured a golden retriever puppy jumping through a hula hoop.

"You ever go anywhere without that dog?" Hung called from the front. He was still bouncing his pencil's eraser against the counter, tap, tap, tap.

Shep stepped out to the parking lot and tore open the bag before he opened the car door and held out the kibble in palmfuls, which Lionel burrowed his nose into, chomping and grunting. He patted the dog's back, soothing himself, drowsing into a reverie of their first meeting behind a diner some fifty miles west of White Sands, New Mexico, and taking refuge together on the road to California.

Shep had risen to pay the cashier following a late afternoon breakfast of biscuits and gloppy white gravy when he was struck by a coughing fit. He dropped his cash, the coins spinning and clattering on the counter, before stumbling out the swinging glass doors and around to the back of the restaurant. He braced himself against a dumpster that reeked of piss and cigarette butts as he doubled over, still coughing, a string of saliva dribbling from his bottom lip.

When he opened his eyes, he was startled to find a little brown dog looking back at him, his wiry tail wagging against the dumpster.

"Where'd you come from?" It came out as a thin whisper from his ripped-raw throat. He looked up to see if there was an owner someplace, but there was no one. The only thing he did see, in fact, was a wall of dust approaching from the north, bulging toward them from the ground all the way up to an opaque ceiling of clouds that made the town, such as it was, feel closed off from time and geography. It was accumulating mass and closing in quickly, winds at sixty miles per hour.

A haboob. He'd been warned about them in Saudi but never experienced one firsthand. Without a second thought, he grabbed the dog and ran to his car. He could hear the wind barreling south, and quickly rolled up all the windows. As the dust storm drew near, Shep closed his eyes and held the dog close to his chest, stroking his soft, collarless throat. The car rattled like a tin can. He opened his eyes, and every window was clouded brown, the car a warm cocoon against the beating wind. He held the dog tighter, and the dog didn't resist.

When the storm had passed with a lowering hush, Shep set him down on the passenger seat, and was taken aback all over again by the clarity of this strange dog's gaze.

"Hello," he said. The dog wagged his tail. Shep continued petting him, and his hands came away greasy and streaked gray. Though the dog's fur was filthy, he was well fed, wherever he'd come from. Shep turned on the windshield wipers, releasing a spray of wiper fluid to clear a semi-circular view outside.

"Suppose we ought to get going," he said to the dog, who was in his lap now, staring up, all wet brown eyes and matted muzzle. "Suppose we ought to find us a place for the night." He didn't call him anything yet, wasn't sure what he was going to do. The dog nudged Shep's chin with his nose as if to say, *The clock is ticking*, as if to say, *Let's go*.

Shep blinked. Lionel had finished off the handful of kibble and was licking crumbs from the webs of his fingers. What day was it? Shep tried to count while Lionel began sniffing around the bag, looking for seconds. Tuesday, the Budweiser delivery came. Wednesday, Lila worked the breakfast shift. Was it still Wednesday? No. He'd spent the night in a motel room. It was morning again. It was Thursday. *Thursday, Thursday*, he thought, imprinting the word into his consciousness. *If the days run together, is there more time or less, and if time is running out, what am I waiting for?* The thought broke in like déjà vu or a shock from the past, nudging him forward as he held onto the ledge. Lionel kept licking his palm, though the crumbs were all gone. He lapped up Shep's salt, and Shep held his hand out, letting him.

"Hey, you," he said, finally pulling his hand away. "Breakfast is over."

He was startled, then, as he glanced out the window to find Eugene, Hung's parking lot antagonist, leaning against the rear bumper of a white SUV. He was staring into the Parkdale's storefront, alone, an ignored cigarette burning between his fingers. Shep looked for Eugene's usual posse, but they were scarce today, no extra cars clogging the lot, no card games or raucous laughter. Maybe he and Hung had come to an agreement. He watched as Eugene let his cigarette drop to the pavement, never breaking his stare.

What was holding his interest? Hung? Or Hung's father? Had he witnessed Mr. Phan's episode? Had he been watching the whole time? Shep squinted—examining Eugene's relaxed but pointed expression, eyes narrow and mouth curled in some private satisfaction—and thought better of his earlier theory. A truce seemed unlikely.

Finally, Eugene stood and ambled back to the water store, propping the door open to let the breeze in. Best not to mention anything to Hung, Shep reasoned. No sense in fueling his grudge.

"What time is it?" Shep asked over the electronic bells as he reentered the store.

Hung slipped his phone from his pocket. "Eight'n' change."

"You okay if I take off? I mean is your dad okay? I got something I've gotta do."

"How many times I gotta remind you you don't work here?"

"I'll be back later, I promise."

Pigeons were clustered outside, having descended on a bread crust that was soaked in spilled coffee, the white paper cup crushed beside them as they bobbed their heads spastically up and down, their prehistoric feet splashing in the puddle. Shep closed his eyes a moment against the sun, listening to the pigeons' scratches and coos with the sound of cars rushing continuously in the background, expansive as the ocean.

He started the car, revved the engine once, twice, and waited. Lionel retired to the back seat. At the other end of the strip mall, a black sports car sped into the lot's opposite entrance and swung in tight beside Eugene's SUV. A pale, scrawny twenty-something with gelled black hair flew from the driver's seat, worrying his keychain in his hand as he hustled toward the water store, where a figure, obscured by the sun's glare, guided him inside by the elbow, shut the door behind him and flipped a sign, "back in 10 minutes," while Shep waited for his car to coax itself back to life.

A third tap on the gas and the Ford's engine purred, robust and ready. He eased out of the lot just as the Cowboy was settling in at the side of the building, arranging his things just so, looking up at the sun, looking back down.

Thursday was Lila's day off from the café. He'd caught a peek at the schedule on the breakroom wall, where he'd taken a detour on his way back from the bathroom, down the rubber-matted hallway and past the bustle and heat of the kitchen. He'd made a mental note of her shifts highlighted in blue and sauntered out with his head down before anyone could notice he wasn't any customer.

Every Saturday he went to the library to check the audition websites: *Casting Direct, Backstage.com* and a few others. He wrote down the days and times of the auditions she was suited for, the girl-next-door parts, the ones that asked for blondes in particular, for women aged eighteen to twenty-eight. He wrote down the days and times of all the open calls and the actors' showcases, where young hopefuls would perform monologues in theaters less than half-full of two-bit agents and managers. Though he wished her success, he hoped he'd have a little more time before she landed a big-time agent who would set up her auditions for her, making it trickier for him to keep tabs.

But there was nothing marked down for today in the notebook he kept under the passenger seat. She kept herself so busy it seemed that he hadn't encountered a day like this before, a blank square on the calendar he'd printed off at the library and glued to the notebook pages, the squares filled with notes and abbreviations in shaky ballpoint.

He drove on toward her duplex, planning to wait and see what she would do. It raised a kind of giddiness in him, a feeling that he was about to see her from a different angle, that the puzzle of her personality would open itself up with a little breathing room. He hoped she would go to the beach or, better yet, the movies. He would buy a ticket for the same show and sit a few seats away, watching for her reactions, what made her laugh, what made her gasp or cry. She was running herself ragged, he wanted to tell her. She seemed anxious all the time.

He parked a few yards down from the bus stop, keeping an eye on her front door from a quarter-block down. Smoothing his hair while the engine cooled, he caught sight of the Wraith sitting at the stop. He'd seen her a few times in Lila's neighborhood. Her hair was white and stringy, her face sunburned to a crisp. She smoked Marlboro Reds while engaging in a fitful argument with herself that would periodically send her flying up from the bench to pace and mutter more emphatically. But her clothes were clean, her shoes in good shape. She puzzled him in the same way the Cowboy at Parkdale's did. He wondered too where she slept at night. In the forty years before he'd moved to California he'd only seen a handful of homeless people. Here there were roaming orphans everywhere you looked. The woman pulled a roll of Necco wafers from her pocket and began chomping them furiously, one after another, while her cigarette burned on in her other hand.

He watched her, mesmerized at her abiding anger. Her body was electrified with it, the veins in her hands and neck popping. Then she noticed him. She stopped her hissing, dropped her cigarette in the gutter, marched over to his window and gave it a wallop, first with her palm and then with her closed fist. She was yelling, but her words came so fast he couldn't make them out. Lionel barked, but Shep sat motionless, avoiding eye contact. He gripped the wheel and stared forward as she rattled the window over and over. She threw the candy against the hood of the car with a hollow thunk, then stood back. She was so quiet all of a sudden that

Shep felt it safe to look again, with lack of focus as protection. He would look toward her, but not at her, not into her eyes.

She was still there, but hung back a few feet, empty hands at her sides. He glanced quickly up toward her face, and his heart jumped. She was staring at him with a look of such disgust, such naked contempt. No one had looked at him like that in years, not since his grandmother's mind had gone completely, when she screamed *Get out get out get out!* until her voice grew hoarse while he laid out a breakfast of sliced fruit and apple juice on her bedside table.

But there seemed to be a lucidity in this woman's rage that made Shep stop and wonder. He'd been watching her as a baffled observer, a garden-variety voyeur, and she knew it. She could see right through him, and for a second, he felt he knew what she was thinking: they were no different. She feasted on anger while he wallowed in fear, but other than that, he was as much an orphan as she was.

After a minute or so she turned around and jammed her hands in her coat pockets. He watched in the rearview mirror as she walked briskly up the street, her head high and gait purposeful. She had other business, and he wasn't that important. But he was shaken. Lionel was shaken too. He growled as if in warning, in case she came back.

"It's okay, buddy. You're okay." He lifted the dog onto his lap and scratched behind his ears.

It was another hour before Lila emerged from the building, fiddling with her hair as she approached the bus stop, as she always did, never satisfied with the style she'd settled on before walking out the door. He started the car as soon as he saw her, giving it time to warm up before her bus came. She checked her makeup while she waited, pressing her lips together and spreading them to check her teeth for traces of lipstick.

The Wraith reappeared like a specter in his rearview mirror, coming back up the street to reclaim the spot she'd decided was her turf today. His heart raced. He could see that Lila's bus was coming from the opposite direction, but the Wraith was coming quickly too, and if she got there first, she'd likely come at him again, and draw enough attention that Lila would surely notice. Or worse yet, she might take Lila for an interloper, a new target.

Shep watched helplessly, his eyes darting back and forth between the heaving, galumphing bus and the whiplash swiftness of the old woman, paralyzed in silent panic.

Miraculously, the bus pulled up just in time, the Wraith still a quarter-block away. Lila climbed up the steps and showed her pass, and Shep peeled out behind the bus.

In the rearview mirror, he could see the Wraith's sandpaper face light up with renewed vengeance as she recognized his car. She stood at the corner, holding it, warming herself with it, while the potholed road stretched out between them.

11

Lila dismounted on a sunny street in Burbank, the sidewalks and buildings cast in an orange light. She walked two blocks to a glassy blue-gray building, the entrance of which was crowded with a lineup of people reviewing the contents of folders and smoothing their hair. Lila took a spot at the back of the line and pulled a folder of her own out of a big suede shoulder bag with fringe hanging off it.

Central Casting, said the big block letters on the front of the building. Shep took a spot across the street, where he could see through its glass doors. The line was moving quickly. Upon entering, people were handed papers to fill out before proceeding to a long table where two women with clipboards took the papers and directed them to a photographer across the room. There, each person stood before a gray backdrop to pose for a series of photos before exiting the building the way they'd come, as if on a conveyor belt.

If this was an audition, it was unlike any of the ones Lila usually went on, where she would disappear into the guts of a multi-story building where he would be lucky to catch a glimpse of her entering an elevator through sun-glared revolving doors. Here he could see everything. It didn't look like any audition. The people didn't all look like actors, either, with their mysterious porelessness, their eyes sparkling with desperation. There were some of those, sure, but some of these people were old, some fat. One woman wore Daffy Duck scrubs, as though she'd just come from her shift in the pediatric wing at St. Joseph's Hospital. He watched Lila, her hair hanging down over her face as she crouched on the floor to fill out papers, then it was her turn in front of the camera.

As she posed for her first photo, her eyes flitted wildly against the flash, her mouth set in a glossy grin. The photographer took several more, and with each flash, it was as though she was steeling herself, her teeth clenched tighter, her veins pulled taut, the camera flash bleaching the bloodshot from her eyes. When she was waved away from the gray backdrop, her face relaxed itself instantly. She glided back into the dimmer light, pulled out her phone and dialed, beginning a conversation that continued as she stepped into a sandwich shop a few doors down and took her place in another line. He watched her tap her foot, cross her arms, stare at the sandwich shop's ceiling fan.

Shep's underarms had grown swampy. He rolled down his window, but still, he felt overheated, trapped in his own body. He tapped his knuckle against the steering wheel, drumming a quickening beat.

"Lionel, will you be quiet if I leave you here? Just for a minute?"

Lionel was asleep in the backseat. Shep cracked the other windows and stepped out of the car quietly, shutting the door as softly as he could, but he could hear Lionel erupt into a fit of barking as he waited for traffic to clear so he could jaywalk.

There were only three people ahead of him in line. The papers he was given included lines for him to fill out his name, contact info, sizes for various clothing articles and shoes, measurements in inches, hair color, eye color, date of birth. He found a pen, but didn't know all his sizes and certainly didn't know any of his measurements. He looked around the room and noticed a pile of tape measures being guarded by another clipboard sheriff. He grabbed one and hid in a corner to size himself up. He still didn't know what this was or why he was doing it as he pulled the tape measure across his belly and wrote down his somewhat depressing waist measurement in fading blue ballpoint.

The woman with the clipboard at the back of the room held out her hand for his form. She frowned.

"License, Social Security card…?"

Shep peered down the line and saw that everyone else had their identification ready in hand. He pulled out his wallet.

"Sorry about that."

"And this is supposed to be in *black* ink. It says so at the top of the page."

"Oh, I thought since I found the pen right over there…"

She rolled her eyes and set his cards on the glass of the photocopier behind her, tapping it with her acrylic nails, painted in a hot pink and gold zebra print that was incongruous with her understated black clothing and fresh-scrubbed face.

"Number two twenty-eight," she said, handing him his cards. She quickly filled out a small piece of posterboard with his name and a six-digit number and handed that over atop a color pamphlet.

Waiting his turn at the photographer's station, Shep wondered how much time he had until Lila finished lunch and moved on to the next thing on her private agenda. He looked at his watch. He wasn't wearing a watch. In any case, he'd better run out and check on her, he thought. This was a stupid idea, not *even* an idea, just a thing he'd done, another pointless activity he'd begun with his brain tied up elsewhere, one that he'd only questioned when he was already knee deep in the middle of it.

"Two twenty-seven," the assistant called, and a middle-aged man with thinning hair parted awkwardly to one side stepped forward in front of the backdrop.

"Hold your card up higher," the photographer said.

The man complied. "Do you want me to do a profile too? Maybe one with my jacket on?"

"Quiet."

The man cleared his throat and grinned, his teeth squat yellow rectangles.

"Now no smile," the photographer said, snapping two more shots with the man staring intensely at the camera, too intensely, it seemed, like he was trying hard not to blink.

"Are they going to call me?" the man asked as the photographer's assistant herded him out the door.

"You have to call in every day you're available to work," she said, indicating the pamphlet he'd rolled up in his left palm. "It's all in there."

"Two twenty-eight."

Shep stepped forward and held up his card. His expression of bewilderment didn't go unnoticed by the photographer, a man Shep's age who styled himself much younger, with a goatee and spiky blond hair and a clatter of silver bracelets around one wrist. He whistled.

"Look at me, bro."

"Oh, uh…" Shep gave a half smile. The camera flashed twice in quick succession.

"Now don't smile, just look at me."

Shep looked at the wall above the camera to avoid being

blinded by the flash. His mouth hung slightly open, making him look either pensive or slow.

"You're done."

As the assistant led him by the elbow—another clipboard woman, with blond hair and inch-long black roots—she asked, "Have you ever done any acting?"

"Huh?"

"You've got a look. You should keep your hair like that. It works."

The woman wasn't smiling as though she'd just given him a compliment. She was squinting at his hair, then his face, appraising him.

"Uh, thanks," he said, and stepped outside. He threw a hand up across his brow in defense against the sun's glare as iridescent spots appeared and dissolved in his peripheral vision.

Across the street Lionel was staring plaintively out the window. A spot in the center was smeared where he'd been pressing his nose ever since Shep left him.

"Hang on," Shep mouthed, and hurried down to the sandwich shop where he'd last seen Lila, so flustered still that he pulled the shop's door open just as Lila herself was pushing it from inside. The two collided, and Lila gasped. Shep's stomach dropped.

"Pardon me, pardon me," he repeated in a quiet panic. "I didn't see you, I didn't mean to…"

Lila smiled and waved off his groveling. She took a sip from her straw and nodded at the pamphlet in his hand.

"You an actor?"

"What?" For a long moment he had no idea what she was talking about. His memory before this moment seemed to him like a disorganized series of flashing lights and sounds.

"You signed up to be an extra?"

"Oh, oh, yeah. Yes, I guess I did." Shep's breathing slowed to a manageable rate, but he was still barely present, his consciousness already reeling at some remote point in the near future.

Lila stepped past him out to the sidewalk.

"You think we're kidding ourselves?" she said.

She fished the big tortoiseshells out of her purse and slipped them on, looking, yes, like a damn movie star. She was the most beautiful thing he'd ever seen, her face like the closing shot of a film both heartbreaking and achingly hopeful, with music swelling as the camera panned across a city of hills and valleys, of traffic dipping and rising like colored water.

"I don't think so..." Shep said, "...but who am I to say?"

She smiled. Oh, how she smiled. "I guess it's too late now."

With that she turned on her heel and made her way back to the bus stop. Shep stared after her, unable to move. When he realized he was blocking the door, he stepped back and pulled it open for a woman leaving the shop with two small kids, a boy and a girl.

"What do you say?" the woman chided.

"Thank yooooouuuu," the kids droned in unison.

The boy trailed a little behind his mom and sister, kicking the plastic bag that hung from his wrist. He stopped in front of Shep and looked up into his face.

"You're welcome," Shep said, still watching Lila as she walked away.

The boy gave a herky-jerky salute, then lowered his hand to rub his nose as he ran to the car.

12

There was hardly any traffic at all. It was as though the streets had cleared for him in acknowledgment of this unexpected boon. Lionel puttered restlessly about the passenger seat, dragging his slightly overgrown claws across the upholstery in a digging motion. At a red light, Shep reached out and scratched behind Lionel's ears.

The radio played "Rhiannon," a song he thought of as one of Lorene's favorites. He presumed it was because she identified with the titular girl, imagined herself as a *bird in flight*, a *cat in the dark*, the kind of girl people wrote songs about. He pictured her closing her eyes when it came on the classic rock station, leaning back on the headrest and rolling her neck from side to side, her clavicle gleaming with late-summer sweat. Though it made him smile, he had a lingering suspicion that this was a calculated ruse on her part to create the impression that she felt music more deeply than other people did. He turned it up now and sank into the sound of Stevie Nicks' voice as it lulled him into a bone-loosening reverie. He thought back to nights on the road in Nebraska, rambling in no particular direction with the windows down, all alone, late into the night.

He wanted to remember a specific night with Lorene, with this song, but he couldn't call up the memory. In fact, he couldn't place it at all, this image he had of her swaying in the passenger seat, whisper-singing, *wouldn't you love to love her.* He didn't know whether it was stuck in some untapped layer of his memory or whether he'd conjured this image out of pure longing. Was it her song, or his song for her, imposed by unanswered desire? His memory or his daydream? He couldn't always tell the difference, and there was no one to ask.

Shep turned the radio off. He wondered what Lorene would think if she knew he was here, that all her efforts to keep his daughter from knowing him were for naught now that the girl was twenty-five and in charge of her own life. She would find out eventually. She'd left Harner when Lila was a toddler, had met a man in the new town and married soon after. But it was only a matter of time until he and Lila would come to know each other. And a person may leave a small town, but the town remembers. Just as news had traveled to him that Lorene's little girl was moving to California to get into the movies, there'd be no keeping word from getting around that Lila Olson—Lorene's husband's name, the name she'd rushed to bestow on herself and her daughter the Monday after the wedding as if to pretend four-year-old Lila was newly born, safely within wedlock, no doubt at Lorene's mother's urging—had been reunited with the man any thinking person had to suspect was her real father.

It didn't give him joy to imagine her horror. But he couldn't help rolling it over in his mind, one memory about which he had no doubts: the look on Lorene's face when he approached her walking to her car after her GED class when Lila was still in diapers.

The parking lot was nearly empty, dirty slush clinging to its corners. Shep had been waiting for her, had parked at the far end of the lot with his head sticking out the window because the windows fogged too quickly when he had them rolled up. When he saw her car, he sprung from his.

"John? What are…how long have you been waiting here?" Her initial confusion turned quickly to hostility.

"It doesn't matter. Lorene, you've got to talk to me. I'm not going anywhere until we figure this out."

She sighed and pulled her coat tighter.

"I know. Lorene, I know she's mine."

"She's not."

"Come on…"

She opened her car door and stuck the key in the ignition to warm up the engine. He could see his breath, and hers too.

"I've got to go. It's freezing out here," she said, rubbing her palms together.

"I know I left you hanging, but I'm here now. I want to help you. You have to let me."

Lorene rolled her eyes. "For fuck's sake."

She looked pale and weary, as though her blood had been sapped of color and now ran clear and cold.

"It was nine months, almost exactly," he said, laying out the irrefutable fact.

"Check your math, John. You dodged a bullet. Most guys would be relieved." She shook her head, sitting down in the driver's seat. She pulled a cigarette from a fresh pack in the cup holder, dropped its cellophane wrapper on the floor.

"Why are you lying to me? Don't you want a fresh start?"

"That's exactly what I want." She rubbed her temple. "Jesus, John, please. This is getting..." She looked up at him as she pulled the door shut and rolled down her window. Her eyes softened.

In an unexpected move, she reached out and squeezed his hand, then gently pulled away. She switched the cigarette to her left hand and let it dangle out the window as she stared out the frosted windshield.

"Lorene," he said, almost a whimper. He'd said the name so many times it went beyond Lorene herself to become a plea to the heavens, a stand-in for his general heartache.

Hearing it seemed to snap her out of whatever sympathy she'd been edging toward. She shook her head and held the cigarette between her teeth as she turned on the wipers and put the car in reverse. He watched it roll down the gravel driveway, bright red against the darkening gray sky, her headlights flicking on just as she pulled out onto the road.

And he couldn't help picturing the way she'd surely have to sit down and brace herself, hold the phone against her chest and collect her thoughts, when Lila asked if she could bring him home with her next Christmas for a little reunion. His mind raced, imagining shopping for gifts for her, accompanying her on a flight, their shoulders and knees touching in the cramped airline seats, the way the world would grow smaller and smaller around them until there was nobody else, and his only name would be *Dad*. But he was going too fast. It was only spring. Today was one day. Tomorrow would be another. He tried to slow his breathing.

It had grown hot in the car again. He rolled down his window.

Or maybe…maybe they wouldn't tell Lorene at all. They could make the world even smaller.

He'd never had a dad of his own, had gotten the brush-off from his grandmother whenever he'd asked about him. He remembered sitting at the kitchen table with his cheek pressed to its surface and his legs dangling from the chair, his grandmother slicing an apple at the counter.

Gran, he'd asked, *was my dad sad? When they told him? Did he cry?*

She didn't look up from the counter. When she was finished, she set the plateful of apple slices in front of him. She licked her middle and index fingers and tried in vain to smooth down his cowlick, pressing it to the back of his head, until she gave up and left the room.

Lionel began to whine.

"Are you hungry already? Settle down, we're almost there."

When he got to his intersection, the street was blocked by three police cars fanned out from curb to curb, with uniformed cops milling about on each corner. Shep went down another block and parked at a meter with a plastic bag tied around the top. He returned on foot with Lionel held to his chest. A long line of cars flashed their left turn signals to follow the detour away from Coldwater.

"Uh," he said to one of the cops on the corner. "What's going on?"

"I can't let you pass just yet."

"But…I live here. Can you at least tell me why?"

Shep looked over the cop's shoulder. At the end of the block there were two fire trucks with red lights spinning. Yellow tape had been spread across the driveways of both strip malls, the one that housed Parkdale's and the one just across from it that was anchored by the H&J liquor store and a Launderland.

He stepped back from the cop and wandered back to the opposite corner, and for a moment tried to figure out how he could get through to his building. He looked through the bars of a neighboring complex and mentally traced the path through parking lots and hedges. But he couldn't get through the fence in the first place. He wrapped his hand around one of the rusted iron bars.

Shep took a seat on a nearby planter and held Lionel in his lap. He could feel panic beginning to rise in his body. Silently he repeated the phrase he'd been taught the first time he'd gone to the ER with a panic attack, a few months after returning from the war: *I am uncomfortable, but I am not in any danger. I am not in any danger. I am uncomfortable, but I am not in any danger.* Sometimes that worked. Other times, he remembered something a fellow recruit had said to him in basic, as they were running an endless round of laps and Shep's lungs were on fire, his legs ready to give out:

Remember, Johanssen had said, slapping Shep's back as he passed, *it won't last forever and it can't kill you.* Shep had wheezed and scowled at the time, but the words had since taken on a meaning for him far beyond what Johanssen had intended.

It won't last forever and it can't kill you, Shep repeated in his head now. But what was *it*? His pulse climbed. Lionel licked the soft skin on the inside of his wrist, which calmed him some.

He got up again to seek answers from one of the cops, but stopped when he saw the Cowboy seated at the other end of the planter. Shep didn't know if he'd been there the whole time or whether he'd just appeared. He sat in his standard posture, one hand slung over the handle of his shopping cart.

"Hey," Shep said, approaching. "Do you know why they've got the street blocked? Were you here?"

The Cowboy looked up at Shep. He pressed his lips together and blinked with heavy lids, like a horse at pasture. He removed his hat, wiped his forehead with a red handkerchief, and put the hat back on.

A siren wailed, but Shep couldn't tell if it was coming from his street or another. Every street held ongoing problems, untenable situations, a grid trembling with the weight of what-if. The siren's whine folded itself into the general traffic noise as it traveled north.

Shep sat down beside the Cowboy. A scattering of people from nearby buildings hung out of doors and windows, some taking pictures with their phones, others watching stiffly with arms crossed. Shep scratched Lionel's head.

The Cowboy gripped the handle of his cart. He tapped his toe in a steady rhythm on the pavement, on a little stream, formed by sprinklers, that ran down a crack in the sidewalk.

"Suppose I'll just wait here," he said to the Cowboy. "If you don't mind."

The panic Shep had felt rising only moments before hit a plateau. It held steady in his breathing, in his inability to take in quite enough air, but he no longer felt it was about to engulf him. He looked down at the water running down all the little cracks and dripping down into the gutter. He could close his eyes and try to imagine he was the water, smooth and viscous, slipping noiselessly through the concrete's grooves and pockmarks. But he could only maintain that bodiless serenity for a moment before the reality of his body intruded, with its overheated flesh, its roiling gut and brittle, clanking bones.

PART TWO

1

1991

IRAQIS! There is no difference between your currency and this piece of paper. Worthless money abounds in your land, and the depravity is increasing, with no remedy in sight. The suffering continues, there is no food, but dirt is all over. There is no soap or water. The darkness surrounds all. The electrical power is cut off, you are in dire straits, you have sexual urges and needs, but your women are not with you. You fear Saddam but do not disobey. Death can be immediate and you can do nothing. WOE the Iraqis ...soldiers, civilians, old people, youth, women and men. The time has come for you to rise up and come into the streets and alleyways...

They'd begun collecting them, the leaflets that were dropped strategically from above. No one knew if they were being picked up, read, or understood by the Iraqis. But Shep—his guard name since basic training, his only name now—and the rest of his convoy, when they found them in the sand, when they had to stop to repair vehicles or refuel, when they wandered away from the roads, the acrid smell of the burning oilfields ever present in the air, they would squirrel them away in their various pockets. Everyone knew the war would be over soon, and they were grasping at every bit of evidence that they'd been there, that they'd done something palpable, even if they'd mostly fought to stay awake as they drove long hours on the main supply roads, as they watched and waited while the real fighting happened overhead, nearby, somewhere else.

The paper was wrinkled, aged by the sun, though it had likely only been dropped a day earlier. Shep folded it into quarters and slid it into the cargo pocket at his knee.

"Hey," said Anderson, approaching. "You ever get used to that smell?"

Shep shrugged. He supposed he was used to it, in the sense that he'd forgotten what fresh air smelled like. He didn't feel he'd experienced the true horrors of war, but he'd had more than his share of the inconvenience, the loneliness and ennui, tinged with the shame of not being on the front line, leaving others to take the real heat. He wanted to feel that he was doing something important, but the war had begun before he'd had a chance to train in any specialty with his new unit. He was stuck, day after day, hauling equipment from one outpost to the next.

"Don't you sometimes wish," Shep started, "I don't know, that we were doing...*more*?"

Anderson coughed and squinted down at the sand. "More liable to die that way, I figure."

"We're liable to die anyway."

Shep leaned back against his truck, its heat emanating through his clothes and deep into his skin. Then, he shifted his weight to the other foot and felt something under his boot.

He crouched down to find a small whitish lizard, dead and stiff like a plastic toy. He picked it up by its tail.

"Hey, check this out," he said to Anderson, who leaned down to look.

"You're fucking gross," Anderson said.

Shep looked at its slick dead eyes and the delicate line of its skull.

"Jeeze, haven't you seen a dead lizard before? They're all over the fuckin' place." Anderson shook his head and unwrapped a piece of gum.

Shep laid the lizard back down where he'd found it, brushing sand over the top of it into a soft little mound.

2

Though it had been a week, Shep still approached Parkdale's with trepidation, as though the yellow tape were still rolled out across all four corners of the intersection, with cop cars splayed end to end. Though the action had mostly taken place across the street at H&J Liquor—where the broken glass doors were still replaced by a sheaf of black plastic that flapped in the wind, secured by duct tape and zealously graffitied—there remained an aura of calamity.

Hung couldn't wait to tell the story to anyone who would listen, further amplifying his role in the shooting with each retelling. Shep glanced side to side and back again as he tied Lionel to the bike rack and walked in on the latest version, which Hung was unfolding for the latest group of teenagers who'd come in for Mountain Dew and stayed for *Scarface* theater.

"I was minding my own, just restocking shelves or some shit, when I heard the first blast. I thought it was just a car backfiring until the first shot was returned with a *rat-a-tat-a-tat-TAT!* A fucking machine gun. I locked up and watched out the window while I dialed 911. Two dudes in sharp-as-*hell* designer suits jump into a black van and screech off into the sunset, and all I can see is that H&J 'cross the way is *tore up*. Glass all over the fuckin' pavement, bodies on the floor inside. I told the 911 lady what I saw, but I didn't see any cop car 'til like eight minutes later. Protect and serve, *my ass*. If it'd been my store, I'd be looking into a case against the city right now, no question."

He punctuated the assertion with a horizontal swipe of his hand. The kids were thrilled, repeating the best bits with more enthusiastic profanity as they collected their various neon-colored bottles and trickled out of the store.

Shep brought his beer up to the counter and poured it into a cup.

"Into the sunset? Didn't it happen around eleven or twelve? And 'designer suits'...you said you didn't even see what they were wearing."

"You know a storyteller's gotta add some flourish." Hung smiled and returned to the word jumble, tapping his eraser rapidly against the counter.

Shep drank his beer in silence, grateful for the numbing effect it had on his nerves. He'd started to call in to the Central Casting hotline for the third time that morning but had once again hung up midway through the recording. He'd held off on Lila too, feeling day after day too nervous to get behind the wheel. He'd spent much of the past week in bed, with Lionel warming the soles of his feet.

"Haven't seen you around in a minute," Hung said, not looking up from the paper.

"Been busy."

"You been reading the paper?"

"Not really."

"Dude..."

Shep finished his beer and tucked the cup back in its spot behind the counter.

"I was right."

"Huh?"

"The water store. Take a look out front. I haven't seen one of those fools all week. They just got one random employee running the place, quiet as a mouse. No sign of Eugene. You know why?"

Hung didn't wait for Shep to answer and continued in a loud whisper, though there was no one else in the store.

"They're saying it was an Armenian mob thing. Dudes walked into the place knowing exactly who they were gonna hit, 'cept it didn't go down as clean as they hoped. I heard there was a damn manhunt 'cause the van had to get the fuck out fast and left one of its crew behind. Cops found him hiding in somebody's backyard, all kickin' it with their golden retriever under the back porch. They're fucked. Now why you think Eugene and his crew might be making themselves scarce, huh?"

"I don't go in for conspiracy theories." Shep got up to get a second beer.

"It's not a conspiracy theory if it's in the paper."

Shep returned, soothed by the cold he could feel through the cup as he poured the beer into it.

"The paper said the water store was involved?"

"They didn't *have* to say."

Shep took a sip and winced as the liquid exacerbated a pain he'd been feeling in one of his rear molars. He'd been tonguing it absentmindedly for days. Three root canals in ten years, and still his teeth felt precarious and prone to ache. He took another sip, winced again. Then it occurred to him what had made him so uneasy outside. The Cowboy was missing, like a piece of furniture removed without explanation, leaving the room too empty.

"Hellllloooooooo…? You there?" Hung had set his pencil down and was looking expectantly at Shep.

"Huh?"

"I said, you did security before, yeah?"

"Uh…kind of. In the Guard. At one point…"

The last sip worked its way down cold but left a knot in his throat, solid like rope.

"You know we used to have a full-time security guard? Juan. Dad hired him after the third time we got robbed. He'd park his ass at the front and drink Lipton iced tea all day. He got killed, though. Not in, like, the line of duty or anything. Car accident. We just never hired a replacement. Hell, we couldn't really afford Juan anyway. Hey—you see any action? Gulf, right? The first one?"

"Not the kind you're probably thinking of."

"But you know how to use a gun and shit."

"Sure, yeah."

Shep looked back to see if he could see Lionel out the window. The dog was asleep at the base of the ancient phone booth that was littered with lost dog and cat signs and flyers for garage sales long passed.

Hung turned back down to the paper, bobbing up and down to a song in his head.

"Hey," Shep remembered, "have you seen that Cowboy around? Where'd he go?"

"Aw, he'll be back. El Vaquero don't stay away for long."

"El Vaquero. That his name?"

"Nah, nobody's gotten a name out of him."

When Shep made his exit some time later, the sky was heavy with smog, but it was warm, a spring day that only looked like winter. Shep untied Lionel from the bike rack and slipped him a piece of jerky. A customer walked into the donut shop and released a near-narcotic aroma. Normally, the smell would have drawn Shep in, but now his stomach lurched. He doubled over and released a torrential stream of vomit onto the pavement.

"Shit," he breathed when it was over.

Lionel wagged his tail and rubbed his head against Shep's pant leg. Shep remained bent over, his palms braced against his thighs.

"Maybe we've gotta go home, Lionel. Maybe this was a bad idea."

Shep coughed a few times and caught his breath, and the two of them made for the corner.

"Hang on, Lionel."

There was a new flyer on the telephone pole, the start of a new row above the other drawings that were growing increasingly weathered, their pigment slowly beaten away by the wind.

This portrait was drawn in red, with narrow eyes and a straight line for a mouth. A line of buttons ran down from the neck—little circles painstakingly colored in—topped by a collar of twin triangles. Perched atop its oblong head was a wide-brimmed cowboy hat with squiggles of hair peeking out from underneath. At the edge of each eye, the artist had drawn three little lines for crow's feet.

Shep stood close to it, running his finger over the pencil lines.

"Come on, boy."

3

Some nights, Shep's dreams were amorphous. Some nights he dreamt a glowing yellow light that enveloped his fetal self, a feeling of warmth so complete that it pulsed through the webs of his fingers and toes. There was no sense of time in these dreams. He named them in his head: *pure light*, or *peace forever*. The feeling was akin to his scant memories of his mother, who had faded to a presence—a scent, a heartbeat—he could remember being near, her arms wrapped around him, the sound of her voice as she sang songs to him in a near whisper. He remembered the intangibles mostly; the shell had cracked long ago, leaving only the hot, runny yolk. But there was a sense of eternity that defined those dreams and those memories, a feeling of knowing an all-encompassing energy field.

When he woke from these dreams, the realization descended like a candle snuffer, leaving him chilled. He would move through space as a clumsy ghost, floating from room to room without purpose, dropping his keys, staring out the kitchen window with the faucet running.

It was on one of these mornings, as he was getting dressed to catch Lila on her breakfast shift at the café, that his phone rang. The only calls he got were from telemarketers. He'd contemplated having the phone disconnected and getting a cell phone instead but hadn't been motivated enough to do anything about it.

"Hello?" he said. Lionel lay on the kitchen floor, chewing absentmindedly on his paw.

"John Shepherd? Hi, this is Lauren, background casting director for *Justice, Inc.*?"

"Uh-huh…"

"I was just calling to see if you're available today. Our guy called in sick for a scene that's shooting in North Hollywood this afternoon, and you're a perfect fit."

"Uh…" He wasn't yet ready to speak or understand logistics.

Lauren's tone shifted.

"Shoot starts at one. You'd have to be there at eleven thirty. I do need an answer right now."

"O…kay."

"Great. Do you have a pen and paper handy?"

As Shep drove to Café Gourmand, he kept looking at himself in the mirror at red lights. It unnerved him to think of this casting director flipping through photos and stopping at his, looking at him, pulling him from the pack. The prospect of his first honest-to-god paycheck in years didn't hurt. There was that, too.

Since their run-in, Shep had decided it was important to take a step back from Lila for the moment, to restore the layer of air between her and his watching eyes. At first that meant staying away entirely, but that didn't last long. Still, he parked a little farther away to make sure she wouldn't see him. He squinted to make out which of the similarly uniformed young women was her. Finally he recognized her profile manning the espresso machine.

Because she was diligently making drinks from the tickets that came up on her screen, she never moved from her spot and hardly interacted with anyone. Shep's mind was still foggy, and watching the mechanical movement of her arms, his thoughts wandered to another day when the sun was in the exact same position, another day spent watching, in another car, on another street.

It was shortly after he'd first gotten his disability. The pesticides and other chemicals he had to use in his landscaping job were making him sicker by the day, not to mention the creeping pain in his joints that had already made the work sometimes bothersome and sometimes excruciating. His working life had been sporadic for some time, between his grandmother's decline and his own sickness. But there was a finality about the letter in his hands, declaring him disabled. He'd spent so many hours on the phone with the VA, arguing over this form or that form he was missing, fuming as he sat on hold through circular voicemail diversions. His grandmother had been gone two years by then. He stood alone at the mailbox, reading the letter in pieces, his eyes ping-ponging up and down the page. So that was it then. He wasn't quite thirty.

For weeks, he'd wandered the house at loose ends, a house too big, decorated decades earlier in a style that made no sense to him. He absentmindedly picked up his grandmother's angel figurines, her macramé potholders, crystal candy dishes that had never held any candy, not that he could recall. What was he to do now, here? He'd put so much energy into securing disabled status, and now he didn't know what for. He may have been too sick to work, but what else could he do? Even worse than the empty days were the red-eyed nights, sleep eluding him in spite of his exhaustion when it wasn't terrorizing him with nightmares and troubling visions.

He stepped out the back door. The spring thaw had melted the last of the snow, but the air was still crisp enough to send a shiver through his skin. He wrapped his arms around himself. One of his grandmother's silver wind chimes was tinkling in the breeze. Such gentility, he thought, in the things she surrounded herself with, gentility she'd never shown him. He'd felt merely tolerated for so much of his life that the brief flashes of love in his memory—the warm vanilla of his mother's neck as she held him, the way Lorene had felt in his arms, open and wanting—burned with such intensity and at such a distance that they merged together, a lost, unreachable light.

Lila. She would be seven now. Second grade. Though he'd made a point of keeping track of Lorene's whereabouts since leaving town, he hadn't seen her or the girl in five years, not since Lila was a pipsqueak in wispy pigtails, dimpled elbows and knees toddling clumsily up the driveway of her grandparents' house. He wondered if he would even recognize her. Even then he'd only seen her face at a distance. Now that he was alone with his days free and rolling out endlessly before him, he was thinking about her more, and the more he thought, the more desperate he felt. Because the only good thing he'd done, the only good thing he'd had a chance to hold, wasn't just taken away when Lorene denied his fatherhood. It was repeatedly taken away every time he was reminded of her, his heart seizing at a glimpse of little girl's hair shining in the noontime sun or scab above a white knee sock. But he couldn't stop thinking of her, like a wound he picked at, aching to go back and do things the way he should have.

He looked out at the muddy field, patchy grass freshly uncovered. He knew where they lived. It was only a two-hour drive, a town not much bigger than Harner, so there would only be one elementary school. He'd thought of it many times, but only now did it seem possible to make the trip. What else could he do?

He finally worked up the courage at the end of the week, setting out early and loading the car with provisions as though he were making a great journey, though he would get there on less than a quarter-tank.

When he found the school, he pulled up beside the playground, engine idling while he unwrapped the wax paper on a ham sandwich. He checked his watch. It would be lunchtime soon. He watched the vacant swings and monkey bars and waited for the bell.

But before the bell had a chance to ring, a man emerged from the school and approached Shep's window. Shep rolled the window down and looked up at him. The man's expression was curt but calm.

"Can I help you with something?" he asked.

"Uh, no, no, I'm fine…" Shep sputtered.

"You sure?"

Shep was confused by the man's pointed tone. "Uh…" he said, looking past the man at the empty playground. *Come on,* he thought, *just come on outside…*

"I see what you're doing, and you'd better get out of here or I'm going to call the police," the man said.

"What? No, you don't understand, I'm a parent, and—"

"I know all the parents and I don't know you, so I'm giving you to the count of ten to drive away and never come back."

"No, no, it's nothing like that at all…"

"You make me sick."

Shep tried to plead further, but the man didn't want to hear it.

"I'm counting now," he continued, "ten, nine…"

The bell rang then, just as Shep had expected, and kids began to trickle outside, running to claim balls and jumpropes. Shep craned his neck to look around the man; if he could just see her for one second, even from behind, he'd know it was her.

"Eight, seven…"

But it was all a blur, he couldn't find her, and the man leaned in closer.

"Six, five…"

In a panic Shep sped around the corner, away from the school. He parked as soon as he could so he could catch his breath and calm down. But the harder his heart pounded the angrier he got. No one would ever give him a chance. He punched the steering wheel, burning tears welling in his eyes.

When he thought of it again now, nearly twenty years later and thousands of miles away, shame burrowed into the pit of his stomach as it occurred to him, not for the first time, that little had changed.

Lionel barked.

"What do you want?"

The dog climbed up into his lap and put his paws on the steering wheel.

"It isn't time to go yet."

Lila had handed off espresso machine duty to another girl and presumably disappeared into the back, because he couldn't find her.

"See what you did? You distracted me. Now I don't know what's going on."

Lionel barked again.

"Hush. You're always interrupting me, making me forget what I was doing." He picked Lionel up under his belly and unloaded him onto the back seat.

He looked for Lila again and found her back at the espresso machine, but the morning rush was already dwindling, so she'd begun to wipe the levers with a damp rag. She was too far away for him to make out her expression, but he always imagined melancholy and imagined it now too in the blur of her downcast gaze.

He started the car.

"I guess it wouldn't hurt to get there early. But you're gonna have to stay in the car. I'll get you some chicken nuggets on the way."

When he pulled off the freeway, following the directions he'd been given over the phone, he saw a yellow sign with "JUST INC" printed on it in bold black letters and an arrow pointing left.

He made the turn and parked in the shade of an elm tree around the corner from the location, a bar with no sign out front because it wasn't a real bar, not since it had closed in the mid-nineties only to be resurrected as a film set, the universes of disparate film-worlds converging in the warm light, the preternaturally sticky floor, and the neon Coors and Miller signs on the wall overlooking rows of bottles filled with colored water.

Shep broke up the chicken nuggets he'd picked up into bite-sized pieces for Lionel and spread them out on the passenger seat. While Lionel ate, grunting and grumbling, Shep took a mini bottle of gin from the glove compartment and drank it down. His jaw ached. He cracked the windows.

"You just sit tight, okay? I'll be back. No reason to raise a fuss."

Lionel ignored him, still diligently eating, and Shep slipped away.

As soon as he walked past the row of trailers and through the door, an assistant descended upon him with a clutch of papers in hand.

"You must be our bartender. That's your time sheet and release. Get dressed, you're late—wait, where's your shirt?"

"I'm sorry?" Shep pulled at the bottom of his white T-shirt.

"You were told to wear a dark-colored shirt. White won't work. Go see if they have something else for you."

And then she was off to harangue somebody else. Had they told him what to wear? He couldn't recall.

Ropy wires affixed with electrical tape were laid out, like a circulatory system across the floor. When Shep emerged from background wardrobe and makeup—where a harried, overweight woman pulled a navy blue Henley over his head and another woman tousled his hair and patted his face down with stale-smelling translucent powder—he stepped lightly between the wires, afraid of disrupting something. Looking around at everybody hustling back and forth, he felt that he alone was in slow motion, not just his movements, but his brain, his perceptions, his heartbeat going thump... tha...thump...while the room swooped around him in an arrhythmic staccato.

Behind the bar, another assistant with a clipboard gave him his instructions while the lighting technicians tinkered with their setups, dimming and brightening the great spotlight that seemed to simultaneously heat and cool him, so close, so enveloping, the crew oblivious to him standing there, save for his earnest instructor, a bespectacled recent film school graduate.

"...so for the first few beats you're gonna have your back to the camera. You're gonna take that rag and wipe down the glasses stacked right here. Got that so far?"

"Yeah, yeah..." He was worried about Lionel. Somehow he'd figured this would only take an hour or two, but he'd been there for what felt like hours already, and they hadn't even begun to shoot.

"And whatever you do, stay on your mark."

Shep glanced down at the day-glow strips of tape on the floor just in front of his toes.

"Hey, uh, do you think I could run out for a minute?" he asked.

"Break's later. We're rolling in five."

Forty minutes later the actors took their places a few feet away from the bar, at a cocktail table topped with a red glass candleholder. The tiny blonde actress held a lit herbal cigarette, though it had been years since Shep had been in any bar that allowed smoking. He wondered if this was a period piece. Across from her sat an actor Shep was sure he recognized, though he certainly couldn't place him or recall his name. Both of them had unnervingly even rows of bleached-white teeth.

When "Action" was called, Shep went into robot mode. The great bright lights were reflected in the glass bottles Shep faced as he worked the glasses with his dry rag. A kind of hypnosis set in as he focused on the glare, bulbous and bouncing across the many planes of glass. He closed his eyes and the glare remained. He swiveled his wrist back and forth. He could hear the lights too, a metallic buzzing that seemed to drown out the dialogue that was supposedly the centerpiece of the scene. In fact, he didn't hear any words at all.

Cut! Take it again.

Shep paused briefly, his eyes open just halfway. Somehow it filled him with a sense of calm, this repetitive motion, this great bright light. He remembered his recurring dream—

Action

—peace moving like liquid all around and through him, of warmth burrowing itself into his tendons. He let out a small sigh, his wrist still moving back and forth, back and forth.

Cut! Go again.

He didn't pay so much attention to the demarcations of one take to the next.

Action!

He kept doing what he was doing even in the in-between, because he had a row of glasses to dry. Some might have called what he was doing method acting, the way he didn't switch on and off. To him it was only natural to stay the course.

Cut! One more.

Shep held his eyes half-cocked, the glare flattened to a line. The buzzing of the lights had died down some, and he listened to what the actors said.

You have beautiful eyes.

Shut up.

I'm serious, Annabelle. Why don't you understand that you're beautiful?

Shep's attention drifted back to Lionel. He felt guilty that he was having something like a good time without him. Shep was hungry, though. He'd felt too queasy to partake of the lunch that was set up in a tent behind the building, and now he could feel the acid rising in his stomach.

How long had he been standing there behind the bar, working his rag, watching the light play against the glass? Shep looked at his bare wrist. He kept forgetting to look for his watch. Save for the spotlights, it was dark and dingy inside, like any dive, the illusion of night no matter the hour. There were no clocks, of course. Could it be night already? How many takes was this?

Thankfully, a twenty-minute break was called before his disorientation could spiral into panic. Shep made himself a sandwich to go and hurried back to the car. It was still light out, but the sun was lowering.

"Hey, Lionel, I didn't forget about you."

He pulled a sliver of ham from his sandwich and fed it to the dog.

"I'm sorry you can't come with me."

Shep leaned his seat back and ate, breathing deeply, eyes closed. What a strange day. It was all too strange.

He couldn't finish the sandwich, so he fed Lionel the rest of the meat and dropped the crust in the street outside his car door. He took a swig of gin and dropped the bottle back in the glove compartment, then let Lionel out onto the grass for a minute before he had to run back inside. The dog licked Shep's fingers as he plopped him back onto the seat.

"Go to sleep, Lionel. Make dreams."

As soon as Shep got back inside, the film school graduate was back with more instructions.

"...so on Annabelle's line, *I'm just looking for a good time for once*, you're gonna turn around, hundred and eighty degrees, and you're gonna approach the customer at the other end of the bar..." The assistant placed his hand on the shoulder of another extra, a man about Shep's age in a trucker hat and down vest.

"...to your marker, no further, and he's gonna be placing an order for four beats, okay?"

"Yeah." Shep nodded to his customer, "I can do that."

The lights were locked into place, setting the room aglow and blinding him to the cameras, the crew, the walls and blackened windows. There was only his spot behind the bar, his marker, his turning radius. He followed his instructions, silently counting as he paced and turned, becoming acquainted with his customer at the end of the bar, or the skin between his eyes at least, every pore and pigment, where Shep's gaze settled each time they repeated their steps. After a few rounds—*Action! Go again!*—as he grew accustomed to the movements and didn't have to count anymore, it began to feel fluid, easy, like a dance. The lights burned on. His thoughts were silenced, his body released.

4

It was just after nightfall when they finally wrapped. As Shep drove back home, the moon was full and tinted orange, a heavy, Halloween-style moon that made the night feel hushed. He switched on the radio, K-EARTH 101. CCR's "Down on the Corner" was playing, and he turned up the volume.

"I'm sorry, Lionel." The dog was pouting, facing away from Shep and letting out a series of sighs and grumbles.

"Anyway, I made us eighty-seven dollars. There are worse things than that."

The moon, the music and the newness of the last few hours had put Shep in something like a good mood. He sang along quietly: *Benny and the poor boys are playin', bring a nickel, tap your feet…*

"Aw, you can't hate me forever, Lionel."

He swung into Parkdale's to say hi and have himself a beer to cap off the day, but the lot was full, the water store lit up and full of people.

As he got out of his car, he saw Eugene step out, sweeping the sidewalk out front. He wore a suit with the tie loosened, sunglasses perched on top of his head. Inside, the usual cast of characters was huddled around a table surrounded by bottles and glasses both empty and full, though now there were women and children present, and extra folding tables topped with picked-over food trays. Shep made accidental eye contact with Eugene and looked away quickly.

"Hello." Eugene nodded.

"Oh hey…"

"Pardon…" he trailed off, motioning toward the winding-down party.

"Oh, no, I don't—"

"We've come from a funeral. My cousin. Too young, too young." Eugene shook his head and leaned his broom up against the wall for a moment. It was brand-new, with a price tag still stuck on the handle.

"Oh, I'm sorry to hear it."

"His heart," Eugene said, patting his chest. "One minute he's talking to his wife, telling her to put on a jacket if she is taking the dog out. She comes home, and…" He extended his hand down toward the pavement, indicating the body on the carpet, then pulled a soft pack of Lucky Strikes from his pocket and lit one.

"Hmm," Shep said. He wasn't sure how to respond. They'd never had a conversation before.

"Like his grandfather," Eugene continued. "He survived the genocide. Just a little boy, he hid in an empty cellar, three days and nights with no food. Then when he's only forty, he drops dead watering his garden."

"That's terrible," Shep said.

Eugene shrugged. "Nobody knows what can happen." He took a step back toward the water store, cigarette dangling from his fingertips, and stopped. "Mr. Phan…he's not doing so well, eh?"

"I'm sorry?"

"Nothing, nothing. You just tell your friend, if he needs anything..." Eugene spread his arms in a welcoming pose this time.

"Yeah, okay, sure thing." Shep nodded an awkward *so long* and Eugene nodded back before stepping through the doorway. Shep watched as a woman silently took the broom from Eugene's hand and replaced it with a coffee cup. She stroked his cheek and whispered something in his ear.

As soon as Shep entered Parkdale's, Hung was on him. He'd been cleaning the handprints off the glass doors, no doubt spying.

"What'd he say to you?"

"Oh, you know, his cousin died." Shep went to the back and grabbed himself a Guinness. He poured the can out into a Styrofoam cup. It tasted perfect, cold and bitter.

"Cousin, eh?" Hung scoffed. "Lemme guess, thirty-five years old and died of *natural causes.*"

Shep was taken aback by Hung's vitriol. He was still rubbing the same spot on the door in a tight circle, staring out the glass.

"He asked after your dad," Shep added in an attempt to tame Hung's pissed-off energy.

Hung froze. "Excuse me?"

"Yeah, he just said to let him know if you need anything, since he knows your dad's not doing so hot."

"He said that? He was talking about my dad?" Hung stared out across the parking lot at the water store. The party seemed to be dispersing, cars pulling out with their headlights bouncing off the glass. "I don't need shit. You can tell him I said that, since you're buddies now."

Without another word, Hung took the rag and spray cleaner to the back room and didn't come back for several minutes. He returned sipping a cup of coffee, intent on changing the subject.

"Where were you this morning? I got donuts for your ass. Still got some." He pulled a pink bakery box from underneath the counter and plopped it down in front of Shep. He selected a maple log, which tasted surprisingly good with the Guinness.

"Had some stuff to do."

"I thought I saw El Vaquero rollin' his cart back around here, but it turned out it was just some other homeless dude." Hung pulled the pink box back to his side of the counter and began picking at a chocolate cake donut.

"I don't think he's homeless exactly," Shep said.

"What? You know dudes with apartments pushin' their shit around in carts they stole from Von's?"

Shep swiveled his stool around, looked out at the fat moon and swallowed, trying to figure out what it was he meant. He licked crumbles of frosting from his fingers.

"I don't know. I think he's got something different going on." It seemed that way to him, anyhow. He put the Cowboy, aka El Vaquero, in a category apart. He seemed to participate in no system but the one governed by his internal compass. "Well, we may never know the truth," said Hung, "'cause he's never been gone this long. I bet Eugene and his crew gave him the spooks."

"Hey, maybe he's on vacation. Maybe he went on a cruise. Maybe *I'll* go on a cruise," Shep said. They laughed.

"I'm serious though," Hung said. "I'd move if I could."

"Where would you go?"

"It don't matter to me. I just want to be as far as possible from that gang shit. It seems funny if you don't think too hard about it, but those dudes don't mess around."

"Which dudes?"

Hung tossed his unfinished donut back in the box.

"Did you live here when they found that fuckin' head half a mile from the Hollywood sign?"

"No, I guess I didn't."

"Man. You gotta get a TV or start reading the paper or something. You're totally in the dark, you know that, right? You got tunnel vision."

Shep rubbed his sore eyes.

"Anyway, some lady's dog found it, came bounding out of the damn weeds with it hanging out his mouth by its hair. When the police searched they found hands and feet, too, but they never found the rest. What does that tell you?"

Hung didn't wait for him to give an answer.

"That shit was a message. Ain't *nothing* colder than that."

"How do you know it was gang shit?"

"It's always gang shit."

"But Eugene hasn't done anything."

Shep glanced back at his car. Lionel was perched up with his paws on the wheel.

"I mean," Shep continued, "maybe he *could* help you out…"

Hung grew quiet. He took the donut box to the back room and returned with a calculator and money pouch.

"I gotta start closing up."

"Oh. Yeah, I guess I'd better take Lionel home…"

As Shep threw out his trash and made for the door, Hung stopped him.

"Hey, you know how many times I've had a gun in my face?" His drawer was out on the counter as he piled bills up by denomination.

Shep shook his head.

"More times than you have, war hero. That I can guarantee."

Shep nodded and waved goodbye, but Hung didn't look up from his counting.

Shep lingered on the sidewalk as he searched his pockets for his car keys. That's when he noticed a little boy curled up against the corner of the water store's glass storefront, reading. The boy looked up and saw Shep watching. For a moment, the two of them held each other's gazes. Then suddenly the boy picked a pencil up from the floor and began furiously scribbling in his book.

With the moment broken, Shep looked back up at the moon. It seemed, as the night grew darker, to be getting lower in the sky, heavier, closer, more insistent upon illumination. Shep unlocked his car door and was greeted by the purity of Lionel's forgiveness, slobbering sweet breath, and little nibbles on the wiry ends of his beard.

5

There were times, had always been times, when the days ran together with such speed that Shep forgot that he was aging.

The years between Shep's return from the desert and his grandmother's death, for instance, felt to him, in retrospect, like one long, confounding month. He could remember those years only in snapshots and clips that ran in a labored circle, scraping like a tire gone flat: the blinding sun as he dug ditches, his breathing getting worse with each thrust of his shovel and each whiff of Atrazine; the lean winters, sitting in front of the TV with his grandmother, spoon-feeding her beef broth, most of it trickling out the corner of her scowling mouth and down inside the neckline of her baby blue nightgown; Lorene, Lorene, Lorene, the way he fixated on her getting in and out of her car, entering and leaving her house, with Lila growing from little cotton bundle to pigtailed toddler in the blink of an eye and then vanishing from his world, their absence only amplifying his fantasies of reunion, building them into the buzzing backdrop of his every action.

Then there were the nights he spent at Cooper's, the caramel-smoke taste of bourbon and the resulting blurred vision that resulted in turn in occasional one-night stands with red-eyed, tequila-breath'd girls he'd avoid thereafter, not that they didn't avoid him just the same in the light of day.

He knew he was lonely. He knew that was the word for it. With no one to talk to—or, more accurately, no one he felt like talking to—there was only the ever-repeating cycle in his head, the constant monologue as his body hobbled forward through time. When his grandmother entered the hospital for the last time, even before she was dead, just that immediate change in the day-to-day made him feel like he was emerging from a fog. Finally, he was somehow, in some small way, free.

And now too—in an entirely, blessedly different way—time began to hurtle forward.

Shep began calling in for extra work every day in hopes that eventually, inevitably, he would wind up on a shoot with Lila. What surprised him was just how well he was doing, with no real effort on his part. Every day he wound up on a shoot was a gift, a new exhilaration he hadn't felt in so long.

He got himself a Thomas Guide and studied routes and backroads, the many methods for cutting through the hills and valleys. He was learning the Southern California landscape as he drove to far-flung locations, unlocking the puzzle of its three-dimensional layout.

Before long he was rarely calling in at all; they were calling him.

In the span of two months he played a reveler at a small-town parade in a police drama; a limo driver on a network sitcom; a restaurant diner in a feature film; a bar patron in another film (this was the most fun he'd had in years, dancing with a beautiful Mexican woman with whom he exchanged few words for six hours straight; it culminated in a sloppy make-out session up against his car before she got embarrassed and ran to her own across the drizzle-slick parking lot, leaving him clutching his pounding chest in the front seat).

He still kept tabs on Lila. Nothing would keep him

from that. But he'd socked away a few hundred dollars and had enlisted Rosa, his landlady, to look after Lionel on the days he was working. The last time he'd felt so *busy* was when he'd first joined the Guard, which he'd done on an equally inexplicable whim.

At eighteen, he didn't know what he wanted to do or who he wanted to be. He figured anyone who did was either lying or lacked imagination. He only knew that he had to figure something out quickly.

He accepted the common assertion that his grandmother had been a saint to take over his care after his mother's death. He remembered hearing it often in those first hazy weeks; *You're a saint,* said relatives who'd come to town for the funeral. *She's a saint,* he remembered thinking as he lay in bed, not sleeping.

What choice did I have? she'd reply.

She wasn't young. His mother had moved back home after a failed marriage he knew nothing of, not even the man's name, when she got pregnant at thirty-six. By the time Shep was a senior, his grandmother was in her seventies, and his mother had been dead twelve years, twelve years he'd spent knowing he was a burden and that putting up with him was a selfless act.

Even as a little boy, he could sense how tired she was. It was in the gray look on her face when she make him breakfast in the still-dark morning, or the way she walked him to school with one hand hanging down limply for him to clutch. It settled in the air during the many afternoons she would sit him down in a corner with a piece of paper and a pencil and tell him to stay there and be quiet. He took her instructions literally and would be as silent as he possibly could, making slow pencil strokes on the paper so it would make no sound at all as he filled the page with houses, trees, cars, dogs and people, all rendered in faint, ghostly lines.

She did try. When he'd squeeze her hand too hard as they walked, she would shake it off. *Come on*, she'd say, and walk ahead of him a few paces. Most of the time she would catch herself. She'd stop and wait for him, take his hand again, squeeze back.

After she'd been forced into retirement from her job at the phone company on a pension that was a severe reduction from her salary, the feeling that he was a burden took on a special urgency. They hadn't had any conversation about bills—she hadn't even told him she'd retired until he saw a pension check on the kitchen table—but though the house was paid off, he knew his part-time job at Ross Wimmer's gas station wasn't enough to cover the difference. Very soon, she was going to need *him*. They carried on as ever, occupying different parts of the house, converging in the kitchen, finding traces of each other, hairs on the soap, shoes by the back door, while he spent each day quietly panicking over the future.

She'd taken to eating breakfast in her bedroom. Many mornings, he didn't see her at all. Their house was on the side of town that had been drying up for some years. To the west, they were surrounded by abandoned farmland where nothing grew anymore and moldering houses sat empty, a warning to the east side of town, though the substance of the warning was unclear. Every morning he walked across the flat plain toward Marty Cumberland's house, using the Cumberlands' family farm's unbroken wave of corn to the east as a focal point. In the wintertime, the division wasn't so distinct. Everything blurred into the periphery, washed away in white.

That morning, he waited outside Marty's house as Marty tumbled out the door chewing a mouthful of eggs. It was the biggest house in town, but Marty was always a mess, jogging down the front steps unwashed with half-done homework falling out of his backpack. They bumped fists and walked to school in silence, taking in the spring tableau that had greeted them since the last snow melted: the first few blocks' green lawns, the *tic, tic, tic* of morning sprinklers, the loose dogs that would follow you a few feet before veering off to unknown purpose, leaving muddy pawprints on the pavement.

As they approached their lockers, he spotted Lorene in his peripheral vision, standing before her own locker, and tensed up while Marty made a show of wagging his tongue and cupping the air a few feet behind her as though he were squeezing her ass.

Knock it off, he whispered, to which Marty laughed and split off toward his class.

While he arranged his books and gathered the day's assignments, all his energy was focused to his left, where Lorene was applying strawberry lip balm, wiping the excess inside the back pocket of her jeans when she thought nobody was looking. When she slammed her locker shut and walked off, the tension in his shoulders released, his head nearly enclosed within the locker's aluminum walls.

On his way to Biology, he noticed a stranger in the front office, not too much older than a student, in his twenties maybe, his hair buzzed, in full dress greens, a clutch of folders under his arm.

Throughout the day, he kept seeing the stranger: taking a sip at the water fountain, exiting the restroom as Shep was entering. He became constantly aware of this man haunting the halls, and because the man was always looking stoically forward and never seemed to interact with anyone, he began to wonder if he was seeing things.

When he saw the man again at lunchtime at a table set up outside the cafeteria, the obvious fact occurred to him: he had to be a recruiter. As Shep choked down his meatloaf and overcooked broccoli at a table with Marty and the Sorensen brothers, he kept glancing back at the stranger just outside, his pamphlets and pens laid out just so while kids swarmed past like he was invisible.

Something cold and limp hit Shep in the face and

dropped into his lap. He picked up the broccoli and threw it back at Marty, who ducked out of the way just in time.

Dick.

When the bell rang and his friends dispersed, he tossed his unfinished broccoli, moving slowly, waiting. He wouldn't have been able to identify it at the time, but the quiet that fell around him in that moment, the way the hallway emptied, leaving him alone with the recruiter, his flat, rehearsed delivery echoing through the space, was the weight of inevitability closing in.

Shep could still remember the moment well, the way his consciousness seemed to leave him as he took the papers, nodding as the man told him he didn't need anybody's signature if he was eighteen, nodding again as the man rattled off a list of jobs he could train for, pay, benefits, scholarship opportunities. He nodded through it all, though he forgot the entire spiel as soon as he walked away from the table. The details seemed unimportant.

Graduation came and went with its accompanying road parties, driving drunk on pilfered Bud Light, and at the end of June, John took his first airplane ride—first to St. Louis, where the sheer number of people in the terminal, and the way the force of the crowd seemed to push him down the cavernous walkways, nearly knocked the wind out of him— and on to Louisville, where he and the other recruits he'd flown with would wait in the USO until enough guys arrived to fill the old green school bus that would take them to Fort Knox. He was the last to take a seat in the bare, windowless room, setting his duffel bag down at his feet, where his gaze remained for some time as he wondered what on earth he'd gotten himself into.

It was nearly two in the morning when the bus departed. Though the recruits had become slightly acquainted during the wait, exchanging the basic facts of their lives—what state they were from, their age, number of siblings, whether they had a girlfriend or no—everyone was so tired and nervous that conversation ceased, and a hush descended. John alternated between watching the blur of headlights and the shimmer of the road, still wet from a summer storm, and scanning the rows of boys like unformed dough, acned and awkward, a bus full of baby birds. Some seemed to be sleeping while others stared out their own windows. John leaned his temple against the cool glass and daydreamed himself back to bus rides of his youth, returning from the cornfields with cramped hands and sunburned ears. He felt the same weariness now, though this was only the beginning. With each bump in the road he traveled deeper inside himself, becoming twelve years old again. He didn't have his Walkman, so he sang a song without words in his head.

Upon arrival, they were immediately herded into a painted brick room to wait for their first drill sergeant, a red-faced wall of age-softened muscle who seemed angry to have been woken up, the side of his face bearing faint crease marks. He told them he would leave the room for five minutes, during which time they could unload any contraband they'd brought with them, and rattled off the list: food, pornography, electronic devices, games. This would be their only chance to do so without consequence. Two silent minutes after the drill sergeant stepped out, one kid stepped forward and dropped a package of Starbursts into the box. Everyone else remained seated.

The drill sergeant shuffled them into a barracks in the dark with brusque instructions to find a bunk, lock their things in a wall locker and go to sleep. Shep lay awake, his breath shallow, aiming for silence. Motionless under his thin wool blanket, he was afraid to fall asleep and afraid he wouldn't. A mosquito began buzzing by his ear, and he tried to slap at it in the air without creating any disturbance, careful not to make the bed squeak.

He must have fallen asleep eventually, because when the fluorescent lights rocketed on amid the hoarse yelling of another drill sergeant bullying them out of bed and into their first formation, he awoke in a panic. And as he marched through the hallway, down the stairs and out into the bright Kentucky dawn with one guy inches ahead of him and another one inches behind, a bead of sweat rolling from his temple down to his peach-fuzzed jaw, he thought:

Am I a soldier now?

Within a few days, once his platoon had gotten their alphabetical order memorized—they'd had to do punishing rounds of pushups and inchworms every time they screwed it up—and once Shep had grown used to five-minute showers and running up and down three flights of stairs several times a day, he began to forget the difference between this, whatever *this* was, and real life. Though he had never before put such demands on his body, this alternate reality was, mentally, a welcome opportunity for surrender. The schedule, the five-fifteen a.m. PT formation, the hours of weapon and vehicle training, running from location to location, all within a small section of the base, the world shrunk down to a manageable size, the sore muscles and utter exhaustion by lights out, even the physical penalties for the slightest failure—a sheet badly tucked or an incorrectly laced boot—gave his body purpose and set his mind free.

By the end of the first week, he could feel himself growing stronger. While the doughier recruits were losing weight, he, having been something of a beanpole, was gaining muscle. He began to relish his new form and the way it filled space. His abdominal muscles held him straight, made him stand taller. His shoulders broadened his shadow under the punishing sun.

Pain is weakness leaving the body, yelled a drill sergeant during one especially trying PT session, when Shep had lost count of the number of sit-ups he'd done but was sure he would vomit if he had to do one more. He remembered the phrase often, when he was on KP duty, his back muscles spasming as he mopped the floor, or on personal time, when he would walk to the PX for a magazine or new socks, his quads burning with every step. Even when he was idle, the weakness within him was evaporating, being replaced by discipline, by confidence, by grit.

By the time he returned to his grandmother's house (she got up and squeezed his shoulder when he walked into the kitchen, convincing him however briefly that she could sense his transformation), he was no longer afraid of the future. He had no better idea of how he would make his way in the world, but he felt that he, or his body at least, was unbreakable. That was enough.

That was the first time Shep could remember time hurtling forward. He got into a rhythm at the gas station, working between four and six days a week, maintaining a running regimen to remain in peak condition for his monthly drills, and earning enough money to make up for his grandmother's lost income.

When he watched her shuffling about in her ratty house slippers, leaving a dripping tea cup on top of the TV set, or when he found a load of laundry in the machine that she'd forgotten and left to mildew, he caught himself having uncharitable thoughts. He wondered if there was only a limited amount of strength and vitality in the world, if his growth had to be balanced by her diminishment. There were moments when he surprised himself with thoughts of fleeing. He knew she had nobody else, but wasn't that her own fault? Driving to meet friends at the D&D or a Friday night house party, he had fleeting impulses to get on the interstate and keep going. And when he was running around the high school track in the early morning, he could picture himself veering off, forging a path through the neighboring wheat field and coming out the other side.

One night about a year after graduation, Shep went out to Howie's burger stand at the other end of town to meet

Marty and some of the guys. Howie's was a trailer with several picnic tables set up in the gravel out front. The smell of sizzling beef and frying onions filled the surrounding air, where pickups convened in the dirt parking lot. The place was lit with a couple of lanterns, the buzzing fireflies lending an added glow.

He sat with the guys over cheeseburgers and onion rings that came to the pickup window so hot they'd burn off your fingerprints. Marty was telling them about how he only needed to save another eighty dollars to finally get that jet ski he'd been talking about for months, to take down to the lake on weekends. It shouldn't be too hard, Shep thought, seeing as how Marty still received an allowance from his mother for doing basic household chores.

Whooooosh, Marty whispered, gazing out into the beyond, reenacting for the thousandth time the feeling he'd experienced on his cousin Travis' jet ski the previous summer.

Shep smiled, weary of all of this, the same people, the same conversations in which his participation was cursory at best, the dullness in Marty's eyes that he didn't know whether to attribute to weed or plain stupidity. Had he known then that Marty, in under a year, would be pinned under 3,000 pounds of metal, slowly bleeding to death in a ditch where no one could see him, Shep liked to think he would have listened more attentively.

He got up to get a refill on his pop.

There at the pickup window, filling up a little paper cup with ketchup, pushing down on the lever with the flat of her palm until the cup overflowed onto her finger, was the girl who'd paralyzed him since the day he laid eyes on her. He looked back with shame at the way he'd always shrunken in her presence, how he'd floated in her periphery, too scared to make his presence known. Immediately, a rush of embarrassment coursed through him; he remained unaware that he was staring.

She turned away from the ketchup pump, holding

a paper fry basket delicately by its edges to avoid getting burned, when she nearly bumped clear into him.

She giggled. "Shit, I'm sorry—guess I was spacing out."

"My fault," he said, swallowing.

"I know you," she said with a sideways glance. "Where do I know you from?"

She wasn't moving. She was standing with him, leaning toward him, digging her toe into the gravel. The shame was gone, all of it, replaced with exhilaration, *weakness leaving the body*. His heart beat wildly.

"Around."

On Howie's radio, the Rolling Stones' "Doncha Bother Me" was playing, the twangy slide guitar flourishes mimicking the lightness in Shep's body, the air lifting through him. He felt weightless, unmoored. The radio station's signal was weak, the song periodically engulfed by waves of static, but he still felt physically connected to it, and to everything else, his body a conductor.

"Where're you going?" he said, his pulse ringing in his ears.

Shep glanced back at the table just as Marty attempted to throw his burger wrapper into the trash can from his seat across the gravel lot, missing by a foot. He thought maybe he ought to tell the guys he was leaving, but he was already climbing into the backseat of Cheryl Baxter's mom's station wagon next to Lorene, who sat in the middle with Cheryl's kid sister on her other side. There were no seatbelts in the back, so the three of them braced themselves with a combination of isometrics and nerve as Cheryl careened down the driveway and out into the muggy night.

Cheryl's boyfriend Ted switched on the radio. Sinead O'Connor was singing *Nothing can stop these lonely tears from falling/Tell me baby where did I go wrong*.

"Change it," Lorene said. Ted complied, though Cheryl weakly protested, "Aw, I like that song…" The car bounced over a bump in the road and Lorene grabbed onto Shep's leg, saying "Change it" again, interrupting a Bryan Adams song. Shep was barely aware of the radio, though, because her hand was still on his leg, which was itself squeezed up against her own. While Lorene continued to crane her neck forward to supervise the radio dial, Shep stared at the seatback ahead of him to keep from staring at that hand, warm through his jeans.

Cheryl stopped the car at the end of a dirt road. In the distance, a chain link fence separated a sprawling cornfield from the adjoining cow pasture.

"Turn it up," Lorene said. Her friend obeyed, the repetitive chorus of The Who's "I Can See for Miles" swelling over the car's rumbling vibration. When the song ended, Cheryl cut the engine but left the headlights glowing.

"I don't like this," Cheryl's sister piped up from the backseat, looking out her window.

"Shut it," Cheryl said, "or you can forget about any more rides."

"You can stay here if you're so scared," Ted said, unbuckling his seatbelt.

"I'm not *scared*, I'm just not *stupid*," the girl huffed. Shep guessed she was around fifteen.

"What're we doing here?" he whispered to Lorene.

Lorene distributed beers from a case at her feet, expertly popping them open with the bottom of her cigarette lighter. She ignored his question; it didn't matter anyway. He took the beer and drank.

While her sister stayed behind to sulk, Cheryl ran after Ted toward the edge of the field. Lorene hung back behind them and Shep kept her pace, though they didn't speak. He kept just enough distance so he could watch her, while she acknowledged him with an occasional, almost wary, glance. The farther they got from the car's headlights, the darker it got, until, to Shep, Lorene was just a presence, jostling hair and hushed footsteps in the dirt.

By the time they reached the fence, Ted was already hoisting Cheryl up, guiding her foot to the top of the post, careful to avoid the electrified wire meant to keep cattle from wandering into the cornfield.

"Teddy, Teddy, I'm gonna fall!" she shrieked.

"I gotcha, I gotcha, but you gotta be quiet," he said. He was holding the neck of his beer with two fingers, both hands supporting Cheryl's back. "Now…jump!"

Cheryl landed ass on the ground, but laughing.

The fence was only chest-high, so long-legged Ted was able to get himself over it easily enough, and soon he and Cheryl had disappeared among the stalks.

"Well?" Lorene looked at Shep.

"Does anybody know whose farm this is?" Shep whispered.

"Don't worry about it," she said, "now give me a boost."

Shep took a deep breath and stood behind Lorene. He took her waist in his hands and lifted. She curled her legs up in front of her, preparing to balance safely on the post, but Shep kept lifting until she was over his head.

"What are you doing?" she whispered. But Shep didn't know. His arms were acting independently. He was stronger than he knew; he didn't know what to do with such strength. He lowered her, his fingers loose and trembling.

"Careful, careful, don't get me shocked," she said. Shep eyed the wires: one along the top of the fence, another at knee height. He was shaking, not from the strain but from the responsibility. It was a relief when she finally jumped down out of his hands.

"Come on," Lorene said, "follow me."

Soon they were wandering between the stalks that stood just above their heads, the stars peeking through between the leaves. The night sky receded; she was the night now. He tried to keep calm. He kept on following even when it became clear there was no destination, only the leading.

"Lorene?" Cheryl's disembodied voice came from somewhere, at least ten rows away.

"Yeah?"

"Just checking!" Cheryl giggled. Then they were alone again.

Lorene turned around to face him. "I think we're in the center," she said.

Shep stood on his toes and tried to peer through the corn. "Do you want to…head back?"

Lorene shook her head. There were crickets somewhere. And somewhere too, Cheryl and Ted were having their own moment. Cheryl's sister was back at the car, stewing or sleeping. And here, for the first time, the two of them were alone together. She grabbed his hand, startling him, kindly ignoring its sweaty palm, and held his fingers up to her soft, cool cheek. "Not yet."

When they dropped him off just before dawn—his car cloaked in dew, his lips chapped, eyes on fire —he climbed in the driver's seat and sat in silence for a few minutes, feeling both fully present in his body and larger than it, his blood running hot and fast.

And time hurtled forward—not just time but he and Lorene too seemed in his memory to have been racing toward something, speeding down dirt roads at midnight with the windows down, getting drunk under the high school bleachers, weeds in their drawers and burrs in their hair from making love outdoors. And when he woke up under those same bleachers, with her still asleep beside him, he would prop himself up on his elbow and watch the rhythm of her breathing, her throat moving under a thin gold chain, her smudged black eyeliner and oily morning skin. He would lean down as close as he could without waking her and wonder what he had to do in order to have her, to own and keep her for good. So lost in wonder was he that he let out a small gasp when she woke up, flinching under his scrutiny. The stare between them shifted back and forth between love and fear. He kissed her to quiet her doubts, and she let him, only barely turning her lips away.

"Morning breath," she said quietly.

One evening he returned home from work to find his grandmother scrubbing the kitchen floor on her hands and knees with a mostly disintegrated paper towel. He dropped his keys on the counter and dove down to help her up. He pulled the sudsy mulch from her fingers and tossed it in the sink, dried her red, peeling fingers with a dish towel. Her knees were like raw meat, scraped and naked.

"What are you doing here?" she said. "You don't live here."

"Huh?"

"Where have you been?" she corrected herself. She turned about the kitchen, opening cabinets, scowling as though she couldn't remember what she was looking for.

Shep felt like a trapped animal. He backed out of the kitchen, went upstairs to his room and changed into his running clothes, slipping out the front door again in silence. As he ran through town toward the pink scrawl of the setting sun, he envisioned himself driving down the interstate, Lorene in the passenger seat beside him, dancing with her eyes closed, performing for him, knowing he was watching her when he should have been watching the road. He ran past her house with half a mind to kidnap her from her parents; her bicycle was parked on the front porch, but her window was dark. He ran in place across the street, hopping from foot to foot.

He'd take her out to dinner the next night, he decided, maybe go into Kearney, take her someplace nice, surprise her when she got home from cheerleading practice. Sweat rolled down the back of his neck.

And if her window was dark the next night, he'd just come back again, every night, until it lit up.

He broke off and continued running toward the sunset, feeling faster than wind and stronger than gravity.

That same vitality returned to him now, like blood returning to tingling limbs, the confidence that's borne of movement.

One night, hours into a difficult shoot, Shep stood a few feet behind the camera while the two leads performed a scene in close-up, a frenzied, whispered exchange in an empty hallway during a party. Background—the party guests—had been sent on break, and most of the others had returned to the green room to read or look at their phones. Shep had taken a seat by himself on a bench outside, pulling at his collar. He felt strangled by the tie a costumer had put on him, but didn't dare undo it since he wasn't confident in his ability to retie it exactly the same way. After sitting there for what seemed like a long time, he returned to the set to see what was going on.

They were still on the same lines of dialogue they'd been shooting when he left, an exchange of a measly two lines, but the director wasn't easily satisfied.

"I thought you said I could trust you," the actress said in a teary hiss. She was dressed in a white evening gown with a slit up to her thigh. The actor leaned over her, bracing his elbows against the wall.

"And I thought you said you could handle this," he said, a vein bulging in his temple.

"Cut!" the director yelled, "No, no, no, I'm not getting anything from you, Harper, I feel nothing. I need to feel *something.*"

The actress ducked out from under the actor's arm and stepped away from the wall. She stood in the middle of the hallway with all ten fingers pressed to her forehead.

"Oh, you need a minute? *Jesus Christ...*" The director dropped his pen on the floor and walked away.

Shep stood back, trying not to intrude while the set

dissolved into casual chaos.

"Uhhh, is he coming back?" someone said.

Shep continued to watch the actress, who hadn't looked up when the director stormed out. Then he felt a movement— or heard it—a metallic wobble, a tiny pop.

One of the massive klieg lights was tilting, leaning, gathering gravity. In a half-second Shep realized it was perched right above where the actress was now standing with a stylist who was busily mussing her strawberry blonde hair. He leapt out and pushed the women out of the way just as the light came down in a hellacious crash, sending pieces scattering and scraping across the floor.

"Oh my god, what the hell!" the actress cried.

An assistant swooped in with a poncho and a bottle of water and led her away while members of the lighting crew descended to assess the damage. Shep took a step back. His heart was beating fast. He swiveled his head around in confused exhilaration. What now? The casual chaos had turned frantic. No one said anything to him. No one looked at him. Once he realized no one was going to acknowledge him, he stepped out of the building. He returned to his bench, where he picked at the leaves of a dried-out hedge until a PA came to tell the background actors they were free to go.

Shep undressed, wrenched himself free of that awful tie. He got back into his own clothes, in something of a daze amid the ambient chatter. He had no clue how many hours had passed. It seemed the sun had always been down.

In the parking lot, he was running through the usual production of getting his car started when a black towncar pulled up beside him and the rear window rolled down, silent.

"Excuse me," a woman's voice said. "Do you need a ride?"

"Oh no," he said, not looking up. "It just takes a couple tries is all."

After a few seconds' pause, she replied, "It's awfully late."

Shep tried the ignition, but it sputtered to life only briefly before succumbing again. He looked up into the towncar's open window. The parking lot was dimly lit. He was only able to make out a curtain of dark hair, the collar of a white blouse. The windows were tinted black, so he couldn't see the driver in the front. The woman tilted her head toward him, and the moonlight caught her jaw, the upturned corner of her lip.

Shep pulled his key from the ignition and sat a moment, looking out the grimy, spotted windshield. It seemed everyone else had gone home. He stepped out of his car. There was a damp chill now, the part of the night that was equidistant between dusk and dawn, its weightless, infinite center.

"Please," she said.

He'd already opened the door.

6

They rode in silence, regarding each other. Shep could see now that she was older than him by a good ten years. Her hair was blown straight, her lipstick a wine-dark red. Pressed powder had settled into the fine lines around her eyes. She wore a diamond pendant that glittered at her thin-skinned throat.

"You're working on the picture, I take it?" When she parted her lips he could see she had a small gap between her front teeth. She had a warm, drowsy way about her, a slowness that made him stare.

"Yeah, just for the day."

"I see."

Shep glanced out the window, the dark made darker by its tint. The ride was preternaturally smooth, as though they were driving through a secret city of unblemished pavement. He watched miles flow past like spilled ink.

"It was very handy you were there tonight," she said. "That was you, wasn't it?"

"Hmm?"

"That damned light...I saw what you did. I wanted to thank you but you'd disappeared."

Shep thought back to the hubbub on set, the swarming crew, but didn't recall seeing this woman. She hadn't stood out, if she'd even been visible. For all the people bustling through a film set, there were as many more watching on monitors in hidden rooms. Perhaps she was one of those. There were always more eyes on you. More eyes than you could imagine.

"Oh, it was nothing. Just luck. I guess." Shep looked out again and ran his finger along the bottom of the window. The stars streaked past. He closed his eyes.

"Is there anywhere in particular you'd like to be dropped off? I suppose I should have asked."

She was smiling, privately amused at something.

"Oh, I should've said." He squinted out the window and tried to gauge where they were exactly. They were winding upward now, hugging a steep hillside he didn't recognize. All the parked cars had their wheels turned out toward the road.

"I think maybe we passed it..." he said, to no one in particular.

"We can turn around if you like."

He sunk back into his seat. He felt comforted, cushioned, but wide awake. The seats were leather.

"Or not," she said. "You look tired. You can stay in one of the guest rooms."

He turned to face her again. He opened his mouth but didn't speak. Even now, he felt she was watching him at a remove, directing him as though cameras were rolling, her words spoken into an invisible headset.

A few minutes later, they pulled through a driveway and came to a stop at a mansion of glass, steel and wood as dark and rich as espresso. Shep stepped out of the car and tried to take it all in, the house's height, its overwhelming slickness, like carved liquid, the surrounding grounds a carefully curated forest. He imagined each bird had been imported, chosen by a hired bird expert, that tending to its hedges was a full-time job with benefits and a 401k.

Were they at the top of the hill? There was no way to tell, no geographic context. It was so dark up there above the streetlights. The car pulled away and disappeared behind the house. He never did see the driver. Had he been kidnapped? That's what it felt like, though he'd gone willingly—was still going, willingly.

"Come on," the woman said, leading him up the wide staircase with a deliberate high-heeled gait. Watching her from behind, from below, he couldn't tell if he was attracted to her or not. But she exerted an authority over him, an authority he felt compelled to keep giving to her, freely. They hadn't yet exchanged names.

She told him to wait by the pool. *You can wait here if you like* was how she put it; he accepted the suggestion as an order. He wandered over to the edge of the deck and looked out over the railing, at the lights way down below. It was bar-closing time. All along the streets down there, people were spilling out, bumming cigarettes, trying to hail cabs. You couldn't hear any of it, only crickets, only the hush of moonglow on the crystalline-blue pool water. She returned with a bottle of wine and two glasses.

"Sit," she said. And again, "You look tired."

"Is…this is where you live?"

She laughed. "For now. I don't know…I'm thinking of selling it. It's too big, isn't it?" She poured them each a glass of red wine.

Shep shrugged.

"It was all my husband's design."

"You're married?"

"Widowed."

"Oh. I'm sorry."

She shook her head distractedly. "Of course I've been saying I was going to move all this time and I've never even called the realtor. Too lazy, I suppose."

"You swim in that pool?" He knew the question sounded stupid as it left his lips. *Do you walk on these floors? The food in the fridge, do you eat it?*

"Did you want to take a swim? You can if you like."

Shep shook his head. "I'm John. By the way. John Shepherd."

"Cynthia."

"You can call me Shep."

"John's fine," she said, and gave him a closed-lip smile.

Shep was unaccustomed to drinking wine. He sipped it slowly for lack of anything to say. He was trying and failing to piece together the moves that had gotten him to this point. He wasn't even clear on what had made him get in the car. It seemed as though mere moments before he'd been planning a night of canned Beefaroni on the couch with Lionel. He worried suddenly about the dog, though he'd already told Rosa it would be a late night. *Relax,* he told himself. He tried to be discreet as he wiped his sweaty palms on his pants.

Cynthia's heels clunked onto the deck. She curled her bare feet up underneath her.

"Are you working on...the picture?" Shep asked, mimicking her terminology.

"I'm a producer."

"Oh, okay..."

"It was a project my husband had committed to before he passed. He left me in control of the production company, so..." She set her glass down and leaned back in her chaise like she was moonbathing, eyes closed. "Soon I'll be able to choose my own."

The diamond at her throat twinkled like a point of light. Shep didn't know what to say, had never encountered anyone like her, been to any place like this. He was struck dumb. She opened her eyes again. Her lipstick was a little faded in the center now, her eyes tired, mascara smudged.

"And you?" she said. "You're new to L.A., aren't you?"

"How could you tell?" he said, not correcting her assumption. Of course it still felt new, everything did.

"Statistics. Background is stocked with actors who haven't given up yet. You are an actor, yes? Aspiring at least?"

Shep found himself nodding.

"Pardon me if this seems rude, I don't know you, but… you're a little older than most actors just starting out. Why now?"

Shep's back was tight. He resisted leaning back in his own chaise, his muscles coiled in anticipation, of what he didn't know, a reason to bolt, a compulsion. He tried to calm himself with a sip of wine. Then he looked at Cynthia and remembered that she'd asked him a question.

Why?

"Well," he began, "I kind of got the idea…from my daughter." The word escaped his mouth and he imagined it sitting there before him, solid. It couldn't be taken back. "I came out here with her," he went on, as though peeling layers of brush off its surface, the word *daughter*, the concept of it, emerging from underneath. "You might say she inspired me." His whole body loosened. It wasn't a lie.

"Oh, that's interesting. To have a father so invested… she sounds like a lucky girl."

Shep drained his glass and refilled it almost giddily, spilling some on the folding table. "Oh no," he said, trying to mop it up with his sleeve, "I'm so sorry…"

"Forget it," she said, laying her hand on his wrist, calming him. "Just sit back," she said, and he did, relieved to be told what to do.

"Your daughter, did she always want to be an actress?"

Shep sank his back into the soft cushioned chaise. "Oh yeah," he said. "School plays. Lila was always the lead." He paused. "I told her if she graduated with good grades, I'd take her out to Hollywood so she could make a real go of it, you know? I wanted her to have a chance to make her dream come true."

"Your faith in her must really help. Most of the young girls out here…they don't have anything, anybody."

"The way I see it, it's the least I can do. She's given me so much." It was true, even if Lila didn't know it. He'd made sacrifices too.

Neither of them spoke for a minute. Shep opened his eyes and looked out at the water. He felt drunk, though there was no way, given how little he'd had. It was the sense that there would be no morning. That he could say and do whatever he wanted without consequence here, in a place that couldn't be real.

"If you don't mind," Cynthia said, "I think I'll have a swim."

Shep took a long sip and watched as she stood up, then nearly choked as she began unbuttoning her blouse. She wasn't looking at him, didn't seem to take his presence into account at all as she dropped her blouse onto the deck and stepped out of her skirt. She stood there, looking down at the water, pale in her black underwear and bra. Shep stared, frozen, at her full, lightly freckled breasts. The skin on her stomach was loose, and he was startled by a long horizontal scar just above the line of her panties, the mark of a C-section long passed. She was shivering, goosebumps rising on her arms, but she didn't get into the water just yet. For a second, he thought he saw her glance in his direction out the corner of her eye. Was this for him? Or was he only watching?

Cynthia stepped into the water then and turned over onto her back, her hair spreading out behind her. Shep quickly poured himself more wine and drank it down, not sure if he should stay or not, though he didn't have much choice. He had no idea how he could find his way on foot. And she wanted him to stay. She'd brought him here for some reason that wasn't yet clear.

She disappeared under the water's surface then, and rose up at the edge with a subdued splash, right by Shep's feet.

"It's quite warm," she said. "Much warmer than the air." She folded her arms on the deck and looked up at him, her feet bobbing languorously beneath her. Her eye makeup was streaked like watercolor down her cheeks.

She watched, smiling inscrutably, as he took off his shoes and socks, then stripped down to his briefs, sucking in his stomach and turning slightly to conceal his stirring erection until he was safely in the water. It was as warm as she said, like L.A. air on its stillest, most weatherless afternoons.

Cynthia floated toward him, un-shy now, as though the water had washed away her inhibitions along with her makeup. Still, when she reached the shallow end where Shep stood, the water up to his chest, she stopped short, staying a few feet away. Without her heels on, she was a head shorter than him, the water just touching her chin.

"It's nice, isn't it?"

Shep nodded. Her eyes were irritated, rimmed in pink. She took another step toward him.

"I didn't swim for a long time. No pools. No lakes. Certainly no ocean. It seems stupid now."

Shep lifted his hands out of the water and ran them through his hair. His knees were loose as leaves.

She came closer and faced him. Who was this woman?

And when she turned her face up slightly to meet his, he sank into her like he'd been waiting for this. His brain went silent as he pulled her in closer, pressing her soft, unknown body against his, his blood running hot as she prodded him backward toward the edge of the pool, still kissing him.

Cynthia pulled away from him and looked in his eyes for a moment, then gently slipped out of his grasp, climbed the stairs out of the pool and crossed the deck to the poolhouse. She turned back and gave him a look that pulled him like a magnet out of the water. He began shaking as he followed in his wet underwear, his hair and beard dripping. She walked several paces ahead, leaving the door open, and pressed a button that activated a fireplace in the corner as he stepped inside. Behind her was a white bed twice the size of his own, with big feather pillows piled against the headboard. The fire was the only light.

Still without a word, Cynthia stared just past him, out the window on the other side of the room, out at the hazy starlight so high above the city, as she unhooked her bra and let it drop to the floor, water rolling from the ends of her hair down over her breasts. His mouth filled with hot saliva as he watched her, a now overpowering ache in his groin. He swallowed. Then she lowered her gaze back to him. She held it as she crossed the room and sat on the bed. Then she smiled, showed the gap in her teeth. She was shivering. So was he.

Shep woke up alone, gagging on the stench of his own body odor in the muggy poolhouse. There were no blinds on the window over the bed, so the sunlight poured in, blinding him and highlighting his clammy, flabby nakedness against the rumpled white sheets. He pulled a feather off his tongue and peeled another, stuck with sweat, off his ass. What time could it be? Where had Cynthia gone? He shielded his eyes and grabbed a towel from a plump stack on a shelf above the ash-wrecked fireplace, wrapped it around his waist and went outside to find his clothes, choosing to abandon his still-soggy underwear.

Lionel, he thought, wracked with guilt. What day was it? What was he doing? How would he get to his car when he didn't even know where he was? There was a ringing in his ears, a rattling in his skull.

He stepped briefly into the house in an attempt to locate Cynthia but only found a housekeeper in yellow rubber gloves, humming as she scrubbed the granite-topped kitchen island. He was too timid to venture upstairs, and in any case, he'd get lost in a house this size. He cringed at the thought of Cynthia finding him hours later, dehydrated and disoriented, wandering around her laundry room. He had to get out.

He stumbled down the staircase he'd floated up, hypnotized, the night before, and sped up to a jog down the driveway, down the hill, his misbuttoned shirt flapping behind him. He was light-headed, his stomach knotted, but he kept running down, down, down, winding past the spray of morning sprinklers, the rumble of engines starting—he had to outrun it all. Unable to stop when he reached the bottom of the hill, he catapulted straight into the intersection, causing a silver convertible to slam on the breaks to avoid him.

"Fucking idiot!" yelled the driver.

Shep kept running until he reached a bus stop and slumped onto the plastic bench, pressing the crown of his head to a graffitied ad for a local realtor, the man's white-toothed smile scribbled black.

He didn't know why he'd run. He didn't know why he did most things, not until much later, when he could delineate and agonize over everything he'd done wrong. He sat up and locked eyes with the realtor's headshot. Not only had the mouth been blackened, but the eyes had been decorated with spirals, converging on pupils enlarged to an LSD-plumpness with scratchy ballpoint. Shep turned away from the ad and glanced down the road in search of a bus.

7

Somehow, amid the valley breeze's barely perceptible shifts and undulations, it was summer. Though it was just past eight in the morning, the sun already felt like it was following him, burning just a few feet above. He held Lionel under his arm, staying close to the buildings to get as much shade as he could from the eaves overhead, and watched his shadow against the shimmering pavement.

When he reached the corner, he was surprised by how relieved he felt to finally see the Cowboy back in his spot.

"Long time no see."

The Cowboy looked at him but gave no outward sign of recognition, same as it ever was. Shep was squinting so hard he could barely see a thing, just a sliver of the squat strip-mall before him. He must have had the time wrong after all. It must have been well into the afternoon, at the sun's merciless climax. He checked his watch; he wasn't wearing it. The disorientation made him chatty.

"Hey, did you see your portrait? On the telephone pole? I guess somebody's got an eye on you."

The Cowboy scratched his jaw.

"I never did find out who was drawing 'em? Did you? I guess you probably know but you're not talking, huh?"

Lionel squirmed impatiently.

"Here, I'll show you."

Shep went over to the telephone pole and scanned the faces. The oldest ones were fairly disintegrating at the bottom, contrasting with the fresh ones at the top. Though the portraits varied in detail—some with tight flicks of hair like blades of grass, others with big loopy curls; some heads oblong, some almost rectangular—they all possessed a common straightforwardness, blank gazes facing outward, both projecting and receiving nothing. He couldn't find the one with the cowboy hat and flat, pinhole gaze. He couldn't make out the top row at all with the glare in his eyes. He returned to the Cowboy's nook.

"Well anyway, there was a picture of you. Maybe I'll see it later.

Lionel let out a little whimper.

"I guess I'd better get going. I guess it's going to be one hell of a hot day. It's good to see you again, man."

He tied Lionel up in the shade of the awning and grabbed a cup of water for him inside, then an ice-cold beer for himself. This was perfect, he thought. This felt good. Though it had been over a week since his night with Cynthia, he was still reeling a little from the experience. Not just the sex but the aftermath too, the hours-long trek on buses and on foot as he tried, parched and woozy with hunger, to find his way back where he'd started. When he finally found the parking lot—and his car, with a ticket under the windshield wiper—he leaned over the roof, stretched his palms up to the heavens, and, though he believed in no creator, prayed to the clouds for the car to start.

When the ignition rattled to life on the first turn, it felt as though fate were making fun of him. Ever since, he'd felt anxious to see her again, though he'd ruined any chances by running before he could get her number. It was better not to kid himself. But at least once on any given day, he'd catch himself staring into space, transfixed by memories of the oaky, amber scent of her perfume, or her stilettos dragging a smooth line up the staircase. He felt pulled, as if by a fishhook in his throat.

Hung stared down at his newspaper.

"N-P-L-E-T-H-O-E-E."

"I'm no good at these, Hung. It's all just a jumble."

"That's the point, son. That's what it's *called*. Here, I'll give you the clue: 'A game of meanings lost and found.'"

"Sounds pretty damn, I don't know, existential, for the word jumble."

"Come on, you've done it before."

Shep tried for a moment to see the letters in his head as Hung had advised, but it was much harder than it sounded. As soon as he'd conjured up one letter, it disintegrated in his mind, replaced by the next one.

After a few minutes, Hung lost patience.

"Dude, you never played Telephone as a kid? One kid whispers 'Laughing Baboon' to another kid, and by the time it's gone 'round the circle, the last kid says 'Stabbing

Raccoons'?"

"No, I guess I never did."

"I thought you grew up in like *America* America. That's some classic American child's play right there."

Hung tossed the paper aside.

"I got the rest of 'em already. They're getting too easy. The jumble editor or whoever's getting lazy."

Shep emitted a throaty chuckle. "Jumble editor..."

"Shit, somebody's gotta make 'em up."

Hung tossed a piece of Chex Mix at Shep's head, and, as though triggered by the action, the little bell on the door sounded, and Eugene entered casually, leading with his pelvis as he always did. He stopped in the entryway, gazing about the aisles, slow and assessing, king of all he surveyed.

Shep and Hung both clammed up, turning their attention to imaginary interests behind the counter.

Eugene walked slowly down the center aisle and disappeared into the jungle of shelves, camouflaged behind family-size bags of potato chips and white cheddar popcorn. After a minute or two—though it felt much longer to Hung and Shep, determinedly puttering—the sound of the opened refrigerator echoed through the store, and he returned to the counter with a Gatorade, electric blue.

"Too hot today," he said, while Hung silently scanned the bottle.

He continued, pointing a finger. "Important to hydrate." And then, addressing Hung, "Your father, how is he doing? I haven't seen him in..." Eugene raised his eyebrows and gave a long whistle. "Long time, long, long time."

"He's fine," Hung said, his eyes fixed on his own hands bagging the drink. Shep watched out the corner of his eye as Hung's jaw pulsed the way it did when he was angry.

Hung passed the bag and a wad of change across the counter. Eugene took it but didn't move from his spot. He stared at Hung expectantly.

"I gave you twenty. Not ten."

"Yeah. My mistake." Hung opened the register and retrieved two five-dollar bills.

Eugene gave a little laugh and turned to Shep.

"This is your dog, yes? Outside?"

"Yeah."

"Cute. He needs water." Eugene pointed his finger again, in a way he seemed to think was friendly.

"Yeah, he's got some," Shep said, but Eugene was already halfway out the door. Hung watched him cross the parking lot back to the water store, then exaggeratedly dropped his jaw and rolled his head back in a circle.

"What the fuck?" he mouthed.

"The place ain't bugged, Hung, you can talk."

"Tell me they don't sell fuckin' Gatorade in his own damn store. All they've got besides a couple of hookahs is fuckin' Gatorade and Powerade and Minute Maid…"

Shep glanced out the storefront to check Lionel's water. He hadn't touched it and was asleep in the shade, against the base of the newspaper box.

"Eugene's got no reason to come in here for any goddamn drink, so what's he coming in here for? Oh, and, what business is it of his how my dad's doing? Am I supposed to be filing reports with Eugene on the whole family's health status? I don't have to tell him shit about who's where and why." Hung stepped back from the register and shook his head.

Shep shrugged.

"I hear things," Hung said. "I been doing some research on our friend Eugene Sandrosyan. You know he did time for aggravated assault in the mid-'80s?"

"What, when he was in grade school?" Shep had assumed Eugene was his age or younger. Maybe he was just fitter, better rested. Wealthier went without saying.

"He's fifty-one! Motherfucker doesn't age, like a friggin' vampire."

"That was a long time ago…"

"But that ain't all. You know he owned that 'supper club' on Riverside that shut down last year, the Silverlight Lounge?" Hung scoffed. "Everybody knew that place was a front, I mean *everybody*. They didn't even have menus, okay? Then it got shot up and never reopened. That shit's still vacant, probably serving *other purposes* if you know what I mean."

Hung was shaking his head more insistently now. "But I keep my ear to the ground. Something's gonna happen real soon. You heard about the identity theft ring the LAPD's been investigating for like years now?"

"Can't say I have."

Hung rolled his eyes.

"I'm hearing they're right on the *cusp* of closing in—"

"—Where're you hearing this stuff?"

"None of your concern. But we're talking, like, *days* until they take down the whole organization. You heard it here first."

"The whole Armenian mob, over some stolen credit cards?"

"Stolen credit cards? We're talking whole fabricated identities, *thousands* of them, we're talking *millions* in fraud. Don't you watch Dateline? My moms can't get enough of that shit, all biting her fingernails over those pedophile stings. But identity theft is for serious. Notice how I watch the ATM like a *hawk* any time anybody's usin' it? Pretend like I'm 'cleaning' near it? 'Cause that's how they do, just act like they're getting cash but really they're installing skimmers to swipe pin numbers and shit. But I'm not such an easy mark."

"I didn't even know you had an ATM."

Hung rolled his eyes and pointed to a machine nestled beside the ice machine in the corner, the letters "A-T-M" glowing green above it. "What are you, new?"

"Okay, but how do you know—"

"You've been in this neighborhood as long as I have, you just *know*." Hung gave a nod meant to punctuate his point, closing the matter to further questioning. He returned to his newspaper, flipping through to the crossword.

"I gotta take a leak," Shep said. On his way back from the bathroom, he stopped in the office for a moment, taking a seat at the hulking metal desk where the Phans kept all their important documents and cleaning supplies. He had to get going soon. Lila was on the lunch shift at Café Gourmand, and he wanted to shower first and get there early so he could get his preferred parking spot. But it was nice back there, quiet, blue-carpeted, and cooled by an ancient but powerful electric fan. He sipped his beer and rocked idly left and right, the chair squeaking laboriously. The combination of the beer and the turning was making him feel pleasantly dopey.

After a few minutes, his head began to ache, and he abruptly stopped turning in his chair. His stomach lurched as he realized the smell that pervaded the back office was a mix of the pillowy dust that collected in the room's nooks and industrial-grade Lysol. He coughed up his sip of beer, and it trickled down his chin. His head was pounding now, and he rose from his chair with one hand clasping his left ear, behind which the pain emanated.

He heard a moan then and for a moment thought that it was in his own voice. He stood still, eyes closed, trying to think the pain away.

Another moan, and Shep realized it was coming from the stairs. He set his beer down on the desk and approached. There on the landing stood Mr. Phan in his white boxer shorts, his pale, sagging chest appearing almost concave. His birdlike legs trembled.

"Mr. Phan?" The words hurt to say, his own voice echoing through his head, vibrating through to his headache's point of origin.

He climbed the stairs to where Mr. Phan stood.

"Mister…"

Mr. Phan spun around suddenly and grabbed the railing

as though catching himself from falling, showing Shep his back, on which was emblazoned a strange scar, like a tree, just a few shades darker then his flesh, with branches that stretched all the way from the back of his neck down his side, disappearing down the waistband of his shorts.

Mrs. Phan, all five foot two inches of her, came tiptoeing down the steps and wrapped her arm around her husband's waist. She took his arm and draped it over her shoulder, heaving his left leg up each step as he dragged his right foot behind. Shep watched until they reached the top. Still holding him tight, Mrs. Phan looked over her shoulder at Shep and caught him off guard with a warm smile before shutting the apartment door behind them. Shep leaned against the wall and caught his breath while the pain in his head pulsed out to the opposite ear.

"You fall in, Holmes?"

Shep stumbled back behind the counter. He didn't answer.

"Yo, you okay?"

Shep's eyes were closed. He rubbed his temple. Outside, Lionel had awoken and was licking the storefront, sensing his master's need through the glass.

He got his breathing under control and leaned his weight against the counter.

"Your dad's got a scar. What is that?"

"The fuck you talking about?"

"He was just…I saw him on the stairs—"

Hung bolted up from his seat and charged toward the back "Your mom's got him," Shep called out.

Hung stopped and turned back, his face grim.

"She took him back upstairs. It's okay," he repeated.

Hung sat down again, his back curved forward like a hook.

"That's the scar you get when you get struck by lightning."

"No shit?"

"He don't like to talk about the war, but that's one story I know. There was some real crazy firefight...he got separated from his boys, and then it started raining so hard he couldn't see shit—it was all just mud and smoke and water. Then all of a sudden he got knocked to the ground, said he thought he'd been shot in the back. Thought his spine was shattered. But after a few seconds he realized it wasn't that 'cause he'd already been shot once before, and it wasn't the same kind of pain. Said he felt like his blood was gone...like he had fire running through his veins instead. And even though the pain was unreal, and he couldn't get up or nothing, he was still, somehow, pretty sure he was gonna live. He passed out eventually and woke up in some, like, makeshift hospital all bandaged up and shit, never figured out how he got there, didn't matter I guess. Anyway."

Hung sat up straighter and began tapping the counter with his pencil eraser.

"He was ARVN? How'd your folks get over here? It was before you were born, right?"

Hung bit his lip, shook his head at the ground. "They never talk about that. I quit asking. They always acted like they didn't hear me when I did. It took me years to drag the scar story out of him, one little detail at a time." He dropped his pencil and let it roll across the counter until it hit the register. Shep wouldn't have said anything if he'd known the scar was war-related; he knew better than to start those kinds of conversations.

"I'm gonna go. I should get Lionel out of the sun."

"That's cool." Hung nodded, and kept nodding to an unheard beat as he took up his pencil, resuming the tapping of his eraser, tap, tap, tap, and Shep wondered if Hung's many tics had been borne of solitude, his brain's response to the crushing boredom.

He untied Lionel and let him walk ahead, but decided not to go home just yet. A nice breeze had kicked up out of nowhere, and the fresh air felt good.

The two of them walked through the tree-lined residential part of Coldwater, crossing muddy, overwatered lawns at the points where the sidewalk receded.

They crossed the street, and Shep let Lionel lead him along the shady jogging path that paralleled the river. He peered over the fence now, down at the skinny stream that had scarcely enough volume to maintain any movement at all. It hadn't rained, really rained, beyond the misty mornings, in months, and the level of the river's valley stretch reflected the dryness. But insubstantial as it was, the water flowed ever forward, dirty runoff from some faraway car wash. He picked Lionel up, carried him across the wooden footbridge, and held him up above the railing.

"How'd you like to splash around down there?" His headache was fading now, turned down as though by a volume knob controlled by the cool, numbing breeze. Lionel wagged his tail.

"Don't know how to get down there. Maybe I'll figure it out sometime for you."

He let Lionel off his leash, and the dog ran through the warm green grass, stopping to drink from a murky puddle, sprinkler water accumulated in a dent in the hillside. Shep walked a little ahead, rubbing the increasingly frayed end of the leash, and glanced at the mural that decorated the length of the river's enclosure. He'd noticed it many times but had never looked closely at it. He looked now at its first panel, labeled "Pre-Historic California," a montage of saber-toothed tigers, woolly mammoths and other ancient creatures that faded into a Native American tableau, a naked woman grinding maize with a mortar and pestle, an Indian chief with an eagle, spreading its wings, sprouting from within his long black hair. Shep whistled for Lionel and the dog scurried to his feet.

They walked a ways down close to the fence, and Shep listened to the traffic on the other side of the hill until, in the distance, he saw a small figure walking toward them in the opposite direction. As the figure got closer, he saw that it was a boy. He held a glossy red school folder against his chest and, with his other hand, dragged a gnarled stick lazily against the chain link. Shep could hear the rattle of reverberating metal growing in volume as the space between them closed.

They stopped and faced each other as their paths met. It was then, seeing the boy's face, that Shep recognized him from the water store, the little boy curled up against the storefront, bespectacled like a little owl. He had Eugene's sharp jawline, striking but incongruous on a little kid, and wore a white shirt flecked with fresh dirt.

"Hey there," Shep said. "Are you…Eugene's kid? I think I've seen you around the store."

The boy squinted up at Shep. He nodded.

"What's your dog's name?" The boy dragged the stick against the dirt now, tracing shapes, a circle, a triangle.

Lionel stayed close to Shep's leg and bared his teeth at the boy.

"Well, this is Lionel. He can be a little bossy, but he's a nice guy. Come on, Lionel, be good."

Shep scooped the dog up and rubbed his head, successfully interrupting his attempt at ferocity. He held him out to the boy.

"Go on, he won't hurt you."

The boy dropped the stick and approached tentatively. Without breaking eye contact with Lionel, he reached up under the dog's chin and scratched at his dripping wet beard. Lionel wagged his tail in spite of himself, his guard dropping.

The boy curled his lip into a lopsided smile. He pulled his hand away and wiped his fingers on his pants.

Shep crouched down and set Lionel on the ground, staying there with him to proffer further pets and ear scratches.

"Hey, what's it like, growing up in a store?" Shep said.

"Seems like maybe it'd be kind of…fun?"

He thought of Hung as a boy, and the stories he'd told Shep about sleeping in a cubby under the cash register while his parents went about the business of running the original Parkdale's, about how his mom would sing to wake him up after they'd closed, lullabies in reverse. He told Shep about how he'd always look over his mom's shoulder as she carried him upstairs to bed, at his father closing out the register, bills stacked in rows on the counter with a pot of pink wax at his fingertips.

When Shep looked up, the boy was gone. He turned around and saw that the boy had continued on his path, trailing his fingers slowly along the fence, stickless now, wandering with the same childlike unawareness of time.

"Was it something I said, Lionel?"

The dog wagged his tail.

The two of them continued along the river, and Shep gazed again at the mural. They'd skipped a few hundred years and were now in line with the Chinese building the railroad, which bled right into the Chinese massacre, anguished faces imprinted in the smoke streaming from the locomotive's chimney. He looked ahead at the winding path and Lionel digging at a patch of earth.

"What've you got there, Lionel?"

The dog kept digging, burrowing soil into his paws and muzzle. Shep picked him up.

"You're just a mess now, Lionel. There's nothing down there. Come on, we've gotta go."

By the time they reached World War II, with a blue-faced, grimacing Hitler spreading his arms across the California Aqueduct, giving way to a wall of green-masked, eyeless soldiers, Shep had cleaned off Lionel's face well enough with the edge of his sleeve.

He carried the dog up the hill, leaving the remaining history behind them, the ghostly Jewish refugees climbing up chains, the division of the barrios, a white policeman holding back an enraged brown woman, her desperation overshadowed by Elvis' hips and the rise of rock 'n' roll, the march of time stopping abruptly with the uniformed runners of the '84 Olympics, bare concrete stretching out beyond the beyond.

He set Lionel down on the sidewalk and leashed him up again, rejoining the traffic, the strip malls and the transmission repair shops. A homeless man slept under a tree where the sidewalk met the grass, curled into it like an animal into its mother's siren pulse.

8

Shep began watching Lila at night. He'd started it as an experiment, after shoots, occasionally bypassing his home to idle across the street from hers. But soon enough, he'd internalized her nighttime rhythms the same way he'd memorized her days. Now he was following her out to nightclubs, where she congregated with friends while he took a seat at the bar and downed glasses of whiskey, near-invisible, frustrated by the impossibility of hearing her conversations but grateful for the darkness.

On the nights she stayed in, he took comfort in her half-open curtains, seeing her in cotton pajamas, drowsily eating her dinner, as he'd never seen her when she was a girl. Even when the curtains were closed, he basked in the warm light at their edges, the occasional laugh track from her too-loud television washing over him like bubbles. If he let his eyes unfocus, he could dissolve the wall between them, putting himself in the room with her. He could imagine their nights together the way he'd portrayed them to Cynthia, a father providing a safety net for his daughter as she explored a strange and exciting new world.

I'm off to bed, he imagined himself saying to her. *Don't you stay up too late now.*

Then one night, while he sat in the car on Lila's block with Lionel sleeping in his lap, she came home as he'd hoped she would, but she wasn't alone. He was already caught by surprise to see her emerging from the passenger side of an unfamiliar SUV that had just parked, its silver front bumper edging ever so slightly into the driveway, and when the driver climbed out and followed her up her duplex's front steps, Shep's throat clenched.

His eyes flitted quickly across the scene: a man much older than Lila, in his thirties at least, dressed in a suit like some kind of banker, was cupping the girl's butt cheek while she giggled, fumbling with her keys. She dropped them on the stoop with a jingling clatter and bent down to retrieve them, while this guy, this man, ran his fingers against the back of her bare thigh and fiddled with the hem of her skirt. Shep instinctively looked away, and when he looked up again, they'd gone inside. The light came on in her apartment. The curtains were closed, but the light at their edges didn't offer its usual comfort.

Where's that roommate of hers, he thought, and the thought beneath that, *to stop this from happening?* But of course, she could be asleep in her own room, or off with her own date. It didn't matter.

For a few minutes he watched the curtain in some vain hope that he could make out the figures inside if he focused his vision just enough, shadows at least, silhouettes against the cotton, but he had to look away again when his face grew hot. He was sweating, now, and pulled at the collar of his shirt, which suddenly felt tight.

He glanced back at Lionel, who slept, who slept through everything, the bastard.

He recognized the shame that coursed through him as it sank in that what he was trying to do was see what was going on in there between his own daughter and this man, that he *wanted*—did he really?—*to watch*? He thought he would throw up, but the relief never came. He sat there reeling, woozy with the feeling of movement in his groin.

As soon as he felt able, Shep started the car and drove away, though he lacked the wherewithal to drive in any logical direction—home, say. Instead he found himself driving down Laurel Canyon. Within minutes, he'd passed through the long, dreary strip mall quadrant, past Ventura, past Mulholland, and down into the titular canyon, Jim Morrison's Love Street.

He pulled off onto a shoulder, a dangerous place to stop, surely, on such an unlit road, but he knew he couldn't trust himself to hug its unrelenting curves; he'd veer right into the hillside given half a chance.

It was dark enough, and quiet enough, that Shep felt safely alone, the dog still dreaming obliviously in the back.

This was bound to happen eventually. She was a pretty girl, on her own, nothing tying her down. It surely wasn't the first time. He couldn't watch her every night, it would be impossible. She was grown, she wasn't any kid. He had to remember that. But the shock—which he now went over and over in his mind in the dark of the canyon, his rapid breath fogging the window against which he leaned his head—took him back to another night.

After he'd confronted Lorene, and after she'd rejected him once and for all, it wasn't as though he could just give up. By that point, Lorene had gotten a job waitressing at the D&D, leaving Lila with her mom at night. After he'd gotten his grandmother off to bed, a process that varied in difficulty depending on what kind of day she was having, he would sneak out and park outside her house, hoping to catch a glimpse of the baby—who was no longer a baby but a full-fledged toddler, fat and unstable, teetering up the driveway in

Velcro sneakers. But the family kept their shades drawn and bedded down early. After a few weeks the hopelessness of the habit, amplified by the all-too-appropriate sound of crickets in the night, forced him to seek another outlet.

He'd never been a regular at the D&D, but it was the only late-night eatery in town, serving a menu that ranged from hamburgers to cheeseburgers, and was thus eminently popular with the young folks. One night, a bad night, one of those rare but not rare enough nights on which his illness and his grandmother's converged—he vomiting a thick, murky substance into the toilet while she scowled, uncomprehending, at the shattered dinner plate she'd just slid off the table—he felt, like a pinprick to his spine, the need to get out.

After the nausea passed, he managed to collect himself enough to guide his grandmother to bed. He sighed at the mush of cold potatoes and peas on the floor, the plate in pieces. He'd clean it later, tomorrow. The house was still. He took the car and drove out into the night, feeling that the distance between himself and that house actually made the surrounding air more agreeable. He rolled down his car window and breathed, long and deep.

When he entered the D&D's saloon doors, he hung back a few moments before taking a seat in the far corner of the room, waiting to make sure it wasn't Lorene's section. The place was bustling enough that she wouldn't notice him right off.

Neil Young played on the jukebox: *I heard you knockin' at my cellar door, I love you baby, can I have some more...*

His waitress, Diane, came and brought him a menu.

"I'll just have a whiskey and coke," he said, watching Lorene across the room as she carried a tray of burgers and fries out from the kitchen, wearing her red D&D T-shirt, jean shorts and the same white tennis shoes she'd worn as a cheerleader, now more grease-stained than grass-stained. Shep tried to squirrel himself deeper into the corner, never taking his eyes off her.

With a drink in hand, he relaxed some. A mild buzz would distract his body from the myriad ailments that came and went in waves, and his mind from the burden of focus. He scanned the room, recognizing roughly half the clientele from his school days. They all looked overgrown somehow, the guys with patchy beards and baseball hats molded to their heads, some now married to the girls they'd dated in high school. The younger girls, though. Where did they all come from, with their overdone eye makeup and overpowering laughter, their milk-fed smiles and endearing baby fat? He didn't remember any of them.

"Shep," came a voice from his left. He set his glass down.

"McNabb? How you been?" The man took a seat across from him.

"Not bad, not bad. You?" They'd been in the same unit, but rumor had it McNabb had gone on to OCS and was now a butter bar, the name given to entry-level officers because the rank was a single gold bar, as worthless and as easy to get as a stick of butter.

"I'm doing okay." Shep caught Diane's attention and motioned for another whiskey and coke. "How about you?" He cringed as soon as he said it, knowing that he'd now begun a loop of pleasantry, repeating the same noncommittal sentiment with which he'd begun.

McNabb laughed and took a sip of his beer. "Well, I guess I could mention I'm a fuckin' father now, what do you think about that?"

Shep could say, *What do you know, me too,* he thought, but wouldn't risk it in the same room with Lorene. He saw her now, leaning across the bar to place an order for one of her tables, not twenty feet away.

"Congratulations, that's great."

"Thank you, thank you. Daniel's his name—Danny—one month old tomorrow. All he does is sleep." McNabb laughed again.

Shep didn't know him all that well, remembering him mainly for the time during a training exercise when he'd tried to do a macho cook-off with a smoke grenade. McNabb took his thumb off the spoon and held on, ready to count to five, playacting as though the grenade was an armed one and that he was preventing the enemy from throwing it back during the interim prior to explosion. But everyone knew you couldn't do a cook-off with a smoke grenade, and it detonated the moment he let go, fusing his hand to its metal body in a puff of white-hot smoke. He was carted off, wailing, to the infirmary, returning that afternoon with his hand mummified in gauze. Shep couldn't believe someone so careless was making a career for himself, commanding respect from younger guys who knew he was an idiot but wouldn't dare say it out loud.

Diane brought Shep his second drink.

"He's all better now, but he was born with one of those... fuck, I don't remember what they called it, that thing where your tongue's set too low, so it's pressed down in the bottom of the mouth? Operation took care of it, pretty much."

"Oh, well, that's good."

McNabb looked back at him with a glassy, expectant stare.

"I mean, I'm sorry."

McNabb laughed. "I'm pretty hammered in case you couldn't tell. I haven't had a drink since before he was born, so I'm making up for lost time. I was just sick non-fucking-stop for...I don't know, stomach flu," he laughed. "Sarah said I could go out with the boys tonight though, you know, since I'm just off for the weekend and all..."

Shep could tell now that McNabb wasn't kidding about being hammered. His stare was glassy because his mind had gone slow. Shep drank some more, not to catch up but because he was so uncomfortable, wondering if there was a polite way to tell McNabb he'd rather be alone.

It was then that Lorene saw him. He looked up and was

startled to lock eyes with her. She whispered something to the bartender and wrinkled her nose, and as though the jukebox knew what the moment was doing to him, the song ended and no other song followed, so the room was filled with the din of chatter and clanking of glasses and silverware, with no soothing rhythm to gloss over the anxiety flooding through him. Lorene and the bartender shared a little glance, and she didn't look Shep's way again.

Now, in his car, on a dark shoulder off Laurel Canyon, Shep felt himself growing hard with the memory of what happened next.

He waited in the parking lot after closing, not with any plan in mind; he hadn't gotten that far in his thinking. He just wanted to see her, see what she'd do, where she'd go, maybe see her greet Lila at her parents' house; maybe he could catch a glimpse of the little girl through the window, even just a shadow against the curtains.

He watched from behind a dumpster as Lorene exited with the bartender, waiting next to an unfamiliar pickup while he locked up the front. Her own car was parked a few spots down. She was going to leave it there. And though Shep knew then that she wouldn't be going home, wouldn't be seeing her daughter tonight, once the bartender climbed into the driver's seat with Lorene beside him, Shep counted to five and followed.

Tucked into the canyon, in his fogging cocoon, in the shadows of multimillion-dollar homes dug precariously into the hillside, Shep unzipped his pants, reached a hand inside, and began to rub his dry palm against his erection. He kept his eyes closed, remembering, not wanting to, but it was too late now.

He followed the bartender's blue Toyota to the next town over, snaking between cornfields, farmhouses and squat yellow hills. He kept a fair distance, but they were the only cars on the road at that point. She had to know, didn't she? She had to have known exactly what he was doing.

jerky for Lionel and held his breath as he exited the store, a squeezing taking hold behind his eye sockets and spreading across his forehead. It could start that quickly.

As he started the car, he was struck by something he thought he saw across the street. It was hard to see in the dark, so he drove up beside it, confirming that it was that realtor's ad, with the black teeth, black eyes, and a new addition now, a bumper sticker for a band called The Dead Weight slapped across the man's name.

He rolled down his window and craned his neck to look up the hill. She was up there now, Cynthia in her empty mansion, moonlight dancing across her pool, heated to the exact temperature of spring air. She was up there, and he…he was all the way down here. Lower. He might as well be deep down in the bottom of the canyon, underneath the streets, in the cold dark earth.

But. If he could go up there again, if he could forget who he was for one more night, if he could let someone believe he was worth something, maybe the belief would rub off. Didn't people go west to reinvent themselves? And couldn't a change in altitude trigger a lifting in the heart?

Lionel climbed up into the front seat and onto Shep's lap. He looked down at the dog, then back up the hill. "Lionel, you're awake. You want I should turn on some music?"

Shep turned on the radio, and a song he'd never heard before was playing, a mournful instrumental, piano and hushed violin. The towering young palm trees swayed overhead, firmly tethered to the earth but terrifically loose in the night sky. Lionel whined in a way Shep might've interpreted as a warning.

"Shhh," he said to the dog. "Shhh."

He eased the car up the hill, taking in every landmark in order to retrace his flight, up this time instead of down. The trees kept dancing, shaking in slow motion under the white moon.

9

Shep tapped lightly on the door. He looked left and right, wary of being seen by some staff member or security guard. He gulped, knocked harder. Lionel squirmed under his arm.

The door opened just a sliver.

"Is that...John?" Cynthia whispered.

Shep took a step back. He could still leave. He should leave, he thought, before he made an even bigger fool of himself.

The door opened all the way then, and Cynthia took a step forward, barefoot in a silk bathrobe, her hair twisted into a low bun. He couldn't tell if she was looking at him with concern or whether it was her face's lack of makeup that made her look sad, pitying, her eyebrows sparse against scrubbed-clean skin.

"Hello there," she said, reaching out to Lionel. The dog sniffed the underside of her wrist.

"I...wanted to apologize for the other night," he said.

"People use telephones for that sort of thing." She let the dog lick her fingers.

"I know, but I didn't have your number, so..."

"Why don't you come in. I don't want to stand out here, do you?"

"I hope I didn't wake you," Shep said, ducking through the doorway.

"Would you mind taking off your shoes?"

He kicked his boots off and left them in a pile by the door, then doubled back to stand them up neatly side by side. Only the living room was lit, seashell-white furniture arranged around a glass-topped coffee table. A steaming teacup sat on the table, a bamboo coaster in between. He held onto the still-squirming Lionel, afraid he'd leave dirty pawprints on the pristine floors. He stopped in the doorway, afraid to sit down himself. He had to be dirty too. Jesus, he hadn't even washed his hands.

"Have a seat. Can I get you anything to drink?" Cynthia took a marked-up script off the couch and set it on the table.

Shep stood still in the entryway, his eyes darting all around at the room.

Quietly, to himself, he asked, "What am I doing here?"

"You tell me." She curled up on the couch, legs tucked like a cat's, and draped her arm over the back of it, and suddenly he felt like he was in a therapist's office. He sat down at the other end but didn't let himself sink down into the cushion. He remained rigid, careful, still clutching his dog with both hands.

"Not now. That's not what I mean." He tried to find the right words. "I mean…why did you stop the car?"

Cynthia took a sip of tea. "You seemed like you needed help. Didn't you?"

"You felt sorry for me."

She laughed. "I felt a certain responsibility to you, true, as an employee of the production. And of course I wanted to thank you for saving us from a massive lawsuit." She laughed. "God knows they pay you peanuts."

Shep's headache burrowed through his forehead. He closed his eyes in surrender to it. "I think I need some water."

"I'll get it. John, relax. I'll get a bowl for your dog, too."

When he opened his eyes again, she was gone. He let Lionel down, and the dog began systematically sniffing every corner of the room.

When Cynthia returned, he downed the whole glass in one go and wiped his mouth on his sleeve. He set the glass down on one of the bamboo coasters and noticed his splotched fingerprints on it. He couldn't touch anything without dirtying it. Lionel happily lapped from his metal bowl.

"My, my," Cynthia said.

"Sorry."

"For what?"

Shep didn't know. But he still didn't feel he'd gotten an answer to his question.

"You said I seemed like I needed help. And that's why you offered me a ride. But why did you bring me here?"

She looked down, smoothed her robe, brushed a speck of lint off the belt that lay draped across her thighs.

He watched her, waiting.

Cynthia looked up at the ceiling fan, its blades gleaming white like the walls. There was no dust in the room, no dust in the air.

"Do you know who my husband was? Of course not, it doesn't matter, but...you know I was never allowed on his sets? He said I was a distraction. I was flattered, at first. I thought he meant I drove him wild or something." She furrowed her brow. "But he needed things a certain way. He needed me to be in certain places and not in others. He needed me to practice...a conditional existence. I can see that now. I can say it."

"I'm sorry."

"Stop apologizing."

Shep repeated it in his head as a means of restraining himself from saying it out loud: *sorry, sorry, sorry.*

"Anyway, none of it matters, I guess. I'm still...I'm getting used to myself."

His headache had begun to fade some. He was listening to her but still didn't understand. "You keep saying things don't matter."

"I suppose we all repeat ourselves." She looked down and fiddled with the hem of her robe.

Shep unclenched, let himself relax against the buttery suede couch cushion. For a moment, it felt as though they were here, together, equal in their uncertainty. Could it be that easy? Shep imagined what it might be like to really be with a woman like Cynthia. To escort her to premieres, cook meals together with wine and a roaring fire no matter the season or weather, host parties on the patio, women in thousand-dollar dresses dangling their feet in the pool. Is that what those people did? Trying to imagine the life she lived was like trying to fathom one part of the city from the vantage point of another. Who could imagine soft sand kissing the edge of the ocean's violent rush when you were under a dying fluorescent lightbulb in a Boyle Heights bodega? Who could think there were mountains, with mule deer drinking from streams, so close to the Hollywood freeway murals, inept renderings of James Dean and Elizabeth Taylor gazing dumbly under the overpass, the sidewalk beneath them littered with cigarette butts and used condoms? You couldn't put together a full picture. It was a place balled up like paper, too many jagged folds between one view and the next. He'd still never been to the ocean, never even seen it from his car window.

Lionel hopped on the couch between them, and Cynthia stroked his chin. Her skin was shiny with some kind of night cream, her eyes small without the smoky eye makeup she'd sported the other night. But she held herself with the same slow grace. She didn't mind being seen, didn't mind letting him see her.

"How's Lila doing?" she asked.

"Good, good," he said.

She smiled politely, expectantly.

"Um, she's a little depressed, I guess…the business, you know, it gets to her."

"Of course."

Shep ran his fingers over the couch cushion, stared at its tiny wrinkles. He didn't have a couch, just his mother's rocking chair, which seemed too old and fragile to sit in, and a chair at the kitchen table, where he ate his quick, unconsidered meals.

"You know," he continued, brushing the suede back and forth with his palm, "there's just so much rejection. And I worry about…the choices she's making. The…people she's surrounding herself with." Shep thought of the sleaze who'd gone home with her, his impression of the man based solely on the fact that he was with her and Shep didn't want him to be.

"Drugs?"

"No, no, nothing like that…" Shep pulled back. He didn't want her to think he'd raised Lila poorly. "I just worry is all. Can't help it." He kept his eyes on the back of his hand. It was easier to talk this way, without looking at her.

"I know. Believe me. Mine are in college. Two Ivy League tuitions and neither of them will so much as tell me who they're living with; it drives me crazy."

There was an awkward pause as Shep struggled to come up with some common ground, some story about young people and their foibles.

"Oh God," Cynthia said, "I know how obnoxious that sounds. Forgive me."

"No, no, I know what you mean. Lila won't tell me anything either." He sighed, relieved to have stumbled on an excuse for any vagueness in his story.

"It's not fair, is it?" Cynthia said. "We spend all those years obsessing over their every move, feeding them, protecting them, loving them so much we can't breathe, and then they just…have no use for us."

Lionel scooted up beside Cynthia and rubbed his head into the crook of her elbow. "He sure seems to like you," Shep said.

She stroked his head. "The kids begged for a dog, and I never got them one. Seemed like too much work."

Shep nodded. He didn't know what to say but didn't want to leave yet. "I got Lila a cat," he blurted, "when she was seven. But it turned out the cat was much older than the lady I bought her from said. Only lived a few months before we found her curled up behind the barn."

"Oh my god," Cynthia winced. "Poor thing. How did she take it?"

Shep's face grew hot as he remembered where the story had come from. It was Marty Cumberland's folks who'd been tricked into buying a geriatric cat, behind their barn that Shep and Marty had found her, half-frozen after a full night and school day. Shep remembered feeling flummoxed in the face of his friend's unrestrained wailing as Marty wrapped the animal in a towel from the laundry room.

"She, uh, she took it hard. Awful business."

"Well, I'm sure this sweet puppy makes her happy now."

Lionel took his leave from her, returning to his master.

"It's late," she said.

"Do you want me to leave?"

"I didn't say that."

Shep sat on her bed while she got ready in the bathroom. He picked up a framed photo from the bedside table: Cynthia, her hair a few inches shorter, beside a man who must have been her husband. They were standing in some sun-dappled meadow with their two children, a boy and a girl in their teens. The husband had one arm thrown around Cynthia's shoulder, the other hand resting on his son's, beaming and proprietary. The girl held her mouth in the same gently amused way Cynthia did, the same curtain of dark hair draped over one shoulder. Did all daughters carry on their mothers' charms? It seemed obvious they would, but it still stopped him, the idea of beauty as a renewable resource.

While the water ran in the bathroom, Shep undressed and continued daydreaming himself into Cynthia's life. Maybe he'd shave his beard. Buy some new clothes. He glanced at the tall oak bookshelves that lined one side of the room. He'd take up reading, ask her for recommendations. Of course, he'd have to figure out how to reconcile his real relationship with Lila and the one he'd invented. But there was time for that. Once he and Lila found their way to each other, he'd make up for lost time. All he needed was a chance, and he could make the lies true.

Cynthia emerged from the bathroom in a white nightgown, considering him from the doorway as she rubbed lotion from her hands up to her elbows. He liked the way she looked at him, liked being the man he'd made himself out to be. He was still so stunned to be in the presence of such luxury, not just the house, with its moneyed air of vigilant maintenance, but Cynthia too; she breathed ease, blinked calm. The fantasy bred more fantasy and lulled him into contentment with himself, whichever self he chose.

In her bed, with the lights out, Shep felt soothed, swaddled. They lay side by side, not touching, but close enough that Shep could breathe in her scent. It was all so clean, even the windows, so spotless that the moonlight streamed in unfiltered. She faced away from him, her hair spread behind her on the pillowcase, and Shep brushed his face against the ends, gently so she wouldn't feel him moving. Emboldened, he inched closer to her and lightly draped his arm around her waist, prepared for her to push it away. But she held onto his hand with her own. He leaned in further, brushing his nose against the back of her neck.

"You can hold me," she whispered, "but—we'll just sleep, okay?"

Shep nodded whispering, *mmm-hmmm* against her neck. Somehow this seemed light years more intimate than the other night, which had happened so quickly it hardly seemed to have happened at all. And in just a moment's reflection, he realized he had never spent a night just sleeping with a woman, had never shared a bed out of anything but post-coital convenience. To choose to sleep, just sleep, with someone was so new he couldn't compare it to anything. He rested against her. He felt her heartbeat against his chest. She let him feel it. Sleep came like warm air enveloping him, swirling up out of the floorboards.

***

A hot afternoon, deep in the belly of the Saudi Arabian desert. Shep was at a dead stop on the Tapline, the road that paralleled the Trans-Arabian Pipeline for hundreds of miles, called "Suicide Road" for thesoldiers, drivers like himself, who'd been killed when the long, flat, one-lane monotony of it made them drowsy, sending them drifting off into the sand or into oncoming traffic. There was some disturbance up ahead, too far up for him to see what it was. The radio was all gibberish. He pulled a small notebook from his pocket. He'd been trying to record things: the subtle shifts in weather, the progression of the fires, the dreams he could remember when he was able to sleep. He hadn't written much yet, but he hoped that slowing down his thoughts would help him write letters that amounted to more than inarticulate cries for help, letters that might be worth sending.

He tapped his pencil eraser against the page, periodically looking up into the oppressive glare to see if traffic had started moving again. Even in sunglasses he had to squint like the sun was six inches from the tip of his nose. He tap-tap-tapped the pencil on the notebook, then tap-tap-tapped it on the steering wheel. Even inside the cab he felt exposed. *Tap-tap-tap.*

Thump-thump-thump

Shep jumped in his seat, and the pencil fell from his hand.

THUMP-THUMP-THUMP

A fist slammed against his window, a bloody fist that left slick red streaks with each *THUMP*. In the spaces between the streaks, he was able to make out a soldier's torso, his BDUs soaked and blackened, one pant-leg ripped off at the groin, the mangled leg inside it gushing blood onto the pavement. Again the soldier thumped the window, harder this time. The other arm was gone; his face, whatever face remained, was blocked out by the sun.

Shep tried the door. He yanked at the handle, but it wouldn't open. He tried the passenger side door, and it was stuck too, as though the mechanism had been soldered shut.

THUMP-THUMP-THUMP

On one side of him: the half-dead soldier frantically punched the window. On the other side: an impassable sand ditch. In front and behind: walls of vehicles, immovable. There was no way to go, no place but here.

Shep pulled with all his strength, his hands now shaking, his sweat causing them to slip off the handle. Finally he gave up and began beating on his own side of the window in some attempt at communication:

THUMP-THUMP-THUMP

      THUMP-THUMP-THUMP

THUMP-THUMP-THUMP

      THUMP-THUMP-THUMP

And he saw that the streaks he left on his side of the window were black, the same color as the sweat that was leaking from his pores. He tried to wipe it off on his pants, but the tar kept bubbling up from inside.

THUMP-THUMP-THUMP—

***

"John, John, wake up."

Shep's eyes were fused shut as he rocked fitfully from side to side in Cynthia's bed. Gradually he realized where he was, but couldn't open his eyes or stop shaking. It was only when he smelled Lionel's muggy dog breath that he was able to calm down, to stop and lie still. The dog licked Shep's upper lip, his tongue flicking against Shep's nose hair.

He opened his eyes to the bright-lit room, the white ceiling, Cynthia's bewildered face hovering over him, puffy with sleep.

"John, are you alright? What was that?"

He propped himself up on his elbows and looked down his chest at the dog, expectantly batting his eyes, curled up between Shep's knees.

"Can I get you something? A glass of water? A cold washcloth?"

He shook his head.

"Do you need an Aspirin? An Alka-Seltzer?"

"No, just—"

"Do you want me to—"

"Stop!" he yelled.

Cynthia shrunk back toward her side of the bed, still staring at him with furrowed brow.

"I'm sorry. Just…go back to sleep."

She nodded okay, shut off the light, but there was a tension in the bed now as they both lay on their backs, awake. Finally, Shep could no longer ignore the pain. He found his way to the bathroom in the pre-dawn pink edging in through the curtains and shut the door behind him.

Slumping onto the smooth white toilet, he breathed in anticipation of the storm brewing in his gut, holding his stomach as though he could keep it under control by any means.

For once, he retained some memory of the hell he'd been plunged into, that had clawed at him, holding him kicking underwater. That was the problem with his dreams. They attacked his body just as they attacked his mind. Before the war he never dreamed, hardly at all, and when he did, it was something innocuous, like he'd shown up to school in his underwear—dumb stuff that didn't matter. But if, as others had intimated, as he reluctantly suspected, the things he'd been exposed to in the desert had changed his body chemistry, then there was something that had reached deep into his psyche by way of his blood. It pulled all the bad stuff to the surface and let it run roughshod, assaulting him as he slept.

Finally: release. His twisted insides unleashed into the bowl—which he imagined was spotless like fine china before he came along—and he wondered what the hell he was supposed to do now. Just climb back into bed as though he hadn't acted like a crazy person and then defiled her perfect spa bathroom with its jacuzzi bath and basket of organic soaps on the marble counter, that she wasn't hearing the whole thing that very moment? Jesus. Or climb back into bed and let her fuss and fret over him like he was a child? What kind of idiot was he, that he let himself imagine she could be his, she who had been married to some industry titan? Sooner or later she would start asking questions about who he was, about his life, about his past and his plans, and he didn't trust himself to maintain the illusion he'd fostered when the sun rose and he returned to level ground.

As he cleaned himself up, flushing several times to clear the crime scene, his frustration turned itself on Cynthia. Who did she think she was, collecting him like some stray animal or wayward boy? To entrap and bewitch him into returning in spite of his better judgment? He washed his hands with a grainy purple soap disc and left it wet and slimy on the counter. It was getting light enough. He could get dressed and see himself out without a word. He could leave and never come back, wind his way back down the hill and forget he'd ever seen the top.

When he opened the bathroom door, he could see Cynthia's form curled into a fetal position, her palm flat against the empty side of the bed. Was she asleep? He stepped as lightly as he could manage, flexing his feet slowly, carefully against the cold hardwood. How long had she slept alone? He wondered if her unconscious would forever drive her body into the pattern of marriage, a hand laid out on her absent husband's chest. He wondered if she wondered the same thing, if she knew her body's secrets.

When he reached the bed, leaning over to feel for his discarded jeans on the floor, he saw that her eyes were open. He stared at her a moment, and in the semi-dark, he was able to imagine that she wasn't staring back. The dog was awake too, watching from the bedroom doorway.

"You're leaving," she whispered, not a question.

Shep sat down on the bed, his back to her, pants in his hands, his resolve already softening. Couldn't he pretend, just a little longer, to be worthy? At least until the sun was fully risen?

"You don't have to go."

She was sitting up now, holding the pale sheet over herself.

He swallowed, turned to face her again. He was so tired. And she smelled sweet, like vanilla or cocoa butter. He couldn't name the sweetness, but it relaxed him. He let the jeans fall from his fingers. He closed his eyes and slowly sank toward her, let his body curl back into hers. He laid his head in her lap, wrapped his arms around her waist. He thought of the homeless man he'd seen at the river's edge, hugging the tree at its base as though he were the tree's own child. Cynthia held Shep's head in her hands and brushed his greasy hairline with her fingertips.

Shhhh, ssshhh, sshhh, she whispered.

He hadn't known he was making any noise.

10

Shep hadn't noticed the night before that Cynthia's bedroom opened out onto a wide terrace. The view was of a lush forest dotted by mansions of wildly varying styles, from clean glass rectangles to faux English cottages. There were no rules, each home crafted to an individual's specifications with no thought to era or place, or to the existence of others at all. Shep looked out over the hillside and wondered who else was looking out at the view, unknowingly looking back at him.

"Do you take cream and sugar?"

Shep shook his head and took the cup Cynthia offered him. He'd woken up alone in her bed, red-eyed and disoriented until Lionel hopped up and nuzzled him back to life.

She set a plate of croissants on the table—a half dozen of them, though it was just the two of them—alongside a carafe of orange juice, a bowl of berries.

"Wow…," he said. "This is…uh…" He wanted to say "too much," but Cynthia had already gone back inside. He took a croissant and began tearing it into fluffy strips.

She returned, tapping on her phone as she sat across from him. She was dressed and made up already, and set her bag down in her lap. It made him uncomfortable to imagine her tiptoeing around him as he slept, exposed and snoring. He'd left a large circle of drool on her pillow, which he'd quickly turned over as soon as he noticed it.

"I'm glad you finally got some rest," she said. "How are you feeling now?"

"Good—"

Lionel, barreling out onto the terrace, began growling and yipping at Shep's ankles. "Shhh, hey, hey, hey," he whispered, scooping him up from under the table.

Cynthia dropped her phone in her purse, poured herself a cup of coffee. Shep was glad; he'd thought she was about to leave. He hoped she'd suggest he stay a while, relax. He pictured himself practicing leisure, tanning poolside with a magazine tenting his face or wandering the grounds trussed up in her dead husband's clothes.

"You look a little pale. Are you sure you're okay? You were tossing a lot in your sleep. Didn't seem particularly peaceful. Have you been to a doctor lately? Had a physical?"

"I'm fine."

"Have you ever tried therapy?"

Shep averted his eyes.

"John, I don't expect what I'm going to tell you is going to hold much sway. I know I barely know you…and I'm probably overstepping…"

Shep listened, but fixed his gaze on the hillside behind her.

"I told you my husband passed away, but I didn't tell you how. I didn't know anything was wrong. He'd always been consumed by work, always half there when you talked to him. I thought he was keeping secrets from me. I didn't know he needed help. Nobody did."

"I'm sorry."

"He thought he was saving us trouble, taking it out of everybody's hands. He thought he could just disappear into the water. He didn't count on somebody seeing him jump off the pier, too far away to save him, but close enough to tell the police. And the press..."

"Oh, Jesus. That's awful."

"I'm okay. It was a long time ago. I'm only telling you this because I can sense that you need to talk to someone. It doesn't have to be me."

"I'm not him."

Cynthia's eyes watered slightly, but no tears fell. "I know you're not, I know. I just didn't want to take the chance of not saying anything. You can forget it if I'm way off base."

She reached out and laid her hand on his, her touch causing the night to rematerialize in his memory: the cold-sweat terror of his dreams, Cynthia's soft lap and cooing platitudes, and the way he felt alternately calmed and trapped by the untold extravagance of her bed, her skin, her scent.

"Anyway," she said, pulling her hand away with a little squeeze, "I need to be going soon, but I was thinking, I'd be happy to take your daughter to lunch some time, if she wants some advice. You can give her my number, or I can call her, either way."

A terrible itch rose up his back. "Uh, she's awful busy these days, I mean..."

"Actually, how old is she? I might have a part for her—a tiny one—but she could at least get her SAG card."

"She's, you know, I don't know..." Unprepared, he couldn't summon enough words to make a sentence.

Cynthia cocked her head, looking him in the eye. "Well, you have my number, anyhow, if her schedule frees up." Her chair made a scraping sound as she got up from the table. "You can see yourself out when you've finished, no rush."

Shep stared after her for a moment, then peeked over the railing as she exited the front doors and stepped into her waiting car. He heard the call of a mourning dove, *coo coo-woo,* and glanced at the tall cypress tree that rose up beside the terrace. The bird was perched on a thin branch, its dun-feathered throat contracting with each *coo.*

He looked down at Lionel in his lap. "Let's get out of here."

Shep could hear the phone ringing through the front door as he wrestled with his keys, still raw and fumbling from undersleep. He grabbed the phone mid-ring.

"Yeah?"

It was Central Casting. Someone had called in sick, and now they were asking him to drive all the way to a ranch off of Escondido Canyon Road that would be standing in for the Old West. His first instinct was to turn it down, but he decided the cash would be nice. When he hung up, he turned to Lionel.

"Can you take care of yourself today? It's too hot to stay in the car."

Lionel looked up at him with those big brown eyes. Shep got down on his knees and picked him up.

"I'll ask Rosa to take you out later, promise."

An hour later he was driving up the 14. On either side of the highway, housing developments—the hulking houses all peach and beige with Spanish tile—crowded the landscape. A stone church at the top of a hill overlooked the houses and the highway too. But before too long, the housing developments were replaced by nothing at all. The plain was all brown, the sky all blue. Minus the mountains against the skyline, it could've been any stretch in the deepest wilderness of Nebraska.

At the bottom of the exit ramp was a yellow sign with an arrow pointed right, beneath the words "Hart's County," the title of the miniseries he was to be filming. He followed the small winding road past farmland, cattle and horses, and through the little town of Sweetwater. In one house's driveway, a little boy was setting up a lemonade stand. He placed paper Dixie cups in even rows while his mother carried a cooler out to him. This too could be confused for Harner, Nebraska. Except for the fact that all the livestock had appeared in countless feature films.

At a stop sign, Shep squeezed eyedrops into his sore eyes and checked their redness in the rearview.

In some kind of unused barn—a wooden structure with a dirt floor but no evidence of animal occupancy—they outfitted Shep and the other male extras as cowpokes in wrinkled Western shirts, boots, vests and hats. He watched as a makeup artist's assistant sprinkled dirt onto a man's neck, rubbing it underneath his collar while he drank a Diet Coke.

Suddenly Shep felt water misted on his face, and instinctively swerved his head out of the way.

"Hold still," the other assistant said. "I've gotta get you looking kind of sweaty, like, clammy. You're supposed to be a drunk."

"Oh, they didn't tell me that," he said, submitting to the watering. Uneasily, he realized he had finished the last bottle in his glove compartment the day before. He'd been planning on replenishing his stash, but he'd been interrupted by the call. A knot formed in his stomach as he tried to settle himself with the idea that he wouldn't be able to go out for a nip at break time. Already the day felt like a trial.

"I'm gonna rub some grease in your hair, okay?"

Shep nodded and bent down so the assistant could reach the crown of his head.

When he was all decked out, Shep made his way to the background holding area. Sometimes he lucked out with a nice air-conditioned room with couches, fresh coffee and pastries piled high. He'd seen some rooms that were less comfortable, but the career extras had told him horror stories of being packed into little windowless rooms with flies buzzing about the waxy American cheese slices and bowls of bruised fruit at the craft services table.

The extras on this shoot were expected to await instructions in an actual corral, like animals. He stepped into the ring and closed the gate behind him. There were droppings on the ground, so there must have been horses here at some point, spirited off somewhere. Shep felt suddenly embarrassed by the line of work he'd fallen into. This wasn't work. Landscaping was work. Driving was work. Dressed up like some kind of gruff, Old West drifter, with dirt spread delicately across his face with an honest-to-god powder puff, he felt less a man than perhaps ever before in his life.

The hat they'd given him was much like the Cowboy's, and he tried to imagine himself in the man's shoes, sitting in the concrete nook. Did he ever sweat, grow thirsty, grow restless? What were those belongings so precious to him that he could never let them out of his grip? He wished he were at Parkdale's now, nodding hello to the man before settling in behind the counter to enjoy a cold beer in peace.

And then, in his customary scan of the holding area, with no beat, no shift in the air to put the moment in relief, there she was: a sunbeam. He squinted at her a few yards away, talking to another girl. He wasn't ready for her, hadn't dreamed this would happen now, today; for a moment he thought he'd somehow conjured her by saying her name aloud to another person. He stared at the contours of her face, incredulous to the point of skepticism that his half-baked plan, if it could even be called a plan, was panning out before his eyes.

She was dressed in some kind of saloon girl getup, a red bustier, ruffled skirt and boots, her hair done up in a pile of curls and lips painted scarlet. He recognized her by her chin first, soft and honey-tanned, her face heart-shaped just like her mother's.

Shep rushed to the buffet spread at the other side of the corral. He squeezed in between people making up plates and a grabbed himself a Styrofoam cup of water, which he drained in one pull and filled up again. The other extras and PAs stepped around him as he braced himself against the table. He breathed in four counts, held for four, then let it out for eight, then repeated for several more breaths, a technique he'd been taught by a VA psychiatrist, the only thing from the six sessions he'd attended that had stuck.

While he concentrated on steadying himself and his breathing, there was a sudden rush of whispering as everyone around him edged closer to the fence, their collective footsteps like a wave of static through the dirt.

She's so skinny, someone said
Her head's, like, too big for her body or something.
I read she only eats three things: sashimi, edamame, and sunflower seeds.
She is pretty, though.
She's not that pretty.
Look at her neck...
Look at her nose...
That wig is not working for her.
I don't think it's a wig, I think that's her hair.
I heard her hair's falling out from being overprocessed...
...Or from anorexia.
What does she use on her skin? It's like she doesn't age.
I heard she's a total bitch.
She looks so much older in person. I mean, look at her hands...

Shep looked up as the actress they were all intently watching while the director conferred with her and her co-star. They were both smaller than average, he only an inch taller than she, and both of them were so heavily made up that they looked clownish in the daylight. The actor wore a hat like Shep's, though he had a badge and a holster at his hip. She wore a modest period dress and apron, the sheriff's good woman.

"I think she's amazing," a voice next to Shep said quietly, and he turned.

Lila was standing a few feet behind the pack, smiling, wet-eyed.

She looked at him and tilted her head.

"Haven't we met?" she said.

Shep's jaw trembled imperceptibly while he struggled to find words.

"Yeah," she said, "I know I've seen you before. You ever go to Café Gourmand?"

"I...no, I don't think I know it."

"That is so weird," she said, "I could swear."

"Well, maybe we've seen each other someplace else," Shep finally managed.

"Yeah, maybe." She shrugged, then nodded toward the throng of extras still huddled at the gate and leaned in conspiratorially. "These jackals...they'd all give their eye teeth to be in her place."

"I don't believe I am familiar with her work," Shep said, cringing inwardly at the stiltedness of his speech.

"Seriously? Yeah you are. She's on the cover of *Entertainment Weekly*, like, right now. Not to mention *Vogue*. And *Elle*."

"Oh..."

"I had a picture of her cut out from *Vanity Fair* when I was in high school, on my dream board that I hung up in my room. I put her in the middle because she was my idol."

Shep turned and took another look at the actress. She was luminous, true, and looked vaguely familiar now that he thought about it. But Lila was more beautiful any day.

"I'm Lila." She stuck out her hand.

"Shep, I mean, John. John Shepherd." He panicked then, thinking he should have given her a fake name, sure that she must have heard him spoken of at one point or another by somebody, if not Lorene then by some mutual acquaintance, but he saw no flash of recognition in her eyes.

"Have you lived in L.A. long?" she asked.

"What, do I seem…green or something?"

"Maybe a little. I can just tell. I've been here, like, forever. Over two freaking years now and I've gotten *one* commercial for a check-cashing service, and it wasn't even national. Oh my god, I'd *kill* for a national."

"I think you'll do okay."

"Aw," she smiled. "You're sweet. You wanna get a coffee?" She leaned in again, whispering, "I am so hung over it's not even funny."

Shep nodded, and followed her like a puppy back to the craft services table. He could feel his shoulders hunched and his head bowed, but couldn't seem to change his posture. He was too anxious. Too reverent.

She handed him a cup and took a sip from her own.

"You have a place yet? A job?" she asked. "I know a place if you're looking."

"No, no, I've got a place," he demurred. "A house in the hills," he continued, then quickly shut his mouth. He hadn't planned on lying right out the gate, but there it was.

"Oh, well," she said, "I guess you don't need my help! I'm still in a little popcorn-ceilinged shitbox in the valley. I'm kidding, kind of. I love it though, I do. Do you know what I did when I first moved in?" She leaned in so close when she spoke, he didn't know where to look.

"I was so freaking excited to be in my own apartment that I actually squeaked after the landlord left me with the keys. I just ran my fingers along the walls, around and around the living room until my fingertips burned. The walls are white, but my fingertips came away black—don't ask me! And then I just lay out on the carpet, splayed like a starfish, just humming and singing songs at the ceiling. I was so happy."

Lila paused a moment to fuss with her nails, and Shep took the opportunity to examine her face. He'd never been closer and was overwhelmed by the texture of her skin, her pores, the peach fuzz on her upper lip, a blemish camouflaged with makeup, her hairline, flyaways and follicles, the black pools of her pupils, her honey-brown irises—there was so much *her*, so much *she* to take in. She took a hangnail between her incisors and tugged, spitting the offending bit of skin onto the dirt.

"Sorry," she laughed. "Sometimes, still, I just can't believe I'm really here. My mom keeps telling me I'll come back to Nebraska one of these days, but I don't think so. I really don't think so."

Shep watched her as though she were a wild animal. He had to step lightly and stay quiet in order not to disrupt her or scare her off.

"Background! Be ready in five!" called one of the PAs.

Lila downed the rest of her little cup of coffee and pulled a tin of breath mints from her décolletage. She popped one onto her tongue and then offered them to Shep.

"Oh, no." He shook his head, though he actually did want one. He couldn't seem to decide what he wanted quickly enough to act. He wanted a day to prepare, to start over with a full night's rest and a clear head.

She pushed the tin back down into her bodice and began chatting with another group of extras.

A minute later a bus pulled up, and they were herded out of the corral and up its steps by a PA. Instead of a prod, he held a walkie-talkie.

"We going somewhere?" Shep asked Lila, interrupting a conversation about headshot photographers. He made sure to stick close by her so they'd wind up sitting together, and followed close at her heels as she selected an aisle, negotiating the ruffled skirts of her petticoat as she plopped onto a seat.

"Oh yeah, we're going to the Vasquez Rocks. You never hiked there?"

"I'm not much for hiking."

"Well if you've ever seen a Western, or *Star Trek*, you've seen 'em."

There was a long silence as Lila stared dreamily, drowsily out the window, her face bathed in sunlight, while he tried not to stare.

The bus stopped at a trailhead lined with juniper bushes, and the extras filed out. Shep followed Lila out onto the trail. The earth was cracked, the wind a refreshing surprise. In the distance, a long wooden facade—a line of backless storefronts—was being fussed over by set dressers, while a cameraman positioned his crane.

Lila took Shep's sweaty hand in her tiny, soft one and led him up a red rock that jutted up at an angle. The suddenness of the movement made his stomach lurch, and he swallowed a mouthful of vomit as he tried to keep up with her. Though she was weighed down by her mass of skirts, she scrabbled up the rock ahead of him, agile like a desert fox. Shep freed his hand from hers and grabbed onto a rock face that seemed damn-near vertical. He kept an eye on the soles of her black boots kicking little pebbles in her wake.

Finally they reached the top, Lila beaming, Shep red-faced and sweating.

"Look!" she said.

Shep struggled to his feet and stood beside her. On one side, rocks, red, orange and brown, stretched out as far as the eye could see, their surfaces marked by millennia of wind and weather. The clouds above were white as cotton, the air clear and cool.

Shep turned the other way, toward the highway, where a nonstop stream of cars flew by. But they were so small they could have been part of the ecosystem too, like insects, or the skinny lizards that ran from rock to brush.

"Oh my god, are you okay?" Lila said. She ran her hand across his forehead.

"I'm fine, great." He concentrated on breathing.

"Here," she said, clutching his arm like a candy striper. "I'll help you down."

Shortly after they reached the ground, Shep was ferried to one area and Lila was hustled off to another with a group of women in similar costume; they were in the same scene, but on opposite sides of the frame. Between takes, he craned his neck to locate her in the sea of bodies, but it was no use. He took solace in imagining the finished product. When it came out on DVD, you'd be able to find the scene and pause it, trace the space between him and Lila with a finger dragged across the screen, the short trip punctuated by static shocks. Each time "cut" was called, he paused the scene in his head and zoomed out until all the people became blurs of color, specks against the desert canvas, she and he and all of them, together as one picture in time.

He realized now, of course, that he hadn't planned anything beyond this, this moment, this encounter, this chance to do... what exactly? His mind raced, not with thoughts but with a stutter of dull panic. He'd had years to prepare, of course, and nothing to show for it but a desperate, gaping hole in his heart that he seemed determined to fill with bullshit.

Another take, and Shep resumed the position for his loosely choreographed wandering. The light had to be just right to get the shot the cinematographer envisioned. Shep looked up at the sun warily; it was still full overhead but would begin lowering soon enough. The time that remained could be measured by a palm held up against the sky. But who could say when the moment was right? Who could recognize the shadows in their proper pattern?

11

Shep got home late and slept in until nearly eleven. He sat up in bed with his legs tangled in the sheets. He'd barely lasted till the end of the shoot, walking back and forth, back and forth across the patch of land they'd made up to be a gold country outpost, then back to the ranch where they'd built the saloon set. He'd been let go before Lila—she'd been chosen along with two other girls for a close-up shot alongside one of the lead actors—and in her swooning excitement, Shep saw an opportunity.

"Hey," he said as he approached from behind. She was anxiously checking herself in the mirror in the extras' wardrobe tent, smoothing her eyebrows with a shaking hand.

She looked up and briefly met his eyes in the mirror.

"Uh," he said, "did you have this on your dream board?"

"Huh?" She wiped a smudge of eyebrow pencil from her temple.

"On your…" Shep realized his opening was nonsensical, didn't know what he meant by *this*, but he had to forge on. "I mean, you still have that dream board?"

"Oh…no, that was just kid stuff. My mom's probably tossed it by now."

"Of course. Yeah, I figured." Lila hadn't looked at him again. It was better to back off, wait for a quieter, clearer moment. "I'll see you around though, huh?"

It was easier to be happy in her proximity when she wasn't looking back at him, when he could let his gaze linger on her face while the makeup artist dusted her closed eyelids with shadow. When she opened her eyes again, Shep ducked behind the wall he'd been clutching. She just needed to get to know him better, that was all. He let go of the wall and shook out his cramped fingers. He *would* see her around, that was a certainty. He knew now what a small and ever-shrinking orbit the two of them could occupy.

With Lionel tied up in a shady spot, as the electronic chime sounded his arrival, Shep nodded at Hung and fetched his morning beer. The routine felt fresh somehow, not rote but cyclical, the most natural thing in the world.

"Dude, where you been?" Hung said. "You missed some *serious* shit yesterday."

"Oh?" Shep cracked his beer, and the popping sound was so satisfying.

"The cops came down on Eugene, boy. You heard it here first."

"Shit. Did they arrest him?"

"No. But they were there for a loooooong time. They were doing some major interrogating."

"Do you...know what it was about?"

"Yeah, it was about the H&J, what else? I told them everything I know, and I mean everything."

"So, they talked to you too? Not just Eugene?"

Hung rolled his eyes with his customary exaggeration, putting his whole body into it, sinking his knees down within the baggy puddle of his jeans.

"They talked to everybody, 'cause they had to, 'cause they got new information. But everybody knows who they were really there to talk to. Trust me, they don't usually go sniffin' around months after the fact for your everyday shooting. They couldn't give a shit less most of the time. It's when rich folks' money is being fucked with, that's when they give a shit. Trust."

"So what did you tell them?"

"I told them the truth: Eugene and his crew have been causing a constant disturbance since the day they moved in, and everybody around here knows it."

"Constant? Really? I don't know about that, Hung."

"You're not here all the time like I am. You don't know."

"Okay, okay." Shep raised a hand in surrender.

"I wasn't telling them anything they didn't already know. If anything I was just confirming their intel."

Shep snorted. "*Intel*. Where do you get this stuff?"

Hung wasn't laughing. "You know how many times I've been questioned by police? Really, guess."

"I didn't mean anything by it—I'm sorry. It was just funny, I don't know why..."

"Guess."

Shep sighed. "I don't know."

"Seventeen times. You know this isn't the original Parkdale's location, right? We used to be in Sun Valley. Sounds cute, right, *Sun Valley?*"

"I've never been there, I couldn't say."

"Biker gang capital of the southland. Now I got another question for you."

He didn't wait for an answer. "You ever been tied up? For real. You ever been tied to a chair, had a gasoline-soaked rag stuffed in your mouth while motherfuckers stole everything you've got? Ever been left like that overnight? No. Really."

"I—"

"We're not relocating again. I'm not relocating again."

"Sorry, I didn't know."

"*That's* why I gotta protect myself." He motioned Shep over. "C'mere."

Hung pushed some rolls of receipt paper aside, reached all the way to the back of the shelf under the register, and pulled out a Beretta 9mm.

"Put that back, man, I get it."

Hung gripped the handle with utmost care and sobriety, cradling the barrel in his other hand. Shep didn't have the heart to tell him it was a shitty gun.

"Loaded," Hung whispered.

"For Christ's sake, Hung, put it back. You don't have to prove anything to me."

Hung complied, arranging the paper rolls to fully conceal its hiding place again. The two were silent for a minute until Lionel began raising a ruckus outside. He was barking with the full power of his little lungs, and Shep could hear the scratching of his claws against the pavement, testing the strength of his leash tied to the bike rack. He went outside to see what was going on.

"Hey, what's the matter? You see a monster? You see a ghost?"

Lionel calmed down as Shep scratched his chin. He smoothed the hair at the top of the dog's head gently with two fingers.

When Shep stood, he felt a pang in his chest, as though something were wedged up against his ribcage. He took a few rapid breaths and rubbed the spot until it dulled enough not to alarm him. Breathing effortfully, he wandered away from the storefront for a moment to soak up a bit of sun. It felt good on the top of his head. He closed his eyes and breathed in the scent of glazed dough from the other corner of the strip mall.

When he opened his eyes, his gaze fell on the window above Parkdale's. It was rare for the curtains to be open, but today they were pulled back as far as they would go, and there stood Mrs. Phan with her back to the window. Her head hung forward, and her shoulders were hunched up at her sides. She wore all black, with no skin showing between her hair and the collar of her blouse, so she was a dark column. He perceived a vibration in her back. The column was quaking. He stood transfixed, in no hurry to go back inside until he remembered the beer that was growing lukewarm behind the counter.

The electronic bells chimed.

"How's your old man doing?" Shep attempted to change the subject.

"Fine."

"He had any more episodes?"

Hung had the drawer underneath the register open and

was counting lottery tickets, ensuring they were divided into their appropriate stacks, the scratchers separated from the Big 5 Lotto slips.

"Nah. He don't even get up."

Shep remembered the relief tinged with shame that he'd felt when his grandmother's fitful roaming and nonsensical tantrums had given way entirely to the near-catatonia that defined the last year of her life.

"I'm sorry," he said.

"Nothing to be sorry for," Hung said, still somehow counting in his head. "You leaving?"

"I was thinking I'd better."

Hung replaced the scratchers and shut the drawer, locking it with a small silver key from the unwieldy chain looped to his jeans, then looked out the window, a quick scan across the parking lot.

"Hold up a sec? I been meaning to ask you a favor."

"Yeah, yeah, anything."

Hung huffed a put-upon sigh. "Listen, I told the cops everything I know about Eugene, but it wasn't enough for them to make an arrest. I been trying to think what else I could give them, but it's like, I can't just go over there and poke around, you know? Eugene's already got his eye on me. He's being careful."

"Okay..."

"So I was thinking, you're not really, like, on his radar, so if you just maybe tried to get close, see what you can see..."

"You want me to spy on the water store?"

"Not *spy* spy. Just see what you see."

"I don't know what you expect me to look for."

"I just need some grasp of the layout, the what and the where."

"What for?"

"Don't worry about it."

"You gotta give me more than that, Hung."

Hung pursed his lips. "Look, before he got sick, it seemed like my dad was having some kinda, like, *rapprochement* with Eugene. They were talking. A lot. He would even go over there some mornings, come back with some of that gunpowder-grade Armenian coffee. I don't know what they talked about and nobody'll tell me—Dad can't, and Mom sure as shit doesn't know. But whenever he came back from the water store…it was like he was shut down. Super-serious, even more than usual. I'd ask him what was up and he wouldn't even acknowledge me. He'd send me off on some errand, almost like he was trying to get rid of me."

"That's it?"

Hung glanced out the storefront. "I don't think there's anybody even over there right now. Haven't seen a one of 'em yet today. Maybe they're in the back."

"Why couldn't you just talk to the guy yourself?"

"Talk to the guy? Do I need to remind you who we're dealing with here? Nah, I'm gonna do this my way. Are you gonna help me or not?"

Shep sighed. "You want me to go there right now?"

"You gotta jump on opportunities when they present themselves."

Shep untied Lionel outside and hoisted him up under his arm. The water store did indeed appear to be empty. There was nobody behind the counter, but the door was open. He crossed the lot, glancing up at the Phans' window as he passed. Hung's mother had vanished, so all you could see were the edges of the yellow curtains and the white wall behind them.

He took a cursory look around. Not only was the store empty, but the shelves were sparsely populated. There was the constant display of hookahs in the front window, but when you took a second look, they were caked with dust.

"Hello?" Shep said. What was he supposed to do? Sneak in the back? Rifle through their books? He took a deep breath and squared his shoulders. If he could just erase his doubts and act like this was some kind of role, that Hung was a PA and "see what you see" an instruction, *blocking*—that was something he could do.

In the back stood a row of water coolers and different-sized refillable jugs, everything marked with peeling orange price tags. Then his attention was drawn behind the counter by a small framed poster on the wall depicting a bleeding forearm with the words *Our wounds are still open* carved into its flesh.

Splayed out on the floor beneath the poster was a little spiral-bound notebook, face down. Still clutching Lionel close, he picked it up and leafed through. The pages featured some pencil drawings, landscapes mostly, some clumsy, labored cursive letters—practice, it would appear—and then, toward the back, were the faces. The giant heads, spindly necks and hanging arms. Shep turned the pages with fascinated delight—he'd wondered, when he first saw Eugene's kid scribbling in the window, if he'd found the artist. What was his aim in displaying his work on the telephone pole? Did his folks know he was doing it, or did he rush out there in secret, late at night? Shep quickly flipped through the pages until he landed on one that was different. This portrait was of a dog, a scruffy terrier with a nose painstakingly rendered, the paper shiny and dented with the effort of coloring it black.

"I think it's you, Lionel," Shep whispered. "I think somebody likes you."

He heard the slam of a car door then and quickly dropped the notebook where he'd found it. Eugene entered through the back door.

"Can I help you?" He dropped his car keys on the counter wearily. The collar of his polo shirt was wrinkled and damp.

"Um, yeah, can I..." Shep scanned the room for a legitimate purchase. "Can I get a Yoo-hoo?"

Eugene pulled out one of the two that sat in a countertop fridge behind him and set it down in front of Shep.

"One twenty-five," he said, without touching the

register. Shep pulled change from his pocket and counted it up in his cupped palm.

"Um," Shep said, "where are your friends at? I usually see you guys over here during the day."

Eugene raised his eyebrows, shrugged.

"It's summertime, huh? Where's your son at, camp or something?"

Eugene held out his hand for the change. "I have three sons."

"Oh yeah? Huh."

"Thank you. Have a nice day." Eugene held eye contact and nodded toward the door.

As Shep departed, Eugene called after him, "S'okay this time, but next time, no dogs."

As he crossed the lot, he saw Hung watching him through his front window. Shep tried to send a message with his facial expression, something on the order of *Forget about it*, or *No dice*, but Hung's encouraging nod led him to believe he hadn't communicated anything at all.

When he reached the corner, he saw that the portraits on the telephone pole were showing their age, rough, wrinkled by the wind, the pencil lines faded to practically nothing, with no new ones added. Some things had even been stapled over the missing persons, an ad for a housecleaning service, and another offering a thousand-dollar reward for the return of an African gray parrot named "Lucky."

As he and Lionel made their way home, he tried to make a plan for the day, remembering that Lila would be starting her shift at Café Gourmand at three, but maybe it was a bad idea to get too close, given that she would recognize him now. He'd have to reassess his approach. He was struck then by a stabbing in his gut. His mouth filled with saliva, which he finally spit into a hedge. He let Lionel down on the ground and braced himself against the wall, abandoning his drink on the sidewalk.

He could feel it coming, the iron body cast of fatigue, the sickness, no telling how long it would last, not again, not now, but he should have known—the ramping up of the sleep paralysis, the daily headaches, it was all of a piece, and it was bearing down.

"I'm sorry, Lionel. You'll just have to hang on. We've got to get back home now. We've just got to get…" He stopped. His lungs weren't up to the task of walking and talking. Perched on the power line overhead, an African gray parrot blinked down at the street below, then lifted off, disappearing over the treetops with a squawk.

12

The morning sun streamed through the window as through a magnifying glass trained on the back of his head, where he lay with his face buried in the clammy sheets. Each breath was painful. The thought of food was anathema. What he really could have used was a drink of water, but still, again, he couldn't get up. That was one thing Lionel couldn't do for him. Though the dog was certainly hungry, and even more certainly had to pee, he didn't whine, but merely sat at Shep's side with near-supernatural patience.

It came in waves, this sickness that defied diagnosis. Sometimes, he could go months, even a year or two with no severe symptoms, long enough that he could start to believe the VA's official position, that it had been PTSD, that it had been psychological the whole time, the pain, the nausea, the night sweats. He'd convince himself it was dealt with. His mind had recovered, and his body had followed in turn, never mind the fact that his stomach was never the same, that even at the best of times he never regained the level of energy he'd had prior to the war.

It was over, he would decide, and now he could focus

on the important things, meeting Lila and starting over—which, up until her marriage, had also included vague ideas of winning back Lorene—finding his way back into some kind of career, maybe taking up running again. He would cut back on the drinking too, just as soon as the time was right. Time and again, he would wait at the brink of a new beginning. He would stand at the tip of the diving board, bouncing lightly on the balls of his feet, readying himself, feeling electricity coursing up his legs, through his joints. He'd finally leap out, leaving the board springing back behind him. But in that moment of floating—exhilarated, finally ready—he would open his eyes and find the swimming pool empty. He'd close them again and mentally prepare himself for the coming blow and the long wait at the bottom.

He moaned into the mattress, the pain squeezing his skull from temple to temple. Finally, he managed to get up onto his hands and knees, then onto his feet long enough to take Lionel out to the strip of grass just outside the building. The dog danced through a sunbeam while Shep clung to the wall. He hid behind a hedge, aware that he must look like some kind of monster, his face pale and damp. He smelled burning and winced—that smell always returned, as though it were *in* him—until he looked up and realized it was the top of the hedge that was on fire, the uppermost rows of leaves already singed black.

He looked both ways down the street and didn't see anybody, so he yelled, "Fire! Hey, there's a fire out here!" hoping someone inside would hear him. He craned his neck to see if he could get an idea of just how bad it was. He supposed Rosa must have a fire extinguisher, wouldn't she? Before he could go get her, a young guy peeked out over the balcony above the hedge, his immediate upstairs neighbor, one of a rotating roster of students at the nearby community college. The balcony was decorated with vertical strips of yellow police tape, hung like a beaded curtain.

"Oh shit," the guy said. He had a cigarette hanging out of the left side of his mouth and wore a white T-shirt so baggy it was hanging off his collarbones. He disappeared then, returning a few seconds later with a pitcher of water, which he casually poured down onto the hedge. Smoke whooshed out from the leaves and got Shep to coughing. He doubled over, a dribble of saliva hanging from his lips. He stood up with his palm over his mouth and nose. Lionel was wagging his tail, circling Shep's feet on the steps of the building. The fire was out now, and the guy upstairs was gone. The police tape swayed in the breeze.

Shep went back in and got a drink of water for himself and the dog, poured some kibble in Lionel's bowl. His head and throat still ached, but the pumping of his heart was robust enough to make him think that maybe he would be okay after all. He'd just go back to the bedroom and rest his eyes for a bit.

An hour later, he was back at the bottom of the swimming pool.

Lionel hopped up onto the bed and nudged his master with his nose. He was breathing but didn't stir. Lionel climbed onto the rocking chair, and from there onto the windowsill that was just wide enough for him to stand on. He pushed the blinds aside with his muzzle and stared down at the sidewalk, pressing his wet nose to the glass. A large tabby crawled out through a fence, and Lionel wagged his tail and danced back and forth on his paws as he watched the cat trot alongside the hedges.

Once the cat had disappeared from view, another figure passed beneath the window, the Cowboy pushing his cart. Lionel licked the window as he watched the top of the man's hat and the skittery roll of the cart's wheels.

The Cowboy stopped and looked up, as though he felt Lionel's gaze overhead, the dog's quivering black nose, the twitch of his whiskers, wiry hair the color of straw, eyes deep, black, searching for his. The Cowboy removed his hat and squinted up, his hairline flattened and sweaty. Their eyes met, and Lionel pressed his nose against the window. The Cowboy wiped his forehead with his handkerchief, put the hat back on. He resettled the contents of his cart and kept walking.

13

Shep squirmed in bed, still half asleep. There was something stirring in him, something that called to him from the surface world. He rolled over on his back, and the sensation localized itself in his groin: a tingling ache, a rush of blood. His eyelids fluttered, and then he felt a hand on his penis. It was soft, dry, just gently stroking him. He blinked and saw the hand, small and pale, a silver ring, almond-shaped fingernails painted with a translucent gloss. He blinked again and saw Cynthia's face, her dark hair hanging down. She watched him curiously, lips parted, her hand moving up and down. Shep closed his eyes again as pleasure surged through his body in waves, building, building—until it stopped abruptly.

"You can tell me," Cynthia's voice whispered. "There's no daughter is there?"

"What?" he gasped. She was still gripping him in her hand.

"You don't have to pretend with me. You made her up, didn't you?"

Shep tried to look her in the eye, but this time her face was in shadow so he could only see her body on the bed, which could be any body.

"Who is it you're following, then?" the voice said, and now he couldn't tell whose voice it was

Shep grunted, finally able to push himself up to his elbows. He patted the bed, then his own body. He was alone. He was alive.

He wasn't sure just how many days he'd been down, but

in all those days he hadn't showered once, and his own smell had grown overpowering. Still, he felt better enough to get cleaned up. Lionel twirled across the bedroom floor, sensing that a veil had lifted.

After a long, hot shower—much of which Shep had spent leaning his palms against the shower wall, the scalding water pummeling his back—he stepped into the kitchen and fixed himself a can of beef stew. He leaned back against the counter and watched the flame from the stove flit about beneath the pot, and his gaze wandered to the phone on the wall and its flashing red light. With no small amount of trepidation, he picked it up and dialed his voicemail.

...Mr. Shepherd, this is Linda Acevedo, background casting for Married Law...

...Hi, Mr. Shepherd, this is Rich Morris, background casting for Under the Gun, *a new reality show that follows...*

...I'm calling on behalf of Californians against Prop 27. We're spreading word throughout the community that...

...This is an automated message from AT&T...

How long had it been since he'd answered, or even heard, the telephone? He only half listened, watching the stove, deleting each message as soon as he got the gist. Then he came to an empty message. He plugged his other ear to listen more closely and was able to hear what sounded like breathing, followed by a clattery hang-up. He played the last message over and made a note of the date spoken by the choppy automated voice: *Monday, June 30th, four eleven, p.m.*

He pulled the phone from his ear, squinted at the smudged screen, and the date he saw looking back at him—Sunday, July 6th—stopped him cold. He'd lost over a week, it seemed, pulling himself from his bed only to attend to the dog's basic needs.

The 4th of July. That's what all that noise had been the other day, the gunshots and the fireworks that sounded like gunshots, both of which kept him jumping and writhing in his bed and kept Lionel barking at the ceiling all night long. He'd thought he was having aural hallucinations. It seemed as likely, anyhow.

The mailbox was jammed full with ads and grocery store circulars, a check from the VA, one from Central Casting—no doubt in a pitiful amount, really, were it his goal to earn money. He dropped it all in a heap on the counter to sort through later. Now he slumped himself against the wall and sank to the floor. Every time it happened like this, the aftermath felt like starting over, but not in the sense of freedom or new beginnings. He was stuck at zero, all previously made progress moot, as though he'd been treading water all his life and would never have the ability to change direction or get out of the water.

Lionel climbed up on Shep's lap and stuck his nose under the lapel of his terry cloth robe.

"Lionel," he whispered, "what now?"

The dog didn't answer.

Shep struggled to his feet and returned to the kitchen. Stew had splattered onto the stovetop, and the pot's contents were bubbling like lava. He could smell the bits that had burned, charred and cemented at the bottom. He turned off the burner and picked the pot up with a dishrag, then dropped it directly into the sink. But his finger slipped as he was letting it go, and the handle seared the underside of his knuckle.

"Goddamnit," he said under his breath, and kicked the baseboard, sucking on his finger. He kicked the wall again, harder.

Goddamnit.

Shep looked for something else to eat and, finding nothing suitable, put on some clothes, leashed up Lionel and stepped outside, still cursing under his breath.

Sun seemed to glow through the hedges and between the ivy that climbed up apartment building fences. He'd left his sunglasses in the car some time ago, so he had to shield his eyes with his free hand. Though he felt notably better, he moved with hesitation, and the sounds of the street—the traffic, the barking dogs and gentle breeze—seemed muffled, warped and slowed.

When he reached the corner, he was struck with an uncanny feeling that something was wrong. He looked toward the nook: no Cowboy. He glanced across the street, and there he was, massaging the handle of his shopping cart and staring out. The man's new position was a strange little jolt, as though a hand had reached down from the heavens, taken the wind in its grip and shifted it to a new angle. Shep scooped Lionel up under his arm and walked to the intersection. With one hand stretched across his forehead, he locked eyes with the Cowboy and gave a nod. The Cowboy looked back, a current of leaves and dust flowing between their mirrored gazes. Shep turned away. As he crossed the parking lot, Eugene appeared in front of the water store and began hosing down the pavement in a powerful stream, soaking the sidewalk and sending little rivers rolling underneath the huddled cars. Shep stepped over the water and approached the Parkdale's storefront.

He tied the dog to the bike rack. The electronic chime sounded.

Hung was working on the word jumble, a ballpoint pen cap hanging from his bottom lip. Too hungry to wait, Shep grabbed a bag of chips and tore it open, shoving them two by two into his mouth as he took his seat beside Hung.

"Where you been keeping yourself?" Hung asked. "I was afraid you'd turn to dust without your daily Miller and sodium injection."

"Oh, no place. You know."

Hung laughed. "Yeah...no place. I been there." He worried the pen cap in his fingers and squinted outside. "Oh, real nice," he said, shaking his head.

Shep wasn't paying attention. He chewed the greasy

chips in a way that felt meditative, eyes closed, listening to his own crunching.

"Real nice when we're in a fuckin' historic drought, just hose down the pavement, puddles everywhere, who cares, right?" His head kept shaking, automatic.

Shep glanced out in time to see Eugene roll up the hose and return it to the side of the building. "Come on, Hung, he's done now, no use getting mad." He didn't have the energy to listen to Hung's paranoid ramblings today, not when he had so much ground to make up, to claw his way back to wherever it was he'd gotten before the sickness found him.

Hung spit the pen cap out into the wastebasket. "Don't tell me when to get mad. Don't you tell me shit."

A knot formed in Shep's throat, and the room seemed to grow hotter.

"You think Eugene's just some harmless local shopkeeper, just running his business, just minding his own?" Hung said. "Then tell me this: How come I walked in on Eugene upstairs in *my* home, talking to *my* mom, huh?"

"What? When?" Shep had never been inside the Phans' apartment.

"Three days ago. In the morning, just after opening, when he thought I wouldn't be there. Didn't come through the store or nothing. He came up the *back* steps. Deliberate. But I'd left my phone up there, so I went to get it, and there they are, all chatting in the kitchen like they know each other or something, 'cept they clammed up real quick when they saw me."

"Did you ask her what it was about?"

Hung leaned against the register, cooling some, grateful to have someone to talk to. "Yeah, and she wouldn't tell me shit. Said 'don't worry, don't worry.' But she was scared. Wouldn't look me in the eye."

"What did Eugene do when he saw you?"

Hung's jaw clenched again. "Fuckin' smiled like the cat that ate the canary, that's what he did. Something's not right.

I knew it before, but now I *know*. There was something about the way he sat. Legs spread wide, elbows on the table. The way you sit at your own house."

There was a gentle scratching at the glass, and Shep peered out to find Lionel on his hind legs, dragging his front paws against the storefront and whining.

"I hear ya, I hear ya, little man, but you gotta be patient," he whispered. He crouched down and touched his index finger to the glass where the dog was mashing his wet nose, then rose slowly, a dull pain spreading up from his tailbone.

When he turned around, Hung was staring open-mouthed down the store's center aisle. There, between the Bud Light display and the Lay's potato chip end cap, Mrs. Phan stood shaking. Her eyes were wide and quavering, her face drained of color. She looked thinner than the last time Shep had seen her, the sleeves of her pilled sweater hanging loose down past her wrists. She looked like a child just woken from a nightmare.

She sank to her knees, slamming them into the shiny linoleum floor. Hung ran out from behind the counter and wrapped her in his arms as she began to sob. He looked up at Shep, his face contorted in confused panic.

Without a moment's hesitation, Shep stood and went to the door. Across the parking lot, Eugene leaned against the stucco wall, hands in pockets. He nodded to Shep, pulled one hand out to offer a two-fingered salute, then returned his gaze to the street and its lazy midday traffic. The blacktop was slick, dirty water collecting in its corners. Shep watched the sun, white and still, reflected in a puddle. He flipped the Open sign to Closed.

PART THREE

1

The lights were off, but every few minutes, a faint buzzing emanated from one of the fluorescent tubes in the ceiling, as though they were readying themselves to be relit. The air had grown stale because the door hadn't been opened in three days. The air took on the scent of the plastic containers, the thin cardboard boxes, bottles and bags, the inks and polymers that lined the shelves.

Every day people would come by, press the edges of their hands to the glass door and look inside. They'd back away, register the Closed sign, and content themselves with an LA Weekly or a coffee from the donut shop. It didn't matter what they'd actually stopped for.

Inside, the silence wasn't silent. The refrigerator echoed, the lights buzzed, the walls breathed.

In the apartment upstairs, thirty people, mostly Vietnamese, were crammed into the living room, which Mrs. Phan, even in the depths of her grief, had spent the previous day cleaning vigorously, scrubbing baseboards, dust-busting the curtains, polishing furniture, while her son made phone calls, wrote checks, found room in the fridge for the pots of food people dropped off. The two of them spoke little, only exchanging looks across the living room, or taking turns, one watching the other. Now he sat on the couch by himself drinking black tea, while his mother sat across the room in a huddle with her friends.

Shep approached, light-footed, and sat down beside him.

The service had been a disorienting affair, held at a funeral home a mile up the road. Surrounding the casket was an elaborate altar bedecked with framed photos of Mr. Phan, burning incense and flowers. Though the casket was open, he was thankful to find that a white cloth had been placed over Mr. Phan's face, a ritual that Hung later explained was meant to symbolize the barrier between the deceased and the living. Shep recalled the shock of his grandmother's open casket—he wasn't sure he'd even been offered an option by the mortuary—her waxen grimace and clay-like eyelids (he'd felt a sick urge to lift them, to see her blank marble eyes), her lips painted a shade of coral she never would have worn, her doll's hair parted on the wrong side.

Shep sat in the back, not wishing to disturb anybody, and watched as a procession of elderly men and women, fixtures of the church the Phans had fallen out of the habit of attending, filled the seats in advance of the family's arrival. Then he saw Hung lead his mom to the front row from a side entrance. Hung glanced around, taking in the room. Mrs. Phan didn't look at anybody. The pastor took to the podium at the front and began speaking in Vietnamese. Shep tried to imagine what he might be saying for a few minutes before zoning out.

"You hungry?" Shep said. "Want a sandwich?"

Hung shook his head.

Shep searched the ceiling, trying to think of something he could offer. The day Hung's mom had come downstairs, he'd felt a rush of exhilaration, shameful in retrospect, thinking he would drive Hung's dad to the hospital and save the day. But when he announced breathlessly that he'd be right back with the car and to meet him outside, Mrs. Phan just shook her head at the ground, tears dripping down her jaw. The only thing he could think to do then was grab a box of tissues off the shelf. He got down on the ground beside her and handed them to her one by one, exchanging them for the used ones she'd soaked through, while Hung held her. They stayed like that for several minutes until Hung helped his mom up and led her upstairs, nodding to Shep in a way he took to mean, *Go on and let yourself out.*

"You want anything stronger?" Shep said.

"What've you got?"

Shep pulled a small bottle of bourbon from his stiff, little-worn dress slacks, unscrewed the top and tipped it into Hung's held-out cup.

"That's better," Shep said. Hung kept staring at the ground.

"You didn't have to come to the ceremony. You could've stayed here."

Shep shrugged. His suit jacket was too tight around his armpits.

"I, uh, I left a card for your mom on the table, with the others."

God, what do you say? He couldn't remember what any of the few relatives and church ladies that had come to his grandmother's funeral had offered in the way of condolences, among them the now-grizzled, lazy-eyed uncle Chet. He hadn't even been listening. And of course he remembered even less about the aftermath of his own mother's passing. On the day of her funeral, he'd been dropped off at a daycare of sorts— the dusty living room of a chain-smoking nineteen-year-old who watched soap operas all day, leaving the kids at a table with scratch paper and number 2 pencils. Some idea of sparing him, he supposed. No one had in fact explained to him that she was dead. He put it together over the weeks that followed through overheard phone conversations and the certainty growing in the dark of his belly that she wasn't coming back.

"Listen," he finally said to Hung, rushing the words, "I just want you to know that I'm sorry, for everything. And I want to help, if I can. That's all." He felt the sweat stains in the pits of his freshly ironed shirt growing under his jacket, dampening his sides.

"You don't have to have a fuckin' aneurysm over it," Hung said. "Chill."

Shep nodded. He gently patted Hung's shoulder and rose to his feet, stopping off at the restroom on his way to the back staircase that led to the alley behind the strip mall.

When he emerged, Hung startled him at the back door.

"If you mean it, there is something you could do for me," Hung said.

"Sure, anything."

"My mom decided she's gonna spend some time at her cousin's place up north, and she doesn't drive…"

"…I'll take her."

"Wait, let me finish. I'm taking her. I got that under control. But, I can't afford to keep the store closed, and I figured you know how to handle the register…maybe you could run it the few days I'm gone? Ten bucks an hour plus all the shitty pizza you can eat?"

"You serious?"

"Hey if you don't wanna do it, I just thought—"

"No, I will."

"Cool, cool. So, meet me down there around eight tonight and I'll show you everything you need to know?"

"You trust me?"

"What?"

"You trust me? Really?"

Hung gave him a funny look.

"Okay." Shep repeated, "Okay," getting used to the idea as he turned toward the stairs, catching a brief glimpse of Mrs. Phan across the room. She was staring at the wall while another woman held and stroked her hand as though it were an injured animal.

"Hey!" Hung called down the stairs. "You'll be a fuckin' expert at the word jumble by the time I get back, I can guarantee that."

Shep nodded while Hung stayed in the doorway a moment, idly scanning the neighboring stairwells and the alley below before returning inside.

Shep tripped on the third-to-last flimsy aluminum step, but caught himself on the railing. His feet tumbled down the last steps, landing hard in the gravel, and he used the railing to pull himself upright. He wiped his palms on the front of his slacks and looked up and down the alley. The only witness was a bored-looking Siamese in a second-story window.

He removed his tight jacket and sweat-stained shirt, draping them over his arm as he continued the walk home in his undershirt.

An ambulance wailed past, its piercing sound somehow crueler in the heat, and Shep stopped instinctively, as though he were a car on the road, making way.

At the apartment, Lionel greeted Shep as he always did, as though Shep were some conquering hero. He gave the dog a scratch on the neck and walked to the bedroom closet, undoing his restrictive dress pants. He slung them onto a hanger and set his black dress shoes—freshly polished the night before—on the top shelf, where they would sit until the next funeral, he supposed with some pause. He pushed the shoes back on the shelf until the heels touched the wall.

Shep's gaze settled for a moment on the bunched and battered old rucksack on the same shelf, stiff from lack of use and lack of cleaning, desert sand still embedded deep in its fibers. It was too boxed in by old junk on either side to extract with any ease, but his eyes went straight to the drawstring hanging down over the edge of the shelf. Like a cat, he felt momentarily compelled to thwack it.

But he pulled it instead and, with both hands, spread the mouth of the sack open. He reached in and withdrew a small first aid kit (a good thing to know he had, so this was a useful chore after all, he reasoned), followed by a musty, mildewed rain poncho and an aluminum camp stove that left a sooty imprint on the carpet when it fell. He dug with one hand, scooping items out onto the floor. Lionel stood watching on the bed, flinching every time an object dropped. Finally he lay down with his paws outstretched, his head turned at an inquisitive angle.

Shep dug his whole arm into the sack and pulled out the thing he'd actually been looking for, a pile of papers so brittle he gripped them as lightly as possible for fear they'd crack and crumble through his fingers. He sat down beside Lionel and held the pile in his lap.

Some of the envelopes were stuck together, and some of the ink was so faded it was almost yellow. The whole stack smelled of something vaguely sweet and vaguely rotten. He could remember, though it pained him, what had held him back from sending the letters to his grandmother, to Lorene. Those were the only two people he'd thought to write to, but each time he completed a letter—and there were many, over twenty in eight months—shame seemed to block up his throat, the thought that no one wanted to hear from him, that his words were a burden he should keep to himself, and every time, he tucked the letter away somewhere to think about sending later.

He opened one of the envelopes easily enough, as the glue was all but disintegrated, one addressed to his grandmother. He turned on the bedside lamp, but still his handwriting was hard to make out. As far as he could gather, it was mostly an accounting of the weather and the food. At the bottom, he'd written something that looked like "Take care of yourself" and on another line, "Don't be shy about asking for help."

He'd signed it "Love, John."

It was bolder than anything he would've said to her in person, the suggestion, though it was true, that she needed help and was too proud to seek it out. He'd known it, and he'd left her alone anyway.

He folded the stiff paper back inside the envelope and set it aside, then one by one opened the others.

In one letter to Lorene he told her about a dream he'd had, a manifestation of his frustrated lust, in which she had crept into his bedroom window back home, slithering nude like an animal under his covers, before evaporating, just as he awoke, into a cloud of vapor that smelled of jasmine and honeysuckle, the signature blend of essential oils that she dabbed on her neck each day. When he woke up for real, he had a hard-on so ardent it was painful. He curled into a fetal position against the wall and jerked off in near-silence.

The letters to his grandmother were short, dull, polite. There was no reason to have sent them, not really. But the letters to Lorene. They were one side of a great love story.

In another letter, he told her of how he would try to call up the taste of hamburgers and beer, and of her strawberry lipgloss, some sensual recall of the night they first got together, something to mask the taste of smoke that now filled his mouth no matter how much time he spent gargling mouthwash.

In another, he told her how he'd thought of her when his convoy stopped at the sight of a half-dozen dead sheep at the side of the road. He'd sat in his truck while they radioed the incident back to base and waited for the chemical investigation team to get there and test the air. He'd closed his eyes and imagined she was in the seat beside him, frightened and disturbed, clutching him for support while he stroked her hair and told her everything would be okay. But when he tried to put himself back there now, the image seemed false. He wondered where he'd gotten it, because he couldn't put her face to the image—only her hair, her shadow, her shape.

He knew now why his longing had been so debilitating: in some pocket of his unconscious, he must have known his child was growing in her, attached to two umbilical cords, the literal and the cosmic, the latter stretched across the ocean to his lonely desert cot.

But the shame was still there, the shame that kept him quiet, that had lived in him long before and ever since everything got all screwed up.

Shep dropped his head in his hands and began to hyperventilate, but was able to get it under control with his breathing trick, breathing in for a four count, holding for eight, then releasing for eight, over and over until he found his way back to a steady rhythm. When he sat up, he looked at the crap all over the floor, which he could either put away neatly, toss, or shove back in the sack as though he'd never opened it.

He heard a tear and found Lionel chewing on one of the letters. He'd ripped the corner off another. Shep stiffened to reprimand the dog, but then he dropped his shoulders.

"Knock yourself out," he said. "They're yours now. I bequeath 'em."

Shep checked the kitchen phone. It was just before five o'clock. He had three hours, then, before he had to be back at Parkdale's. Three hours was enough.

Lionel bit down on a piece of brittle, yellowed paper, tore it off, and mashed it to a pulp between the tiny points of his teeth.

2

Shep idled kitty corner from Lila's duplex and contemplated knocking on the door. He could come up with something to explain how he knew where she lived, couldn't he? Maybe he'd seen the address on her time sheet at the shoot and, you know, accidentally memorized it? Or maybe he could wait around the corner until she came out, then bump into her crossing the street, tell her he had an appointment in the neighborhood, and what was she up to? He cringed a little more with each bad idea, and finally began circling the block, glancing up at her window each time he cruised past, until it started to feel less purposeful and more like a ride he couldn't get off.

He finally came to a stop back where he'd begun, noticing a dented black van that had parked up ahead. On the back of it, the words *"Follow me to..."* were printed in white cursive, but whatever attraction had been advertised underneath the words had been painted over in a dull gray that stood out against the shiny black, a tour van that had been repurposed, and hastily, it seemed. If you looked, there were vans like these all over the valley, these ports in a dust storm, with clothes hanging in windows and bicycles wedged in front seats, emanating scents of tobacco, patchouli and weed. He'd recently seen one with duct tape-covered windows, plastered with handwritten signs: *Stay Back; You Are Under Video Surveillance; Will Refuse All Medical Care; You Are on the Internet Even if You Can't See the Cameras; Report Any Trespassers Hanging Around this Van.*

He heard a disturbance then, and rolled down his window to hear the yelling that seemed to be coming from inside the van's tin-can walls. Its door slid open, and a woman hopped out, her tennis shoes giving her a little bounce as she hit the pavement. Shep was startled to recognize her white, witchy hair, her identity as the Wraith confirmed when she swung around and gave the side of the van a swift karate kick as it sped off in a cloud of exhaust, her leathery face defiant, a Marlboro Red gripped between her front teeth. She'd shed her black coat and now revealed her ropy red limbs in shorts and a tank top.

"Aw, get the fuck out!" she yelled after it in a pained rasp.

Before she could spot him and redirect her rage, Shep pulled away from the curb and drove around the corner, winding up beside a vacant lot that was overrun by weeds and littered with broken chairs, mattresses, and drawers yanked from dressers, as though a tornado had hit with unprecedented specificity. He looked behind him and saw that the Wraith had turned the corner too and was now coming up behind him. He imagined her reaching in and yanking him out of his car, shoving him up against a wall and blowing smoke rings in his face. He was struck by the notion that she was a scarecrow warning him away from Lila, a snarling dog at the girl's gate.

His pulse quickened as the Wraith got closer, and he peeled out, figuring that Lila probably wasn't home anyway.

The digital clock on a bank's wall told him it was six fifteen; just under two hours to go.

"We haven't got much time, Lionel."

Shep pulled up to Café Gourmand, thinking that if she wasn't working today, at the very least he could sneak a glance at her schedule for the next week. Even if he was stuck at the store, he would at least have an idea of where she was on any given day. He needed that much. He found a shady spot to tie Lionel and, after quickly confirming she wasn't there, ordered a passion fruit iced tea, then cut past the back office to the restroom, where he found to his surprise that he actually did have to take a leak.

But when he returned the way he'd come, someone was standing just inside the office door, a manager type flipping through a stack of receipts, blocking his access to the staff schedule. He lingered a few moments in the rubber-matted hallway, pushing himself against the wall as busboys charged past hoisting heavy trays, but the manager remained. He'd missed his window.

He went to get a straw at the milk and sugar station at the other side of the café when a flyer caught his eye: an eight-by-ten color flyer for *"Scars," a new play by Xander Michaels*, and, beneath a poorly lit tableau of a man with his head buried in his hands and a girl—Lila, there she was— looking wistfully past him, was the cast list: starring *Xander Michaels and Lila Olson*. Shep took it down from the bulletin board and folded it into his pocket.

When he exited the café, a figure passed him on the sidewalk; his body tensed at the sight of gnarled white hair and the overbearing smell of cigarette smoke. The woman stopped at the crosswalk, and Shep let out a grateful breath as he caught sight of her young face half-turned in his direction and her hair—blonde, not white—that was only windblown. The walk signal came on and the young woman dropped her cigarette butt in the gutter, flip-flopping away in her flimsy sandals. Shep watched her cross, wondering with a shiver if she might change back when she reached the other side.

3

It was his fourth day behind the counter, and the days' rhythms had settled into Shep's unconscious so he could predict the waves of activity moments in advance: the commuters; the man in the cheap suit who never removed his sunglasses and bought two energy drinks and a bag of Doritos every morning; the kids on summer vacation; the shaggy-haired twins who did skateboard tricks in the parking lot until one of the neighboring shopkeepers chased them away, who flipped through all the magazines but never bought any; all the old men, black, white, Armenian, Mexican, retired and aimfully aimless, all dressed for a bygone era in starched collars and close-cropped hair, all loyal to a different brand of cigarette; the bikers from a few miles north in their leather vests with cryptic insignia; the frazzled mothers grabbing some approximation of dinner on their way home from office jobs, in tennis shoes for the bus ride, pumps sticking out the tops of their fraying, overstuffed purses.

He was weary by eleven. Lionel slept on the floor beside him—that was a condition he'd insisted upon, that the dog be welcome. Shep was so tired, he wanted to curl up beside him, there on the nubby black floor mat. Instead he leaned his elbows on the counter and whistled a few bars of "Hotel California" to nobody until the bells chimed.

A man entered, his blond hair so close-cropped it was nearly invisible, like peach fuzz on a baby. Shep recognized him from the water store; he was the one Shep saw coming and going the most out of any of them, his car keys always dangling from short, stubby fingers since he was always on his way to or from the car. Hung referred to him as "Tubby," as in, "Tubby really parked for shit today, son of a bitch takin' up two spots." The man browsed through magazines for a minute, then stopped at the sunglasses. He turned the cylinder slowly with an index finger, watching his reflection in a row of mirrored lenses.

"You work here?" he said. Though Shep recognized him, they'd never spoken.

"Not officially, as such. But, uh, can I help you?"

Lionel growled, and Shep shushed him under the counter.

The man shrugged. "People...they're wondering."

"Wondering...what people?"

Again the man shrugged, and Shep couldn't tell if it was a tic or a performance. "Just wondering if they're coming back, your friends."

"'Course they are."

"So, you know where they went?"

"Just to see family, you know..." Shep watched the man toss his keys gently between his fingers and palm.

"North, yes?"

Shep straightened. "I'm sorry, is there something I can help you with?"

The man smiled, seemingly amused. "Not now. I already have sunglasses." He approached the exit, cupping the keys in his palm and wrapping his fingers around them. He stopped in the doorway. "We're all very sorry. You tell Mrs. Phan."

Shep puzzled a moment and began to say okay, but the man was already gone, the door swinging behind him. The bells that weren't bells made a noise that was beginning to sound to Shep like a malfunctioning smoke detector. Lionel rubbed his head against Shep's shin and growled under his breath.

By eight, Parkdale's was a ghost town. Hung had given him permission to close early if he needed to, but he was saving the option.

As he had several times a day since he'd picked it up, Shep pulled the flyer for Lila's play out of his pocket and spread it out on the counter. He ran his finger underneath the pertinent information—eight thirty that Friday night at the McCadden Place Theater, *World Premiere, reception to follow.* In the photo, Lila was staring off to the side with photogenic sadness in her eyes, and Shep traced the direction of her gaze with his thumb, running it off the page and along the counter. His thumb stopped.

He imagined spotting her in a lobby, a foyer, a parking lot, and orchestrating a collision. He'd wait for the right moment and come around the corner with just enough speed, enough force that she'd be jostled into him. He'd get a sweep of her hair against his neck, a whiff of her scent. If he did it just right, he might throw her off balance and be in place to catch her in his arms. Over and over he practiced it in his head, the slow-motion topple of her, limbs akimbo, her mouth forming a perfect "o" as she landed in the cradle of his grip…

He stared down at his dirty thumbnail up against Lila's face on the page. He'd carved an indentation in the paper that looked like a slice in her cheekbone. What was wrong with him? Was something wrong? He had to take a step back. There were days to fill between then and now, and the pressure of anticipation would kill him if he didn't calm down. He picked Lionel up and cuddled him to his chest, and the dog licked his stubbly jaw. Lionel was a good boy, but Shep needed someone to talk to, someone who could talk back. He was too alone. That kind of aloneness could poison an otherwise pure heart.

Ever since he'd clawed his way out of his sickbed, Cynthia kept reappearing in his mind. True, her bedside accusations had all been in his head, but he could still hear them in her voice. Sometimes, when he let his mind wander, her questioning continued, alongside a tightening hold on his crotch: *What are you doing, John? What is it you think will happen?* Though he had her phone number in his wallet and had dug it out many times, he'd never called. He thought about her plea at breakfast that he "talk to someone," but he couldn't bring himself to make that call either. The fear of having to explain. Fear of exposing too much of himself. He didn't need that kind of stress.

Shep pulled his wallet from his jeans, took out the receipt on which he'd written Cynthia's number, and threw it in the wastebasket before he could change his mind. The door jingled, signaling the entrance of a customer, a young guy with intricately sculpted facial hair who made a beeline for the condoms. Shep took a long breath and spread his fingers out on the counter.

At closing time he began counting out the register, an endeavor that required his utmost concentration. He scratched out numbers on a strip of receipt paper, double- and triple-checking every addition, and when he put the money pouch away in the safe, he pulled hard on the handle to make sure it was securely locked. The fact that he'd been entrusted with this degree of responsibility seemed like a terrible mistake on Hung's part.

A motion sensor light flicked on as he stepped out the back to take the trash out. The alley was carpeted with bird shit. He swung the bag over his shoulder into the teeming dumpster, where it settled into the pile with a satisfying splat. He looked up at the glowing splinter of a moon, and then his gaze fell on a cubby just to the left of the back door, a multi-level maze of pipes and sooty concrete, where the neighborhood's pigeons were all huddled and still.

The light blinked off and Shep waved his arm in the air to reactivate it so he could get a better look. He counted upwards of twenty birds, some leaning against the walls, some against each other, tucked away from the street. He stared at them, trying to catch the rhythm of their breathing. He had never wondered where pigeons slept, or when. He'd taken their ubiquity for granted. He tried to match his breathing to their barely discernible movement, his breath to theirs.

Shep's calm was interrupted by a series of loud noises coming from a few doors down—a muffled crash, a thump, and then yelling. He stepped back closer to the wall and craned his neck to listen, though it only took a few moments for him to realize the yelling wasn't in English. He'd thought it was Russian the first time he'd heard it, but Hung had corrected him.

"Do *not* let them hear you say Russian, dude. They're Armenian. Big fuckin' difference. You call an Armenian Russian, you just found your way onto his shit list. Same goes the other way 'round."

The yelling stopped, and a door swung open. A figure in shadow came tumbling out and landed hard in the gravelly, bird shit–encrusted alley. Shep watched, half inside the door and half out, as the guy pulled himself up onto his hands and knees, then slowly stood, brushing his hands off on his pants. When he turned, it looked like his left eye was puffy, the side of his face lumpen and slick, but he turned away again so quickly Shep couldn't determine if it was just a trick of the light. The guy bent over and breathed heavily, resting his palms on his thighs. Suddenly, the motion sensor light flicked off.

"Uh, you okay there?" Shep called out into the darkness.

No answer came. Shep listened, but all he heard was a cough, followed by hurried, lumbering footsteps in the gravel. He glanced up to where he knew the pigeons were slumbering, then pulled his head back inside and shut the door.

Lionel stood alert at the other end of the aisle. All the closing chores were done. Shep scooped his dog up under his arm, hit the lights and locked up. As he checked the door—pulling and pushing to make sure it was really and truly locked—he could see a figure out the corner of his eye in the doorway of the water store. The store was dark, closed as it had been, but was now barely illuminated by light streaming in from the back room.

He heard something, a lip smack, a sigh, a rustle, and looked back.

The figure, Eugene, had stepped out into the light of the streetlamp and was now leaning against the concrete column beside his storefront, sipping a drink. When Shep made brief eye contact, Eugene took a few steps closer, taking up a new leaning position against the hood of an SUV. He jutted out his chin and raised his Styrofoam cup in greeting. Shep returned the gesture with a vague nod, and gave the door handle one last yank.

4

The night was merciful. Shep's dreams came as a soft hand, petting him. As he lay under the creaking ceiling fan, the dreams led him down a garden path he'd never seen before. It was early morning; he could tell by the light and the chill in the air. A red-throated hummingbird fluttered about his head, following him, it seemed, bobbing ahead and then circling back to guide him. *Where are we?* he wanted to say to the hummingbird, but when no words came to his lips, he understood it was because no words were needed.

The path opened onto a field. It wasn't corn or wheat. It wasn't any crop at all, just wild grass, untended, weeds so rampant they were barely distinguishable from the grass. The hummingbird swooped down to his eye level, a blur of metallic red, then took off across the field, disappearing into the clouds with its speed. Then he was alone.

In the distance, he saw the grass move, and a woman rose from the ground as though she'd been sleeping there. He watched from behind as she smoothed her long hair and carefully rose to her feet, brushing dead grass from her skirt.

He began walking toward her and, in keeping with dream logic, assumed that he would make no progress, that she would remain at the same distance no matter how long he walked. He continued, at peace with the thought of walking toward no end. So it was an exhilarating surprise when he found he was getting closer to her, that her shape was coming into focus. He could even hear her whistling a soft tune as she stretched her arms over her head. He quickened his pace and felt his heart begin to race. He imagined the hummingbird hovering in his chest and felt weak.

She was close now, just a few feet away, but still didn't see or hear him.

Hello, he called out, and found that the word came out too loud, as he'd assumed himself incapable of making a sound.

The woman froze, but didn't turn. He watched her shoulders hunch, her back tense, her head lower—like a flower trying to reverse her bloom.

No, he said, confused. *I'm not...I won't*—

Shep woke to sheets stuck to his back, a fire in his throat. The phone was ringing. It took a few seconds for his mind to climb out into reality. He fumbled toward the kitchen and poured a bowl of kibble for Lionel as he picked up the phone.

"Hey," said Hung, "I was—I was thinking I was gonna leave a message."

"Sorry to disappoint."

"You gonna be ready to open in fifteen minutes?"

Shep pulled the phone away from his ear and looked at the digital display.

"Fuck. I must have turned the alarm off in my sleep. I'll be there. Just walking out the door."

"So, listen," Hung said, breezing past Shep's excuse. "I gotta stay here a little longer than I thought. You cool with that?"

"When do you think you'll be back?"

"Not long, not too long. I got some stuff I gotta take

care of. And it looks like mom's gonna stay a while longer, so. You know how it is."

"Oh." Shep nodded, though he realized Hung hadn't actually given him an answer. "Oh, hey," he started, remembering the message he'd been asked to relay. "The guy from the water store, the, uh, the heavyset guy with the blond hair, he wanted me to tell you and your mom they're all real sorry, you know."

Hung didn't say anything for a moment.

"You there?"

"What exactly did he say?"

"Just that they're sorry is all."

"I'm asking you for his exact words."

"I…I think he just said 'We're all real sorry'? And to tell your mom?" Lionel whined. "Go eat your breakfast," he whispered to the dog.

"He specifically said to tell my mom?"

"Well now I forget, I didn't know I'd be getting the third degree about it…"

"Listen to me, Shep. From here on out, any of those dudes say *anything* to you, you write it down."

"You serious?" Shep buttoned his shirt.

"Yeah, I'm serious, is that too hard?"

"No, uh, okay I guess…" He shushed Lionel, who was dancing and yipping at the front door.

"And…could you do me one more favor? If you talk to Eugene, or if anybody else comes sniffin' around, just don't tell 'em where I'm at. Don't tell 'em anything."

"You never even told me…"

"Thanks," Hung said. "Gotta go."

"Alright, alright," Shep said to the dog as he hung up the phone. "We're going, have a little patience, would ya?"

A sense of disquiet caught up to Shep as he approached the strip mall. If Hung wouldn't tell him when he was coming back, maybe he didn't know himself. And if Hung didn't know, then Shep's predicament was indefinite. Though he was chained to the counter, he was beginning to feel untethered from himself. He tied Lionel up outside and grabbed a bear claw at the donut shop as a means of procrastination, knowing that as soon as he unlocked Parkdale's, he'd be stuck again, breathing and re-breathing the same trapped air. As he shook the key from his chain, he heard a familiar squeak and looked over his shoulder to see the Cowboy pushing his cart up the street. Shep nodded, but the Cowboy didn't nod back.

After the opening chores were done, Shep settled in behind the counter with the word jumble. He managed, finally, to solve the riddles to get the letters V-N-A-H-E-A-C-L-A, and started writing out *Havana* but was stumped by the leftover letters. *Haven, Vehac, Lachan*, he scribbled freestyle, word after non-word, until suddenly the right one came sputtering out of his pencil: *Avalanche*. Shep took a big bite of his bear claw and washed it down with milk.

He'd been trying to stay calm, to distract himself from the fact that he'd be seeing Lila again that night. It had been so long he felt he was beginning to forget what she looked like outside of the grainy Xerox of the flyer. Staring at it again now, he practiced what he would say to her under his breath:

You mentioned you worked at Café Gourmand, and I thought it sounded real good, so I stopped off for lunch and saw your flyer...

I go to plays all the time, he'd say. *It's kind of my thing...*

He imagined the whole theater darkened, little specks of lint dancing like stars through a beam of light running between them. She'd look out into the audience and there he'd be, brimming with pride. She'd see him, and she'd feel his protective reach. He wanted to be fresh and alert for it. He took another sip and pictured his bones growing stronger and whiter as the milk traveled, ice cold, down his gullet.

He didn't start watching the clock in earnest until a little past six, when the sun was just starting to slip down to eye level. The portable fan had crapped out a couple hours earlier, and he couldn't figure out how to fix it. The muggy air was sapping his energy. Even Lionel was splayed out on the ground panting.

So it was in a state of breathless confusion that Shep reacted to the great rat-a-tat-tat that shattered his eardrums and sent him catapulting out of his daze. It was so loud that Shep felt his ribcage rattle, and the next thing he knew he was down on the floor, belly to the ground and face to the cruddy linoleum. He squeezed his eyes shut and wrapped his arms over the back of his head while Lionel ran in circles, barking like mad.

His eyes were shut so tight that bubbles of white light traveled beneath his eyelids, spreading and receding, and Shep was transported to a night in the desert—after the lizards and before the sheep—when he'd just come off guard duty. He was on his way to get a coffee when an explosion shattered the night air, sending a flash of red across the starless sky, starless because the smoke from the oil well fires had layered itself between heaven and earth. He ran back to his tent and got into his MOPP suit with everybody else, those who were awake and those who were fighting through the fog of sleep as they fastened themselves into the protective gear while the chemical alarms blared. By the time he got his gas mask on, his jaw was numb. He rolled it around and around inside the mask, momentarily panicked as the numbness spread to his lips but too generally rattled to think much about it. They all headed for the bunker, waited, and kept waiting, their hearts in their throats.

When the noise stopped, Shep opened his eyes and found that, without realizing he was doing it, he had grabbed Hung's Beretta. He held it in his right hand, his knuckles regaining color as he loosened his grip.

Shep rose to his feet slowly, gun still at his side, and scanned the store. He stepped out from behind the counter and sidestepped his way to the storefront, his eyes flitting across the aisles, and pushed the door open with his shoulder.

Though he didn't know what he was expecting to find, Shep immediately looked to the water store.

He smelled an acrid odor, sulfur and smoke, and saw three kids—Eugene's son included—standing over the smoldering remnants of firecrackers.

"Hey!" he yelled.

Two of the kids laughed and took off running, but Eugene's son froze, his owl's eyes open wide. Shep tucked the gun away in his rear waistband and crossed the parking lot to him.

"You can't just do that in the middle of the day, it ain't the Fourth of July," he said, softening some, taken aback by the boy's apparent fear of him.

"Hey, hey, it's okay. You're not in trouble. You just gotta be careful, is all. You could hurt yourself. Where'd you even get those?"

The boy rubbed his eyes with a closed fist, then wiped his nose on his forearm.

"What's your name anyhow?"

"Eugene," the boy said quietly.

"Eugene Jr., huh? You should go play somewhere else. All the cars and traffic, it's not safe."

Eugene Jr. looked down at his shoes and kicked at the firecracker remnants, then looked up warily.

"You listening? Why don't you go on home?"

The boy kept his eye on Shep as he readjusted his glasses.

"Hey," Shep said, crouching down to his level. "I didn't mean to scare you." He put his hand on the boy's shoulder. "I just want you to be safe. You and your friends."

The sun shined right in Shep's eyes. He squinted and remained still. Warmed and enclosed in the light, he had an impulse to hug the boy but gave his shoulder a light squeeze instead.

"Evgeny!" called a woman's voice.

The boy shook Shep's hand off and turned. Shep rose and shielded his eyes with his hand. A woman he believed to be Eugene's wife stepped out of a silver Mercedes that had just pulled up in front of the water store. She slammed the car door and stood with her hands on her hips. Eugene Jr. shrank and stared at the ground.

The boy's mother held the water store's door open as she lifted her sunglasses onto her head, pushing back her curly black hair. She whistled and called out something in Armenian that shook Eugene Jr. out of his frozen state. He trotted toward her, leaving Shep standing in the middle of the parking lot with the firecrackers still smoldering at his feet.

The woman looked impatient, even a little angry, but when Eugene Jr. reached her, she knelt down and, rather than greeting him with a harsh word or a swat like Shep had expected, she stroked his cheek and straightened his collar. She noticed Shep watching then and whispered in the boy's ear, her eyes fixed on Shep as she tapped her son on the back to guide him inside.

Shep gave a hesitant wave. Eugene's wife pursed her lips and returned the wave before following the boy inside. She clicked the remote in her hand and the car beeped twice.

What time was it? Shep patted his wrist as if his watch might somehow manifest there. He was sweating. As he hurried back to Parkdale's, his foot stuck, and he discovered he'd stepped in a glob of fresh bubble gum.

"Goddamnit," he sighed, and tried to scrape it off on the curb.

Inside, Shep paced in front of the counter. He couldn't remember what he'd meant to do now. Lionel followed close at Shep's heels, pushing off with his paws, grumbling and whimpering.

"Not now, Lionel," he pleaded, and went behind the counter, where he grabbed three mini bottles of Jack Daniels, downed one and shoved the others in his pockets. The dog barked. "Leave it, come on, settle down," he whispered, as the liquor warmed his raw throat. He paused, then pulled the second bottle from his pocket.

He was always doing things like this, making plans and forgetting them, giving in to his momentary weaknesses. There was no point in trying to be any better than he was. He squeezed the back of his neck and tried to transport himself back to that morning, when he'd felt confident, benevolent and sane. Hadn't he? He wished Hung were there to give him some kind of point of reference, to remind him where he was. He rubbed his eyes and was reminded of how Mrs. Phan would peek down the stairs and call for her son in a high, lilting voice, the way Hung would roll his eyes and follow, dragging his feet up the stairs as he'd no doubt been doing since he was a boy like little Eugene. To call and be called in that mother's way—what did it feel like?

The sun was lowering. Shep drank the second bottle, then covered the empties in the trash with crumpled newspaper pages. He always went for the little bottles for discretion, but for whose benefit? He took one more off the shelf to even out his pockets, then two more, so he'd have two on each side, then grabbed the broom from the back and gave the floor a cursory sweep, giving up halfway through. He had to hurry now. He'd lost track of time. He left the register uncounted, the trash full. He remembered the Beretta in his waistband and put it back in its hiding place behind the rolls of receipt paper.

Shep hurried toward home, stopping short as he realized Lionel wasn't with him. He'd neglected to leash him up, he realized, swiveling around in dismay. Probably left the leash inside, though he couldn't remember if he'd even had it that morning.

"Lionel!" he called. "Lionel!" and soon the dog came barreling up the sidewalk in response.

Shep picked him up, all wagging tail and claws climbing, and noticed as he stood up again that the Cowboy was standing too. His face was in shadow, so Shep couldn't discern whether the man was looking at him or past him. But he was overcome by a strange understanding. He called out: "Thank you."

5

Shep hid himself in a corner of the theater lobby and studied the flyers on the bulletin board, which was littered with ads for acting classes and improv troupes, one for a "free personality test," flyers for upcoming productions, and a card that simply stated, "Lose your accent – 6 weeks or less!" with a phone number.

The lights in the lobby dimmed and brightened, and Shep hurried into the theater, taking a place in the rear, a few rows behind the rest of the sparse audience. He leaned back in his seat and felt unnerved by the thumping of his own pulse. The theater was much smaller than he'd expected. He was relieved when the room went black, plunging him back into invisibility.

The stage lights rose on a young man in James Dean drag, blue jeans and a white T-shirt with the sleeves rolled up, though the effect was somewhat diminished by the obvious cheekbone-mimicking bronzer on his face. The actor rose from a crouching position up onto his feet, but before he said a word, the lights dropped again, a screen was lowered behind him, and a quick sequence of images was projected: vintage footage of Manson family–esque hippies crowded into a cluster around the body of a woman who was either dancing or convulsing, her fine, greasy hair whipping across her face, flash cut to a view of a blue sky, with white clouds passing across the screen. After a few seconds the sky was burned through the center, the image seeming to melt away like wax, and then flash cut to a pack of lions in the Sahara, huddled over the carcass of a gazelle. That image was quickly replaced by a close-up of shoes shuffling on pavement, the staggering of a drunk or a ghost, then a reprise of the clouds on blue sky and a fade to black. Silence.

The lights rose again, with the actor in the same position downstage, but now, upstage, curled up on a chaise longue, in cigarette pants and an angora sweater, with black eyeliner and her hair done up like Ann-Margret, was Lila. Something the lights were doing made the stage appear shrouded by a pale mist, and the actor looked directly into the audience, as though it were understood that a statement had been made. Upstage, Lila stared out a window, which was merely a window frame hung on wires from the rafters. Shep was stunned, and not a word had yet been spoken.

Throughout the first act, the action alternated between vaguely poetic arguments between Lila and the man—*Don't you want me anymore?/I don't know what I want/You don't know who you are*—and video montages depicting hurricane patterns on weather maps, funeral processions, brief graphic sexual images—Shep was startled when an image of a beach at high tide faded into a full-screen shot of an erect penis in black and white.

The whole thing was mystifying. Though Shep's gaze was trained on Lila, she was always upstage, with the actor dwarfing her by way of perspective. Her role required her to watch him, alternating between anger, plaintiveness and lust, interjecting only when he addressed her, dancing morosely on top of her chaise longue when the video accompaniment included music. After a while, it became clear this was more rambling monologue than anything else, a vehicle for this Xander Michaels person, and Lila was little more than set dressing.

Shep tuned out everything that was going on downstage and watched her face, wondering how she knew when she was supposed to look sad, when she was supposed to smile, sneer or pout. Outside the context of the play, she looked like a little girl practicing expressions in her bedroom mirror, brushing her hair over one shoulder, then over the other, trying on exaggerations of adult emotions. Shep imagined walking in on her doing just that as a teenager, interrupting to tell her to come down to dinner. He would've been a firm but caring father. He'd have said things like, *I'm not gonna say it again, come down to dinner before it gets cold*, and *Like hell you're going out on a school night*. But he'd be understanding too. He'd say things like, *I know you're young and just trying to figure out who you are*. He'd strike that elusive balance if he had the chance. His gaze drifted upward so he wasn't watching Lila anymore but letting himself be carried away by the lights.

Shep realized his mind had been drifting for some time. He refocused his attention on the stage just as it was suddenly enveloped by a red glow. The actor was perched on the edge of the stage like a gargoyle, making eye contact with the audience members nearest to the front as he spoke slowly, em-pha-siz-ing-each-syll-ab-le. But Shep didn't hear a word he said, because at the back of the stage, a noose fell from the rafters, right above Lila's chaise. She slowly rose to her feet and slipped it over her head while the actor kept talking and talking. *Shut up*, Shep thought, watching Lila with growing discomfort as she stared defiantly toward the back wall of the theater, and suddenly, as though he had heard Shep's thoughts, the actor stopped, Lila jumped, and the stage went dark. The sound of rope swinging from a wooden beam squeaked over the speakers for nearly a minute, then the lights rose on an emptied stage, and a ten-minute intermission was announced.

Shep sank into his seat, reeling while the rest of the audience trickled out into the lobby for wine and crumbly store-bought cookies. He couldn't figure out what had just happened. Was she wearing some kind of harness? Had she been wearing it the whole time? While logically he knew she was perfectly fine backstage, watching her jump with the rope around her neck for that split second before the lights went out had shaved years off his life. He needed air, but his legs felt so weak he didn't think he'd be stable on his feet. He forced himself up, supporting his weight on the armrests, and slipped out the lobby's swinging glass doors.

It had cooled down a great deal since the sun had gone down. The street was a dark one, but the lights on Santa Monica Boulevard were bright enough to lend a glow to the end of the block. He leaned against the wall of the theater and worked on catching his breath. He felt lightheaded, and remembered that he hadn't eaten anything since the bear claw that morning. He didn't know if he could make it through the second act. He could go home. But when would he see Lila again? He had to stay strong. The lobby lights flashed, but Shep couldn't bring himself to move just yet. He listened as the lobby chatter subsided, waiting until all was quiet to lay his cheek against the cool concrete wall and close his eyes, steeling himself with a memory.

It was during one of the dark times, after his grandmother's death, when his health ranged from precarious to abject, when his days were spent vomiting or waiting for the next miserable wave, sleeping or trying to sleep on a threadbare orange couch in the basement. He'd been delirious, hearing the revving of the neighbor's lawnmower as a skeleton-shaking rumble just beneath the earth's surface. In a panic he'd crawled on the shag carpet and grabbed onto a table leg to have something to hold onto when the crust split. He'd passed out there and woken up under the table, thick saliva gluing his face to the floor. There was no point in pursuing anything anymore. Even if he could muster an aspiration, his body would never be up to the task of realizing it.

But eventually, though he'd held out no hope, some modicum of strength returned. One day, he remembered he had an appetite. His stomach was twisted with hunger, and he walked across town to the store for provisions. It was a beautiful spring day and hushed in the way particular to small and smallish towns on Sundays, when most everything is closed, when everybody is either in church or at home relaxing under ceiling fans. The only place open, in fact, was the little grocery store. He bought himself a loaf of bread, a bottle of milk and a carton of eggs and tore into the bread as he walked back home, feeling instantly nourished and calm.

He walked alone, slowly, down the street, and when he got back to the house, cheeks full and chewing, it looked… small. And more importantly, it looked unfamiliar, the door shorter and squatter than the image he had in his head, the lawn a different shade of green. In fact, everything—the roof, the doorframe, the mailbox—was just a shade or two off.

It was only after staring for a long moment that Shep realized he was standing before the wrong house. He was looking at the Hansens' house, two doors down. He shut his eyes tight and opened them again, and it was so obvious, of course it was the wrong house, but his perception had already undergone a fundamental change. He walked the rest of the way to his own house, his grandmother's house, and—though of course it was as familiar as his own body—it was just a house. He realized with total clarity, the most clarity he'd felt in years, that this house had no power over him. There were no ghosts in the eaves. The breath of the dead didn't hang like clouds from the ceiling; it had gone out the window with the breeze and was as gone as gone can be, as gone as a cloud he might've seen as a child, gone back to the sea, wherever that was.

Of course, it took him a few more years to leave, but that had been the first step. He'd lost Lorene long ago, though in the back of his mind he dwelled, wondering what she was doing now, and now again, and what about now? But, gradually, his focus shifted. He wondered if Lila needed braces like he did, though there had never been money for them.

He wanted her to have everything he didn't. He wondered if she took swimming lessons. Or gymnastics. Did she ever fight with her mother? Did she ever think about him, staring out her bedroom window, wondering where he was, what she would say to him if they met? He and Lila had no past to taint their future. He was free to dream about it unfettered.

Following her to California had been step two. He'd sold the house along with virtually all his belongings. As he drove west, he knew he was traveling toward an endpoint. Now there was only one step left. What happened after that was a question he couldn't yet consider.

A gale of laughter burst out from the back of the building. Shep's eyes popped open. He pulled his face back from the wall and listened as the laughter swelled.

Ssshhhhh! someone said, and the laughter devolved into quiet, fitful chatter.

Shep followed the sound, dragging his fingers along the wall until he reached the back of the building. A group of young people in fifties costume were crowded around the back door, smoking and whispering animatedly. One of them let her cigarette dangle from her bottom lip as she refastened her dark blonde hair into a bouncy ponytail and brushed a wet leaf off her saddle shoe, and for a moment, Shep thought it was Lila. But when she moved and an overhead light hit her face from a different angle, the girl became a stranger again. He peered around the corner and tried to figure out what to do next. The decision seemed to be made for him when the whole group ground out their cigarettes and grab-assed their way back inside for some cue or another. Shep stepped out from the wall; there was no one around, not a soul, not a sound but the traffic on Santa Monica. He waited a few beats and followed.

The backstage area was a maze of dark hallways with duffel bags, shoes and hair products dumped all over the floor, a cloying mix of powder, mold and body odor in the air.

He crept through it like a tunnel, looking for the light.

When he found it in a quiet dressing room, he poked his head just barely into the doorway. There were mirrors on opposite walls, so the room repeated itself in both directions, the room growing smaller and smaller the deeper one looked. And the only figure in the successive reflections, the only shape breaking up the infinite perpendicular lines, was Lila. In a polyester dressing gown, she sat with legs folded beneath her, the filthy soles of her feet peeking out. She was intensely occupied with writing in a small spiral-bound notebook. For a second he contemplated approaching her then and there—they'd never been alone in a room before—but instead he just watched her, with her head down and brow furrowed, and wondered what it was she was writing. What he wouldn't give to get a look at that notebook. When she stopped writing for a moment and looked up at the ceiling, Shep quickly ducked away. Now that he'd located her, all he had to do was wait, circle, watch.

He retraced his steps back out to the alley behind the theater and paced agitatedly until he heard applause coming from inside. He returned to the lobby and blended in seamlessly with the other audience members, his attention piqued when cast members in garish makeup, transformed by the absence of the stage lights, began to trickle in to receive flowers and hugs.

Eventually Lila wandered out among them. She'd changed into jeans and a gauzy blouse, but her hair was still teased, and she'd touched up her eyeliner. She looked around the lobby a bit sheepishly as she figured out that no one had come to see her. Shep recognized his opening and slipped through the crowd to her like jumping into a cold pool, without giving himself a moment to think.

"Lila," he said.

She turned to face him and looked confused as she tried to place his face.

"John Shepherd. Remember? We met on the shoot with

the rocks, in, uh, up north a ways, you remember?" He blinked fast, knowing he was making no sense. "I saw you were in this play."

"Oh, right," she said, not quite making eye contact, and he couldn't tell if she really remembered him or if she was only being polite.

"It was real good," he soldiered on, "I mean, your performance was…yeah, wow."

Lila smirked, leaned in a couple inches and whispered, "Be honest. It's a piece of shit."

"Uhh…" Shep smiled, his mind racing for a way to continue the conversation.

"It's okay, I don't ca—"

"—so how did they rig the rope thing, anyway? 'Cause it looked really real—sorry for interrupting you."

"Uh, there was a thing under my sweater…" Lila was looking past Shep now, scanning the lobby for anybody else she might know; then, disappointed, she returned her gaze to him. "You know, stage magic." She smiled, and Shep was dazzled by the symmetry of her features, the slick white shine of her teeth.

She eyed him nervously, and Shep realized he was staring.

One of the actors grabbed her elbow.

"You coming to Barney's?"

She nodded.

Shep looked at her expectantly.

"Do you…uh, wanna come?" she asked. "I mean, it's just a few of us. Nothing big."

Shep would have wagged his tail if he had one. "I could give you a ride, if you want."

"It's like four blocks."

"You sure? You must be tired after all that."

"No, I'm fine," she said firmly, and Shep's heart sank as he put it together: he was a stranger—a strange *man*—to her, inherently unsafe. He smiled with teeth, his eyes desperately searching her face for any recognition of his goodness.

Shep tried to keep up with Lila and her friends as they walked down La Cienega. He felt numb, wooden, preoccupied with his appearance, though he lagged behind and no one was paying him any attention. He forged onward, compulsively running his hands through his hair. The star of act one, Xander Michaels himself, wasn't part of the group, which seemed to be by design, given the way they were talking about him.

"Did you know he has an MBA from UCLA? He decided he was an actor like six months ago, now he thinks he's the first person to ever hear of Uta Hagen," said a small brunette with a booming voice.

"He spent three thousand dollars of his own—I'm sorry, his *parents'*—money on the show."

"How do you know that?"

"The owner of the theater told me!"

Shep listened but had trouble hearing underneath the traffic noise.

"I'm not positive, but...I think he might be a Scientologist," Lila contributed. "He was telling me about the acting classes at the Celebrity Center, wouldn't drop it until I took a brochure."

"Of course he is!" the small girl cried. "He's got the look, you know? Like he probably doesn't have genitals, and he's really proud of how pure that makes him or something."

"He might not have a dick," Lila yelled through her laughter, "but he definitely has an asshole, because he never stops fucking farting in the green room."

Shep was taken aback by her crassness. It seemed uncharacteristic of Lila, though, he worried, maybe that was just the Lila he'd imagined, the personality he'd extrapolated, watching her like a silent film. He walked faster to get up beside her as a guy on a bicycle pedaled past, with speakers rigged on the handlebars to blast intense, pounding dance music.

"Awhoooo!" the small girl howled after the cyclist. The

others joined in, howling not at the moon but at the traffic, the colors streaking by in the darkness.

"Awhoooo! Awhooooo!" they cried, collapsing in laughter as they hurried down to the hill. Shep watched them like the animals they were.

At the bar, Shep managed to stick close enough to Lila to wind up seated beside her at a table that was plastered with photos of the Doors, Jimi Hendrix and other legends of the sixties and seventies. They were just old clippings under glass, though you could see some paper edges curling, some fading newsprint. He wondered if the clippings had been old when they were glued down, or if they went on aging, traveling down the path toward decay in defiance of attempts at preservation.

He ordered a Coke and insisted on buying Lila the drink of her choice, a lemon drop with sugar encrusted around the rim of the glass like crystal.

"Aw, thanks," she said, as the waitress placed it before her on a little white cocktail napkin. Shep moved his finger through wet rings left on the table by the previous party, keeping his eyes on her hands, her drink, anything but her face lest he lose nerve.

"So, uh, you mentioned—that you were from the midwest?" Shep said, his eyes now fixed on the tabletop at a picture of David Bowie with orange hair, flashbulbs rendering his skin a sickly white as he exited a nightclub.

"Did I?" With a finger, she swiped granules of sugar off the edge of her glass and licked them off.

The small girl with the loud voice squeezed Lila's shoulder and headed out to the patio for a smoke.

"Yeah, you know, I'm from there too. Nebraska, actually."

"Shut up." Lila coughed and set her drink down.

"Yeah, yeah. Uh, why? Are you...where are you from?"

"I'm sure you've never heard of it—Upton?"

The answer jarred him. He'd expected her to say Harner,

but of course, he remembered, she'd been so little when she left.

"I don't meet ANYBODY from Nebraska," she said, excited now. "Fuck, I don't meet anybody who could pick it out on a map. You a Husker fan?" She poked his chest with a chipped pink fingernail.

"Of course, yeah."

When he saw the waitress he flagged her down and ordered a Jack Daniels to mix with his Coke.

"I miss it sometimes," Lila said. "I'm not going back though, hell no."

"Never? Not even to visit?"

She shrugged.

"I miss the seasons, I guess. The thunder storms, the way you can smell them coming. And the way you can feel sort of small, with all that flat land on all sides of you..." she tipped her head and squinted at the ceiling "...but only sometimes. It's not a part of me, you know? It's just a place I've been. I know my parents wish I'd move back. I feel bad about that..." She paused, taking a long drink. "Do you, I don't know, do you see your life as some, like, line that makes sense, some... *grand arc?*" She said it like it was a joke, but he could tell this was something she'd been thinking about.

He opened his mouth as if to speak, but his thoughts hadn't caught up. The word "parents" was a stab in the gut; that husband of Lorene's was no father, couldn't be. But he couldn't let on.

"'Cause I really don't," she said. "Not anymore. When I first came here, it was like I kept waiting for the ground to click under my feet. But that's all faded away now. Maybe because I've got a rhythm going. Now that I'm not listening for the click...I just am where I am. And I don't really think about whatever came before. I'm *here* now. You know?"

Shep looked at her face. She was so close to him. He smelled coconut, different flower scents, and chemicals, the things girls slather and spray all over themselves, layer upon layer, to feel good. She spoke as if she'd unlocked the secret of being, but he remembered the way she'd cried in the alleyway. It hadn't been so long ago.

"I mean, maybe that's why I'm an actress, you know? Like, I'm just my instrument. I'm just this." She patted at her chest, her face, her leg. "Who I am, what's in my head, what I feel…it's vapor, I can shift it anytime, any way I want."

"Do you…like acting?" he said, hoping to steer the conversation to territory he could grasp, knowing the question was asinine.

"Yeah," she said, "most of the time." The waitress came by with a shot for Shep. He poured it in his Coke and stirred it with a finger. Lila motioned for another lemon drop.

"I mean," she continued, "I'm excited all the time. Hopeful all the time. You need to hope. You need to hope beyond all logic, beyond any kind of reason. You need to believe in yourself in a way that doesn't even make sense."

Shep nodded, and Lila leaned in, startling him.

"Like, I can't even sleep half the time, I'm so excited. You ever try to count sheep? I've tried. But I even get excited about them! I picture one of them jumping over a fence and then the angle changes and I'm watching from above, like I'm up on a cloud. And then it's a different sheep, in a different field, maybe there was grass before, but now it's snow, and now it's a black sheep instead of a white one. And maybe then I'm looking from underneath, watching the lamb's hooves fly overhead. Who can sleep when there's so much going on, when everything changes all the time?"

"Sometimes I have a hard time sleeping too," Shep said.

"I've always been like that," she said, "not just at night. My mom's always telling me how I was impossible to feed when I was a little baby. I'd stare at the wall, obsessed with the shadow of the spoon coming toward my shadow, like I was hypnotized. She could never get me to face her and actually *eat*."

The small girl came back to the table and summoned

Lila to the ladies' room, her chunky metal bracelets clacking into each other as she waved her over. Lila squeezed Shep's hand as she hopped up from her seat and followed the girl past the shuffleboard table and down the hall.

Shep took a long drink and looked down at the clippings on the table, a picture of Elvis in the black leather jumpsuit from his comeback special, pointing across the tabletop at Janis Joplin, who grinned with her eyes hidden behind the round lenses of her sunglasses, her mass of hair floating upward as though she were in the act of falling.

Over the sound system they were playing an R&B song he'd heard a lot on the radio, in which a woman sang over and over in a sad vibrato that she'd found love in a hopeless place.

It seemed like Lila had been gone a long time. He looked around. There was no clock anywhere in sight. He went to the men's room.

After taking a leak, Shep waited for the frat boy types to leave and stood before the mirror. He washed his hands and ran them, still wet, through his hair, looking at his face.

"Lila," he whispered to his reflection, "I came here for a reason tonight, and I don't mean to alarm you..."

"Lila," he whispered, "there's something I have to tell you, and I have to tell you now."

He repeated "*now*," watching the crooked edges of his teeth behind his lips.

"Fuck," he whispered, tears forming in his eyes. He wiped them away and rubbed his palms up and down his face.

When he got back out to the bar, Lila was sitting with her friends, wedged between the small girl and one of the guys who'd accompanied them, who had half his head shaved, the other half of his hair long and black, and had a tattoo of an ankh on the back of his neck. They were all huddled so closely together that there was no opening for him, no angle of approach. By the time he'd mustered the courage to try anyway, the whole group had scooted away from the bar and trailed out to the patio. Shep followed, trying to look nonchalant.

"Hey!" Lila said brightly when he stepped outside. She threw her arms around him, coming close to singing his collar with her cigarette. "Where'd you go?"

Shep just smiled as she pulled away from him. Liquid jostled in his stomach like stagnant bog water.

By the time he regained some composure, she had turned her attention away from him again and was listening intently to something ankh tattoo was whispering in her ear. She didn't seem to be smoking. She was just holding the cigarette aloft, letting the smoke sting her eyes.

The small girl slunk up to Shep.

"So, are you, like, Lila's boyfriend or something?"

"What? No, no, it's nothing like that—"

"But you want to be her boyfriend, right?"

Shep shook his head but was too horrified to think of anything to say.

"How old are you, anyway? I knew she liked older guys but..." she laughed, and rubbed her nose, the nostrils red and peeling at the edges. Shep realized suddenly that this was the roommate he'd seen coming and going from Lila's apartment. He'd never gotten a real look at her face before.

"Listen," she said, yanking at his sleeve. "I don't have any money. Do you think you could buy me a vodka soda?" She rubbed her nose again and fluffed her bangs.

"No, I can't." He was watching Lila, who was talking animatedly, but he couldn't hear her over the drunken voices that were building all around him. Her pupils were huge, and the cherry of her cigarette was moments away from burning her fingers.

The girl let go of him and snorted.

"Jeez, I thought you were cool, my bad." She went inside in search of somebody else to buy her a drink.

Shep leapt forward and grabbed the cigarette away from Lila, singing his own fingertips. He sucked on them as he dropped the cigarette on the ground.

"What the fuck?" she said.

"You were gonna get burned," he yelled over the noise.

"Ummm, okay." She made a face for her friends' benefit and laughed.

"Never mind," he yelled.

"Sorry, that was so chivalrous, really."

"I just didn't want you to get hurt."

Lila stepped up closer to him, taking on a totally different posture than she had before. She seemed to be reprising the character she'd played onstage, all vulnerable eyes and pouty lips, her hips jutted toward him, prior caution dissolved by a few drinks, or whatever she'd done in the ladies' room.

Shep recoiled. Lila laughed.

"I don't bite," she said, and then bit her thumb. Shep noticed the redness that cobwebbed across the whites of her eyes.

"It's not that," he said, thinking *tell her, tell her, tell her, tell her.*

But before he could say anything else, she reached an arm around him and stuck her hand just barely inside the back of his scratchy dress pants, patting her fingertips against the waistband of his underwear.

He yanked her hand out and reared back, bumping into the wall.

Lila looked back at her friends, laughing again. They were all laughing.

"You're *jumpy!*" she said. "What did I do?"

He was squashed between strangers as more people poured out onto the patio, and the cigarette smoke on all sides of him was making his throat raw. Bile roiled in his gut.

"I, I—" he said, but the bile was rising, and he knew he had mere seconds to get away.

Shep pushed through the crowd and ran to the nearest alley, unleashing the contents of his stomach, all colorless liquid, behind a trash can.

6

John tried to be quiet as he came in through the back door. His back was slick with mud since he'd been way out in the tall grasses behind the house when the rain started. His wet, misbuttoned shirt clung to his chest. He slipped off his tennis shoes and began wiping them down with paper towels, letting clumps of mud plop against the laundry sink's metal basin.

His grandmother was in the living room watching TV. She often fell asleep in front of the evening news, and remained otherwise hypnotized by whatever she watched. He crept up the stairs in his stocking feet, slowly, slowly, taking special care not to let the steps creak.

She was watching an old movie, an MGM-type musical in fuzzy black and white, the orchestra at full swell. The screen glowed into the darkened living room, like a fire without warmth. It was hot outside, and the rain had stopped, but moisture still hung in the air, heavy and waiting.

"Hey," she whispered.

John stopped on the stairs. The orchestra had quieted, and a woman sang, her trilling voice light as a ribbon in the wind, singing something about love.

"Hey," she said again.

He remained still, head pointed toward his room, and tried to conjure camouflage somewhere between the banister and the wall.

"What are you doing?" she said.

"I...I've gotta go, Gran. I've got drill this weekend, remember?"

She looked back at the TV for a moment before her expression soured.

"Of course I remember. You think I'm stupid?"

"No, I just…" He turned his face to the wall, focused on his shadow and breathed.

"You left the kitchen a mess. I know you left your room a mess. You leave everything a mess."

John swallowed his indignation, knowing none of this to be true—he hadn't even used the kitchen that day.

"I'm sorry, Gran, I am, and I'll make it up to you as soon as I get back Sunday night, but I can't—"

"Why are you yelling?"

John looked down on her from the stairs. He didn't know if she was angry. She looked hurt, truly. Had he been yelling? These exchanges were slowly grinding him down. He didn't know whether to beg forgiveness or do nothing, nothing at all, whichever tactic would get him out of there faster. Every time he returned to the darkened house, he instantly reverted to a scared, shamed, childlike state. And why? Because of this little old woman, muttering in her half-sleep. He looked down at the top of her head, the greasy gray hair at her crown, and he thought:

Please God, don't ever let me get old.

What was the difference between a passing thought and a prayer?

John hurried up the stairs. He couldn't tell the difference between the dampness of his shirt and his own sweat, and peeled it off like a shed skin. He put on a fresh T-shirt and jeans and threw his things into a duffel, his uniform, boots, shaving kit and toothbrush, his belongings pared down to the barest minimum.

As he was passing through the living room, he stopped and watched a minute of his grandmother's movie, standing over her with his duffel swung over his shoulder. A man in black tie and tails was doing a tap routine with a little girl. The man stopped with an exuberant *tap-tap* and spread his arms to better display the girl's perfectly practiced steps, her stiff crinolines bouncing as she tapped across the stage, bright and grinning.

"Okay," John said. "I'm off."

He watched her for an acknowledgment, but she was transfixed by the film again, the light from the screen flitting across her glasses. He passed behind the couch so as not to disturb her and stepped out into the night.

The ground was still wet. He threw his duffel onto the passenger seat of his car and drove to the bus stop with the windows down, because there was no smell lovelier than the post-rain summer air. He pulled out an apple he'd thrown in the bag and ate it while he drove one-handed through the near-empty streets, the juice dripping down his chin. Just the breeze of movement lifted the humidity.

He felt something then, tickling his lower back. He reached down the waistband of his jeans and pulled out a long blond hair; must've gotten stuck to him when he was with Lorene, clinging to his body despite the rain and the change of clothes. He stuck his arm out the window and worked the hair off of his fingers.

He came to a red light and, presciently it seemed, turned his palm upward, catching a few drops of newly falling rain. The light turned green. The rain picked up quickly. He barreled forward blind, his dull wiper blades barely keeping pace with the deluge.

7

Shep spotted the Cowboy's shopping cart in front of his nook, but the Cowboy was nowhere to be seen. But he was running late getting the store open already; there was no time to worry about it.

Once the lights were on and the register set up, Shep parked himself behind the counter and poured a Miller into a Styrofoam cup, stopping just as the foam crowned, a perfect pour.

It was a Saturday, so there wasn't the usual glut of commuters, there were no deliveries, and there were long stretches in which Shep and Lionel were alone with the merchandise: canned sodas chilling in rows; boxes of Rice-a-Roni pressed against each other on the shelf, butting up against soup cans and brightly packaged cookies and snack cakes; the magazines splayed against the register, women's painted faces peering out from the stacks, gazing meaningfully at nothing, the whole room and its contents still. Shep felt compelled to remain still himself, so as not to disturb the tableau. He leaned back against the rear counter and sipped quietly until his beer was drained.

Lionel began to whimper.

"Hnnh, wha…" Shep muttered with a start. "Oh shit…"

His cup was on the floor, his neck ached, and a string of drool connected his bottom lip to the front of his T-shirt.

"Lionel, why didn't you wake me?" he said, scanning the aisles and patting the register as though he were checking it for tampering.

Lionel whimpered again.

"What is it? You can't be hungry. Your water's damn near full…"

Lionel yelped and danced back and forth on his paws.

"Alright, alright, hang on."

Outside the back door, Shep led Lionel to a little patch of grass and leaned against the wall while the dog purposefully sniffed each blade. Kitty corner from the doorway, at the end of the alley, a figure was crouched low to the ground, a figure he recognized by the cowboy hat. His back was to Shep, but he seemed to be holding something, rocking gently from side to side.

"Hey, Lionel, don't go anywhere."

Shep kept his back up against the building as he approached, careful not to startle the man, and when he reached him, he walked a wide circle to see what was going on without getting too close. Beside the Cowboy was a paper bag with peanut shells spilling out, and in his hands was a little brown squirrel who appeared completely docile as the Cowboy petted its head with his index finger. Other squirrels were gathered close by, some chewing on peanuts while others hovered expectantly.

The Cowboy didn't look up, and Shep watched as he gently turned the squirrel around to face him and rubbed the underside of its chin. He was some kind of squirrel shaman, a rodent mystic.

Shep thought it better not to interrupt, so he made his way back to Parkdale's, where Lionel was digging into the patch of grass with his little claws.

"There's nothing down there, kiddo." He scooped up the dog and glanced back at the Cowboy, who, gripping the bag of peanuts, had risen to a half-crouch, the squirrels still congregated at his feet.

When Shep returned, he was startled to find ol' Tubby using the ATM. Hung had more than once made snide comments about the man's frequent visits to the donut shop moments before biting into his own maple log. Shep watched from the other end of the aisle as the man stretched his neck from side to side and rolled his shoulders, taking his time at whatever it was he was doing. The man had never frequented Parkdale's before. This was his second sighting in...how many days? Shep couldn't recall. The man finished his business and exited the store without making a purchase, lowering his sunglasses to nod at Shep as the little bells jingled in his wake.

Didn't the water store have an ATM? Shep could've sworn he saw one in there, beside the rotating rack of car fresheners. He watched out the storefront as the man climbed into the passenger seat of a white BMW, the driver invisible behind tinted windows as the car eased out the driveway and joined the traffic on Coldwater.

Shep walked back to the ATM, the ice machine chilling and rumbling beside it, and tried to remember if Hung had given him any instructions as to its maintenance. He couldn't remember. But he did remember Hung's warning, the way he watched "like a hawk." If some kind of skimmer had been installed, what would it look like? A little camera? Something plugged in? Shep got down on his knees and ran his hands down either side of it like he was embracing the thing. He stood and ran his fingers over the keypad, wiggled the card slot. Would it look like anything at all? Finally, Shep went into the back office with Lionel trotting at his heels. He found a yellow legal pad and wrote *"Out of Order"* in ballpoint, then secured it to the ATM's screen with a strip of duct tape before unplugging the machine from the wall, then paced ineffectually, consumed by the irrational fear that some alarm would go off, that a credit union representative would rappel down from a helicopter and handcuff him. He had to get a hold of Hung.

While the phone rang, Shep ran through the litany of stories Hung had told him, a growing list of boastful warnings: the nineteen-year-old who'd been shot in the back of the head in the Sears parking lot, supposedly over a misunderstanding via text message, though no one would say for sure; Eugene's old spot, the Starlite Lounge, that got shot up with only a group of six Sandrosyan family associates inside, commiserating after a wedding. And the shooting just across the street. Did anyone besides he and Hung even remember it had happened? There were never any answers, only Hung's cryptic pronouncements, his ever-ready reminders about bodies found in the trunks of abandoned cars and heads found in the canyons, the way he would nod knowingly while drawing a finger across his throat.

"Come on," he whispered anxiously into the receiver. He waited one more ring and hung up.

Shep tried to calm himself, remembering the less

menacing things he'd been warned about, the insurance and credit card fraud—criminal, sure, but not *severed head* criminal.

He began tidying shelves, and when that didn't calm his nervous energy, he retrieved the push-broom from the supply closet and imagined himself into a different circumstance entirely as he swept the aisles. Maybe he could get a job at Café Gourmand, as a dishwasher or a busboy. Then he'd get to see Lila all the time, but in a safe way, not like the other night, away from those friends of hers and the booze and the noise. Maybe they'd get to have some private jokes or nicknames for each other. He'd be cleaning up in the back and she'd playfully bop him with a dishrag, call him 'Pops.' And he'd call her 'Kid' or something, foster a paternal relationship to ease her into the idea, and then... No. That was too much. There had to be another way to start over. It had been so much easier before they'd met, when he was still a stranger and everything was possible.

Lionel kept getting in the way of the broom, lunging at the fraying bristles.

"Come on now, the broom didn't do anything to you."

The dog bared his teeth and let out a quiet growl.

He leaned the broom against a shelf, picked the dog up and touched his nose with the tip of his finger.

"I'd get a hell of a lot more done if I wasn't always looking after you, you know that?"

Lionel licked his nose.

At the end of the night, when Shep was locking up in the back—his diligence verging on the absurd as he pushed and pulled, pushed and pulled before turning the key to lock it all over again—he felt a presence over his shoulder. He turned around to find Eugene standing behind him with a trash bag slung over his shoulder, a cigarette burning low in his other hand.

"Oh—" Shep started.

Eugene dropped the butt on the pavement and ground

it out with his tennis shoe. "Slow in summertime. Slow, slow, slow." He pulled his foot away, but an ember still burned orange.

Shep nodded, noncommittal.

"They left you all alone, your friends?"

Eugene was standing so close Shep could smell the trash he was holding, bitter coffee grounds and the dry remnants of sweet pastries, a hint of banana peel and emptied ashtray.

"They'll be back soon," Shep said. "I talked to Hung today, actually." The lie uttered itself, and Shep was pleased with his quick thinking.

Eugene chuckled softly and switched the trash bag to his other hand, the plastic straining under its weight. "It's very quiet without him." He laughed again.

"Yeah," Shep laughed back, but it was just a laughing sound, a mirroring.

Eugene stopped laughing. "The father, always very nice. The son…he likes to give me trouble. But he must trust you. Strange." He sucked his teeth.

Shep squinted, unsure what response was expected.

"I don't trust anybody like that. Not my brothers. Not even my wife." Eugene seemed to eye Shep up and down now. "It's very dangerous to trust."

Eugene held eye contact for a moment before sauntering over to the dumpster. He tossed the bag over his shoulder, his muscular arm flexed in a white T-shirt. On his way back to the water store, he pointed back at Shep. "If you speak to Hung again, you'll tell him I say hello."

Lionel growled, baring his little teeth. Eugene laughed as the water store's back door swung shut behind him. Shep scooped the dog up under his arm, whispered in his ear, *hush now, you hush.*

It was ten o'clock but felt so much later that it seemed the sun might peek out above the hills at any moment. Time could lose meaning so easily. It was a made-up structure anyway, meant to conjure order out of chaos. He hugged Lionel to his side. Here, the seasons were made up too. The climate could change between noon and three, and the only thing that defined "winter" was a faintly grayer sky. And what did Eugene even mean by it being "slow in summertime"? People still went to work in the summer, still stopped off for coffee, newspapers, candy. Or did he mean things felt slow: the smoggy heat, the melty blacktop, the way summertime was signified by the sun's subtle sharpening?

Shep was growing short of breath. He stopped and leaned his palm against a telephone pole that was littered with dispatches: a "Black Cat Still Missing" flyer with not a photograph but a drawing of a cat's silhouette, and the plea "needs medicine," was new, having replaced a simpler "Missing Cat" flyer that had grown weathered; a handwritten 3x5 card said simply, "Need help with housework, yard work, cleaning, pet care? CALL ME," the last bit underlined with a fading black marker. The phone number was written beneath it in shaky blue ballpoint.

There was desperation everywhere. Knowing he wasn't alone in it wasn't a comfort, not quite.

Shep set off again, quickening his pace. He was getting angry—not at Eugene, per se, but at everything—and anger always manifested itself in the body. His lower abdomen tightened into a knot, and his footing grew wobbly. He tried to take in more air, great gulps of it, but he wound up hiccupping, his body never fully under his control.

Could he blame it all on the war? Everything that had gone wrong in his body and mind? He remembered it all so vaguely—flat desert, black sky, hours on the Tapline, trying to stay awake until the next convoy support center, the reality of warfare mostly tangible in sounds and smells—the planes, the burning oil—the weeks and months punctuated by horrors that felt unexpected, though they shouldn't have, though they weren't.

He swallowed, his throat parched and raw, as he remembered watching from several car-lengths back, idling in a line of vehicles outside Kuwait City, while Marines examined the charred remains of an Iraqi tank. He'd been staring out his dust-speckled window, trying to make out the shapes of the buildings in the distance, when he felt a shift in the air, a hottening that pulsed in his brain as the Marines appeared to move in slow motion. After a second, not even a second, an explosion sounded, followed by a piercing wail. When he jumped from his truck, what he saw was chaos, everyone rushing around in the smoke, a stretcher loaded onto a field ambulance. Finally, he climbed back into the truck. The traffic didn't move. A piece of unexploded munition, he heard later, had blown off the Marine's foot. Then it was the whole leg, he heard, plus an undetermined portion of his groin. Then, days later, he was dead, it turned out. Had died within hours of the blast.

How could Shep tell anyone what he'd felt the moment before it happened? He didn't even know the Marine, had never even seen his face, but he'd felt inevitability taking hold. Could he have stopped it, if he'd recognized it for what it was? Even if the answer was no, it didn't temper the feelings of culpability that kept him quiet, that mutated the memory as it churned through the years.

But his experiences weren't the stuff war films were made of. There had been no ending, for one. He hadn't saved any lives. He hadn't taken any. Could he even say he'd been ruined by an outside force, be it psychic or chemical? Did he have a story or just a list of complaints?

He still wasn't getting enough air. His nostrils flared as he leaned against a building, and Lionel squirmed.

"Alright, alright, alright," he sighed. He set the dog down.

They'd reached an intersection, and Shep realized he'd passed his building, so lost was he in the struggle to point a finger at something. The building he'd braced himself against turned out to be a 7-11. A man with long, greasy white hair was sitting outside on the ground, but Shep didn't have any change to give him. He was bent forward, his muddy hiking boots splayed out into an empty parking spot. In the spot next to him, a woman sat in the front seat of a gray Mazda, scratching the silver boxes of a lottery ticket with her fingernail.

For a moment, Shep fantasized about continuing his walk until Coldwater descended into the winding hills. He would wander like some wise medicine man, collecting wild herbs along the way, whistling a tune he'd heard in a dream. He'd wind up in Beverly Hills, gliding placidly past gilded mansions with twigs matted in his hair, his wolf-companion bringing up the rear.

But when he pushed himself off from the side of the building, he knew he was too weak to continue. He stepped around the corner of the 7-11 and slid down the wall, rested his forehead on his knees, and Lionel joined him, pushing his snout against Shep's rib.

I'm too young to feel so old, he thought, but he wasn't sure what that meant either. Age was just time in the body, and if time was made up, then the sentiment was meaningless. There was no use in getting worked up. These feelings were just words, after all.

8

It was early yet when Shep was overtaken by the sense of something amiss upstairs. He was at the back of the store restocking bags of potato chips when his head began to ache, and he became aware of an odor that reminded him of potpourri gone rancid, if such a thing existed, or perfume on a corpse. The odor came and went over the course of the morning while his headache pulsed, steadfast, intensifying as he got closer to the staircase that led to the Phans' apartment.

He'd lost track of how long it had been since he last spoke with Hung, but it was deep summer now, a fact betrayed by the even greater dearth of people on the sidewalk. It was the time of year when people cowered in their air-conditioned homes, offices and cars when the sunshine felt malicious. He was cowering too. When he wasn't at the store, he was holed up in his bedroom, drinking from the bottle of whiskey he kept in the freezer.

He knew there was a key to the apartment somewhere on the cumbersome chain Hung had left him. He posted the "Back in 10 Minutes" sign on the door and locked it, beckoning Lionel to follow as he climbed the stairs, breathing through his mouth as he tried each key until he found the one that opened the flimsy front door.

The apartment was dark, all the curtains drawn. Shep patted the wall in search of the light switch. When he flipped it, a ceiling fan over the kitchen table lit up and began turning slowly. He took off his shoes. The cream-colored carpet was so clean and brushed in a single direction—Mrs. Phan must have shampooed it after the funeral reception—that he was afraid even his socks would sully it somehow. He stepped into the living room and turned around.

The smell was stronger inside, as he'd expected, but there was still no apparent source. In fact, it took him a few moments to notice that there was virtually nothing in the living room. The sparse furniture—a couch and a recliner sunken with the indentation of Mr. Phan's body—was sheathed in plastic. There were no lamps, no end tables or trinkets. The framed photos he'd seen on the mantel after the funeral were gone, the polished wood now layered with translucent dust.

He wandered into the kitchen and found the cupboards bare of both food and dishes. In the fridge all that remained was a little orange box of baking soda on the bottom shelf.

This was as far as he'd ever gone into the apartment, but the smell was somewhere deeper. He lifted the bottom of his shirt and used it to cover his nose and mouth as he stepped slowly down the hallway, as though the family were asleep and he had to be quiet as a ghost not to wake them. He came first to what must have been the parents' room and found the bed stripped down, just a bare queen-sized mattress and box spring, and there it was, the source: heaps and heaps of dead flowers on the dresser and surrounding floor, some wrapped in paper with petals wilted and brown, others drooping over the edges of vases filled with grungy water. The sight was as overpowering as the smell. He imagined Mrs. Phan couldn't bear to throw them out and had left them there fresh, thinking there was some chance they would remain so. Stacked beside the wreckage were dozens of condolence cards. Shep opened the one on top, but the writing was all in Vietnamese. It filled all the white space, wedged around the English message, *Our thoughts and prayers are with you at this difficult time.* He found a box of trash bags under the kitchen sink and held his breath as he filled it. He poured the swampy water out into the sink and lined up the rinsed vases on the counter.

"Lionel," he called. "Where'd you go?"

He found the dog in what must have been Hung's room, laid out on the twin bed, his belly in the air and tongue lolling in the heat. Unlike the rest of the apartment, this room felt recently occupied. A seasons-old Kobe Bryant poster hung over the bed, its corners curled away from the wall, the tape that secured them yellowed. Otherwise, the room itself was as meticulously clean as Hung kept the store. His shirts, even the T-shirts, were wrinkle-free, arranged in a perfectly spaced row in his closet; even the issues of *Maxim*, *Playboy* and *FHM* he kept in a stack on the bottom shelf of the bookcase by his bed appeared untouched and were organized by month. It occurred to Shep that, with the demands of the store and helping his parents, Hung couldn't possibly spend much time in this room. The only lived-in touch was the poster, the decorating choice of a teenager, now in his twenties, having never had the time or chance to move on. He wondered if Hung ever watched basketball anymore. He had a Lakers keychain, but Shep had never once heard him mention a game.

Shep sat on the bed and ran his hand over the duvet, navy blue with a red stripe around the bottom. He scratched Lionel's belly and gazed out the window, which looked down on the parking lot. A car idled outside the water store for a long time before Eugene stepped out the passenger door and rapped his knuckles on the roof, which seemed to trigger the car's departure. A younger man came outside and brought Eugene a Styrofoam cup as he sat at the folding table where the other water store associates were having their morning coffee and cigarettes. Shep watched dazedly, imagining what they were saying, where Eugene had come from. No wonder Hung had grown so obsessed; even in his own bedroom, he wasn't free. Shep felt suddenly very sad and very close to him. A disturbance grew in the back of his mind, questions of why the Phans' apartment seemed so utterly vacated, of how long he would be trapped in this holding pattern with no guidance from the outside. But the disturbance was hushed, held at bay by Lionel's soft snoring at the end of the bed, by the muggy air and hot white sky. Shep wanted Hung to return and relieve him, true, but more than that, he missed his friend.

9

It was always in the dead of night that Shep's panic came roaring back to the forefront. He lay in bed, back sticky, heart racing. He was afraid to fall asleep, of the landmines his dreamlife had waiting for him, but equally afraid of the madness that would overtake him completely if he didn't get some rest. He forcibly slowed his breathing, keeping his eyes closed. He breathed

in on a four count, breathed out on eight, visualizing a wave
of blue, then repeated, and repeated, and repeated...until the
wave became nothing, and nothing descended.

A ringing pushed through the darkness and Shep sat up,
blinking. He got up and fumbled around the kitchen in
search of the phone, unable, in his sleep-daze, to locate a light
switch. He stubbed his toe on something and, as he braced
himself, his hand fell onto something vaguely phone-shaped.
    "Hello?"
    He heard breathing on the other end.
    "Is somebody there?"
    The breathing seemed to grow labored then, devolving
into a wheeze.
    "Hello?"
    The wheezing voice let out a single, plaintive groan then
Shep heard a click followed by a dial tone. He hung up the
phone, but the dial tone remained and then grew louder,
filling the air. Frantically, he patted the walls, looking for the
damn light switch, but there was none to be found as he grew
dizzy with the sensation of spinning through the darkness,
the dial tone droning in his ears.

Shep's eyes opened. He sat up on his elbows and searched
the walls, realizing he was in bed but not knowing if he'd
returned or had never gotten up, if the phone call had been a
subconscious reminder of his own failing health or a real cry
for help from an unknown source. He spent an inordinate
amount of time these days trying to distinguish what were
dreams, what were memories, and what were just thoughts,
the line blurred by the heat. He still heard a dial tone; though
faint, it felt wedded to his ear like a seashell to the sound of
the ocean, but the fact gave no insight into its veracity or lack
thereof. Was this what going crazy felt like? A fading of the
grid that separated the real from the unreal?

The dial tone receded to a soft hum as he watched the ceiling fan above his bed. It had always wobbled, but now it seemed to be taking the corkboard with it, so the ceiling panels shifted with each turn. If the fan fell one of these nights, and the ceiling came tumbling down with it, would he have any chance of escaping it? If he continued to lie there doing nothing, night after night, it seemed inevitable that this would be his end. At least he would be found before his corpse began to rot; Rosa would surely notice if the roof caved in.

He could turn the fan off and melt in the heat. Or he could get out, now.

Minutes later, Shep sat with his car running in the carport, his hands gripping the wheel. There was only one place to go. He squeezed his fingers around the wheel once, twice. It was foolish, but he had to try. He had to see Lila again. He was crawling through the desert of her absence with a potent, scraping thirst. He squeezed the steering wheel a third time and released the parking brake to back out of the driveway into the pre-dawn mist.

At a red light, Shep imagined himself on the water with Lila. Maybe on a fishing trip, she in oversized rainboots, he showing her how to bait a hook, holding her hand as they stepped off the dock and onto a fishing boat. Maybe one of these days he'd buy a fishing boat. He'd say, "Be careful" and "It's awful slippery," and she'd roll her eyes the way girls do. She'd be wearing those big sunglasses of hers, and he'd smile watching her cast the line. "What?" she'd say, noticing him staring. 'I'm just proud of you is all,' he'd say, and then—

The words, he'd have to say the words sometime. Even in his imagination he could never come out and say it. He hoped she'd guess, say something like, *On some level I think I've known it since the day we met...*

He parked in his usual spot across from her apartment and a couple of buildings down. Lionel was asleep beside him. It was just beginning to get light out, and the only sounds were those of the sprinklers activating up and down the block and the straggling crickets that overlapped the waking birds.

Shep reached into the glove compartment quietly so as not to disturb the snoozing dog and pulled out a mini bottle of whiskey. He drained it, though it burned all the way down, and tucked the evidence in the console.

"Jesus," he murmured, clutching his stomach.

He turned the ignition halfway so he could switch on the radio, and found a station on the second half of "Peaceful Easy Feeling." He turned the volume down low and stared out the windshield.

Because his nights were so strange and sleepless, the days had grown indistinct. He had to stop a moment to remember what it was he was supposed to be doing—not just now but at the store too. He'd try to make change for a customer and realize with a start that he was just turning the coins over and over in his palm.

And some days, it felt as though dreamlife was encroaching. On the walk to work he'd see something out the corner of his eye, something bright and glittering, something floating like gauzy fabric, and he'd swivel around, but there was only the breeze. It didn't feel as unsettling as he supposed it ought to. He had to get some sleep. He was trying, if trying meant getting into bed, assuming the position, tossing fitfully while his mind wandered and weaved into crevices.

He had to come here because his mind wandered again and again to the girl's face, her hair flapping in the wind, with the sun beating down and reflected up from the water, encircling her in light.

He hummed along with the song on the radio

   ...But this voice keeps whispering in my ear, tells me I may never see you again...and I got a peaceful, easy feeling, and I know you won't let me down, 'cause I'm already standing on the ground...

But when the song ended, transitioning into an ad for an Indian casino out in the desert, he heard it start over again, faintly in the background. He turned the car off.

It was a raspy female voice singing, *And I found out a long time ago what a woman can do to your soul, oh but she can't take you any way you don't already know how to go…*

He couldn't tell where it was coming from. He turned and looked out the back window, checked the mirrors. Lionel burrowed deeper into his seat and began to snore.

"Shh-ssh-shhh," Shep said, and scratched the dog's rump.

The voice stopped singing. He rolled down the window and leaned his head out just in time to see a gnarled curtain of white hair whip around the corner at the end of the block. He ducked back inside and sealed the window shut again. It was the Wraith, had to have been her. But where had she come from? How had she been close enough for him to hear her but far enough to remain out of sight? He closed his eyes and replayed it in his head, her hair swooping around the corner, knotted and white as bleached wood.

Or: was her hair like the colors that sometimes floated in his peripheral vision, just for a split second, long enough to make an impression but not long enough to question too closely? Suddenly every encounter he'd had with the Wraith came back to him, seeing her charging up and down the street, sunburned limbs pumping, menacing him with her hateful stare, emerging unbidden from vans and bus shelters, singing her siren song—his memories of her were so heightened, so imbued with toxicity that he couldn't place her in any realistic context. If he ever described her to anyone, it would sound like a tall tale: the Wicked Witch of his subconscious.

His hand trembled as he reached for the glove compartment and drank another of his bottles. The compartment was full enough now that the bottles didn't roll. The full ones sat snugly atop the empties. He supposed he would have to clear it out one of these days.

The sun was inching upward in the sky, spilling orange all across the hilltops. It was going to be another hot day in a long line of them. It could go on like this for months yet. Everything could go on for months like this, Hung staying away, dodging his calls, he waiting in cars overnight, watching out windows, sitting alone, his breath purposely shallow and hushed.

"Shhh sshh sshhhh, Lionel," he whispered, though the dog had already stopped snoring. He climbed out of the car and shut the door softly, pushing it in with his hip to make it click. He glanced both ways as he crossed the street. There was not a vehicle stirring, though some curtains had been opened, some windows lit. The sprinklers and crickets had quieted, clearing the way for birdsong, clock radios and the whirring of coffeemakers. He stepped up onto the porch and rapped his knuckles on the metal cage in front of her door; he was beyond excuses and explanations now. It didn't matter how he knew where to find her, and she'd see that too, he knew she would, she had to, and then they could both stop pretending.

The door swung open, and the brunette roommate blustered out, her eyes puffy and makeup-smeared. She wore a satin bathrobe with Japanese characters running down her breast.

"Hang on two minutes, I just have to—wait, you're not Chazz…"

"Sorry to bother you." He had already backed one step down from the stoop. "Um, you remember me…?"

The girl stared at him blankly.

"No, no, never mind. I was just looking for Lila because—"

"She moved out last week—I gotta go." The girl began to swing the door shut again, but Shep ran up and smacked his palm against the metal cage—it rattled louder than he'd expected.

"What do you mean? Where'd she go?"

The roommate paused, seemingly about to tell him, but thought better of it. "Wait, why should I tell *you*?"

"Please—"

The door slammed shut. He heard the lock turn behind her. His heart pounded in his ears.

The sun was rising fatter in the sky now, and Shep swung an arm over his forehead to block it as he ran back to the car.

"Come on, come on, come on" he muttered into the steering wheel as the car sputtered.

He got onto the 101, though he was supposed to be opening Parkdale's soon enough. Rush hour was only just beginning, and he eased into it like a river to the ocean, one stitch in a seam. It was a comfort he'd found in Southern California, the anonymity of the freeway, the feeling of smallness as the city unfurled before him. Lionel woke up and climbed into his lap.

He was reminded of their early days together, two strangers hurtling toward California.

"What am I going to do with you?" he'd said then.

The dog panted.

"I wish you could talk. I wish you could tell me I'm crazy.

"I never had a dog. So, don't be surprised if I don't know what I'm doing.

"I wish you could tell me what your name is, if you've got one.

"Aw, hell."

The one-sided conversations kept him going through the multi-day drive, made the time go faster. Within three nights, he was waking up to find the dog nestled in his armpit or cradled between his bare feet, snoring. Even if he couldn't sleep, he'd avoid changing positions so the dog would stay.

"When did I say you could sleep on me?" he'd yawn in the morning, rising in another cold motel room.

It felt good to talk to somebody. He found himself rambling in the car, telling the mutt all of his stories, and of the things he hoped would become stories. He talked until his throat dried up, and when he stopped talking, the dog was still there beside him, listening.

But in the present traffic, Shep said nothing. His mind was an expanding blank, a flat, white plane extending in all directions. Only the sunlight registered, bright and dense, needling him. He pulled down the window shade and fumbled around the console and under the seats in hopes of finding a pair of sunglasses, finally just driving in a half-blind squint.

But though he had no thoughts, though the verbal part of his brain was temporarily silenced, when he got to Café Gourmand, he patted Lionel's head in a way they both understood to mean that he would be right back, so there was no point in raising a fuss.

The café had just opened, and a girl about Lila's age was behind the counter, starting up the house brew. Without even making a show of looking at the menu or ordering a drink, he went straight to the back, stopping short of the restrooms and swinging the office door open to get a look at the staff schedule, with its usual chart of young people's names like "Madison" and "Dakota."

But adjustments had been made. Every "Lila" on the board had been crossed out in red and replaced by another name, a "Skyler" or a "Shay."

"Can I help you?" A bewildered manager in shirt and tie entered the office with a money pouch in his hand.

"No, no, thank you, just looking for the bathroom," Shep stammered, and ducked back out of the office.

Something's happened, he thought. *She's gone.* He searched the walls until his gaze landed on the bulletin board where he'd seen the flyer for Lila's play. Now there was an advertisement for guitar lessons, a flyer for an open mic night at a bar down the street, an ad for a headshot photographer... He didn't even know what he was looking for. The first customers began to trickle in for to-go cups of coffee, and he shrank further into the corner.

He looked back over his shoulder at the folks lined up in suits and dresses, women with wet hair, everyone fiddling with phones. He hadn't showered, hadn't slept. He hadn't looked in a mirror in days, but he could smell himself, a sharp, metallic odor emanating from somewhere underneath his wrinkled clothes. His breath, too, smelled—he recognized with some dread—like blood. And it tasted like blood. He felt around with his tongue and winced as he landed on a sore right behind his rear molar, deep and raw. He couldn't stop burrowing into it with his tongue, no matter how much it hurt. He tried to disappear into the corner, imagining himself an ogre, hulking and wretched.

Finally, he sat down in a booth. Lila had slipped through his fingers, and it was his own fault. He kept jabbing the sore with the tip of his tongue, churning the wound of unknown origin. His eyes filled with tears. He was so tired of trying to start over all the time. He had absentmindedly pulled one of the phone number tags off the ad for guitar lessons and was worrying it with his thumb and forefinger, rendering it illegible with his sweat and grease.

Some time later, a busboy brought him a glass of water and a menu. He pushed the menu aside and chugged down the whole glass, wiped his mouth with his sleeve.

"Can I help you?"

Shep looked up at a young man's face. He was holding a notepad in one hand and a pitcher of water in the other.

"Uh, no, I'm not hungry."

Shep watched him go and looked around the room again. He caught a glimpse of the manager through the smudged kitchen window. The girl who'd opened the store had been joined by another girl who was checking a monitor overhead and calling out names as she arranged cups on the counter with the Sharpied names facing out.

He recognized her. She'd started working at Café Gourmand the same week Lila had—they'd done their training together, hands clasped behind their backs while the unsmiling manager showed them how to operate the espresso machine. She looked enough like Lila too, with her honey-blond hair, that Shep had been fooled a time or two when watching from afar. Not only that, he realized that he'd seen her at the theater. She'd been one of the actors smoking outside the dressing room, the one he'd taken for Lila for a split second, the night he'd been so incautious. This flood of connections caught him off guard—he'd been feeling so slow, thick-tongued and fuzzy-minded that he immediately questioned their reliability.

She saw him staring. He looked down at the table. He looked back up. She was occupied now, rinsing out a smoothie blender. With just a few alterations, she really was a dead ringer. Her nose was a bit longer, her eyes set farther apart, but it was easy to gloss over those differences, attribute them to the light or the angle. He was staring again, but this time, when she noticed, he didn't look away.

He fantasized then that it *was* Lila, that they'd crossed over into a reality that was slightly askew. Maybe he too looked different, his hair a little darker, his eyes hazel instead of blue. If he stood up, he might find himself a couple of inches taller or shorter.

When the girl came out from behind the counter and approached his table, Shep felt suddenly giddy, like she'd read his mind and was about to assure him that it was all true, that this was their chance, everyone's chance to start over, that he should pull up the car and meet her out front.

"Can I help you with something, sir?"

"Oh, uh, no," he stammered, the fantasy evaporating as he looked at her up close and noticed more differences: the shape of her jaw, the smattering of freckles across her cheeks.

"More water?" She tilted her head sympathetically.

Shep gripped the empty glass in his hand. He nodded.

"Actually, you know what? I will get something. I'll have a coffee and…and a bagel and cream cheese. Just regular cream cheese, no infusions, nothing…pickled or anything…"

"Alright," she laughed as she refilled his glass. She turned to go.

"Wait—one more thing."

The girl swiveled around again. The tag on her shirt said "Chrissie."

"Do you know a girl who works here, or maybe used to work here? A girl named Lila? Lila Olson?"

"Uh-huh." She nodded.

"I'm a friend of hers," he said, "and I thought maybe you could help me?"

"Um, maybe…I'm gonna go put your order in, 'kay?"

Shep nodded, and Chrissie disappeared into the kitchen. He had to get back to Parkdale's. He'd have to take his food to go. He regretted ordering it; the thought of eating anything now made him nauseated. He drank down the second glass of water, but the taste of blood remained. He drove his tongue into the sore again, a slave to all his worst instincts. The pain radiated through his jaw.

Shep turned around in his seat looking for Chrissie, hoping he'd find her just far enough away that he could look at her and see someone else again, just for a second, and imagine that he was someone else too.

10

The ancient desktop computer at Parkdale's took several minutes to boot up, and he'd had to dust the screen, but he knew where to look to find what he needed.

…and then Trevor told me she got cast in a show called Perfectly Pauline, *a network sitcom,* Chrissie had said as she brought him his bagel. He'd left his legal pad in the car, so he asked to borrow her pen and wrote the name down on his hand.

She's not, like, playing Pauline or anything, but still, I mean, she's got lines and stuff, and it's, like, a multi-episode arc…

The unsmiling manager was watching from the kitchen doorway. Shep scribbled *Not Pauline* on his hand.

There were only so many networks, only so many studios. The bells chimed. Lionel barked. Shep set his legal pad down on the desk and went back behind the counter. A woman was browsing the medicine aisle. While he waited for her to select her purchase, he ducked down and took a swig of a beer he'd poured while opening up and forgotten under the register. The cool but no longer cold liquid soothed the sore behind his molar for a second, but when he swallowed, the pain returned.

The bells chimed again. Lionel barked.

"Goddamnit." Shep sighed and rose again, the blood rushing back through his legs a little too quickly. He braced himself against the counter.

A line formed, trapping him, people buying tissues and frozen burritos, energy drinks and lottery tickets. While he was ringing up one customer, a man came from the back and interrupted, holding his wallet aloft.

"Hey man, how long is that ATM gonna be out of order?"

Shep shrugged a wordless apology and pulled a plastic bag off the dispenser, noting that it was the last one. Were there more plastic bags in storage somewhere? Where did Hung order them from? He'd have to tell people he was out of bags for the rest of the day at least, one more thing out of order. And if deliveries stopped coming, would the store eventually be bought clean, a room of empty shelves he would dust to a shine every day? Did the Phans own the place, or did they rent it along with the apartment upstairs? If those payments stopped, who would come calling? None of these questions had been addressed in Hung's training session.

When the store cleared out, Shep returned to the back with Lionel trailing just behind. He was eighty percent sure he'd already managed to figure out where *Perfectly Pauline* was being filmed from the websites he used to frequent to find Lila's auditions. But you couldn't just wander onto a set. You had to be on a list to even get in the parking garage.

Two viable strategies flashed through his mind: He could call in to Central Casting every day until they were casting extras for *Perfectly Pauline*. Or he could get a job as a delivery driver, keep working day in and day out, driving packages all over town for weeks, maybe even months, until he was assigned to make a delivery to the studio, then "get lost" until he found the right set. Both options would take time, could in fact take so long that her "multi-episode arc" would be long over by the time he got in.

Shep picked up the cordless phone and dialed Central Casting, pacing through the aisles as he listened to the long recording listing the types that were needed in the coming days, the genders, ages, races, sizes and "looks" needed to fill out every movie and TV show in production.

He stared idly out the window as a white SUV pulled into the Parkdale's lot and eased backward into the handicapped spot in front of the water store.

Shep listened to the recording: *two women, eighteen to twenty-five, needed to play prostitutes, any race, possible nudity, no tattoos; three to four white males needed, ages thirty-five to fifty, must bring own tuxedo.*

The tinted window of the SUV rolled down, and Shep saw that it was Eugene in the passenger seat. He dangled a lit cigarette out the passenger side door, letting his ash hang over the pavement while the driver climbed out and entered the water store. Eugene was wearing a suit and a gold watch that caught the light and reflected it like a beacon. A minute later, he got out and leaned against the car door. He'd removed his jacket and rolled up his shirtsleeves. He tilted his face up toward the sun, eyes closed, soaking it in contentedly, like a lizard on a rock.

The recording came to a call for males aged twenty-five and up, no other requirements, and Shep pressed the pound key, still watching Eugene from the doorway as he sunbathed. When prompted, Shep entered the last four digits of his Social Security number and waited. Shep smoothed his hair back and squinted his tired eyes open and shut. When he opened them again, Eugene's wife and son had come outside. She kissed his cheek while the boy threw his arms around his dad's thighs. His wife said something to him, but he didn't seem to be listening, instead looking at his watch, at his ash on the ground. How could a man be so bored when he had so much?

The recording clicked over to hold music, an instrumental version of "Saturday in the Park." Shep watched the boy climb onto the back of Eugene's SUV and bounce on the bumper until his mom snapped her fingers at him. He returned to his parents and began playing with his dad's belt buckle until Eugene brushed his hand away. Eugene's associate, also in a suit, returned. Eugene tossed his cigarette butt toward the curb, gave his wife a limp hug and got back in the car. The SUV pulled out of the driveway past the Cowboy, who appeared asleep sitting up in his shaded nook, Eugene's tinted window gliding upward at identical speed.

Shep watched as Eugene's wife pulled the boy by the hand to her own car, leaning over into the backseat to get him situated. If she were his wife, he thought, he would look at her when she spoke to him. He would return her kisses. He would appreciate her, he thought, seeing the back of her bra through her thin blouse as she stood up to get in the driver's seat. Why did a guy like Eugene have all the love in the world? Why did love seem to be hoarded by the undeserving, while people like Shep had to fight for scraps? If there was only so much love to go around, what did a person have to do, how far did he have to go, to get his share?

Three teenagers were gathered in front of the donut shop, sitting on the curb drinking from little milk cartons and passing around a bag of donut holes, the sweet aroma wafting around them, a sugary cloud. Shep glanced over at them. He crossed his arms, the phone wedged between his ear and shoulder. Their laughter was melodious, impenetrable, inexplicable to anyone outside their little group. He could still hear them laughing as he stepped back inside, even over the rush of traffic, over the hold music and his own hard breathing.

Little feet came clattering behind him, and suddenly Lionel was headbutting his shins.

"What the—you scared me, boy."

The hold music stopped abruptly and a voice came on the line. While the casting assistant rattled off the requirements and call time, Shep climbed the stairs to the Phans' apartment and leaned against the banister. He scanned the ceiling from the vantage point of the stairs, the cobwebbed corners and intermittently flickering fluorescent tubes, eyes flitting around like gnats.

Shep interrupted the man on the phone, "Hey, where is it, the address."

"I just told you," the assistant said. "Sunset Gow—"

Wrong studio. Shep hung up and dialed again as he wandered back down the stairs. He tongued the sore at the back of his mouth, wincing in pain, but not stopping. He imagined the wound swirling and black. The recording began again, and Shep half-listened to the parts he'd heard before. He ran his finger across a spot of dust he'd missed, staring at the dull light of the computer screen. He pulled his dusty fingertip away from the screen and rubbed it in a circle against his thumb.

The same hold music came on again. Shep paced the aisles while it droned on endlessly. The taste of blood, thick and sour, filled his mouth, and he swallowed it down. He hung up the phone. He didn't have time for this shit. His car was littered with drive-on passes from previous shoots, and the security guards never seemed to look that closely. If anyone questioned him, he'd figure it out then. All he had to do was get on that lot.

11

Shep drank a neon-orange Gatorade as he drove around the perimeter of the lot to get a sense of the space. There were no windows to look into. The high exterior wall protected the enclosed soundstages from prying eyes and hid the constructed city streets, suburban neighborhoods and carefully decorated three-walled living rooms away from the dull and polluted outdoors. On one of those soundstages, Lila, that very moment, could be sitting on a stylish sofa with a layer of pancake between her skin and the hot lights above, her hair smoothed to the consistency of velvet, a production assistant waving a light meter all around her face like a magic wand.

He started to turn into the driveway but thought better of it. If the garage attendant turned him away, he'd have no recourse but to bust through the boom gate, and he didn't think his car could survive the impact. He found a strip mall with an underground lot because it was too hot to leave Lionel out in the sun. He took a spot between the wall and a dark-red van, killed the engine and cracked the windows.

"Lionel, you've got to be quiet."

He set a little paper plate of kibble on the back seat and poured water into a plastic dish.

"Just sit tight," he whispered, and took a last swig of Gatorade, swishing the sweet, lukewarm liquid around in his mouth.

Shep headed back to the studio lot on foot, holding his breath as he crept down the exit ramp. Pressing himself to the wall, he imagined himself invisible, all the while eying the guard in his booth, who was eating pasta salad from a Tupperware and bopping his head to the music playing on a tiny radio. Shep reached the P1 elevators, blending in with a pack of deliverymen as they entered and rode up to the ground floor.

When the elevator arrived in the lobby, the deliverymen dispersed, and he didn't have any idea which way to go. But everyone around him was walking, so he figured he'd better start walking too.

He walked in a straight line, looking to his left and right for some kind of sign. Some clouds had gathered overhead, softening the sun's edge. Then a sudden coughing fit overtook him, and he grabbed onto the back of a bench for support. He leaned over it, hacking as tears rolled down the sides of his face. When he looked up again, the place looked even more confusing and unknowable. Everyone who passed him had a headset or a walkie-talkie. They had clipboards and toolbelts. Shep wiped the tears from his cheeks. No one stopped or looked at him as they passed. This place was a gigantic maze, covering two square blocks and containing multitudes. He'd never get his bearings, let alone find Lila, if she was even here. He should have found out what kind of show *Perfectly Pauline* was, so he'd know what kind of set he was looking for.

Then he spotted a golf cart across from him, beside a row of trailers. If he had one of those, he could cover more ground. Shep crossed the way and found the key in the cart's ignition. He looked around. Nobody was watching. Before he had a chance to talk himself out of it, he sat down and started the cart up, its tiny, battery-operated engine purring to life. After he'd gone a few hundred feet, he heard a voice in the distance yell, "Hey!" but Shep didn't look back. He pressed the pedal to the floor, pushing the cart to the upper limit of its power.

The cart didn't go all that fast, but it was enough to kick up a breeze that set his hair fluttering against his neck, and when he turned a corner, he found himself barreling up to the driveway of a high school set, presently deserted. A hand-painted sign for a Homecoming dance was stuck to the front doors, and a row of classic cars from the '50s were parked at the curb. Were there classrooms inside, or was it just a hollow exterior? Was there a football field in the back or just a wooden stand that could be kicked, sending the building toppling over like posterboard? He didn't have time to investigate.

He pressed the pedal hard against the golf cart's base again, sending it whirring and careening past the driveway, and turned down a long alleyway surrounded on either side by walls so high they sunk him into a deep, cool shade.

When he reached the end of the alley, blinking and disoriented by his sudden reemergence into the sun, he stopped just short of plunging headlong into a pool of water rendered a murky greenish blue, a color that approximated the ocean when shot through a particular filter. Behind the water stood a massive wall that was painted sky blue with white, cottony clouds. Shep stopped a moment and took in the view: the real sky, bright and hazy, surrounding the fake sky that looked more real than the real one, the image that comes to mind when you close your eyes and think *sky*. The longer he looked at it, the less he could tell which was which. The water, too, looked more and more like the ocean the longer he sat with it. He imagined little wisps of seaweed, slimy sand at the bottom, tiny schools of fish weaving through the depths. On either side of the water were fans the size of jet engines that would be positioned and switched on to make waves when they were called for. But now the ocean was dormant, the tide on standby, the sky still.

Shep heard movement in the alley, either a car or another golf cart, and moved on, turning around the back side of the sky wall—naked, splintered wood with splatters of blue at the edges.

After driving around lost and circling for what felt like an hour, he found himself driving along an exceptionally clean New York City street, rows of brownstones with wrought-iron staircases, bright yellow fire hydrants and storefronts of frosted glass. And when he saw, across the block, a group of trailers with *Perfectly Pauline* signs hanging from their doors, Shep parked the cart, abandoning it in front of a subway entrance that stopped short five steps below street level.

Each sign had a name underneath the pink cursive *Perfectly Pauline* logo: *Darla, Evan, Pauline, Mr. Wells, Traffic Cop*—the names of the show's characters. Could Lila be *Darla*? She wouldn't be *Traffic Cop*. He walked down the line, imagining the trailers' interiors, foldout beds and makeup mirrors, delivered food in little plastic cartons. He stopped and held onto a streetlight—was it functional, or hollow and bulbless?—and contemplated Lila's rise. In just over two years she'd gone from café waitress to TV star. Maybe she'd moved from her old apartment to a house, or a condo in a high-rise. It could happen that fast. So many people came to Hollywood and never made it. They gave up, chose other professions, settled into the background, but not Lila.

Someone tapped him on the shoulder.

"Background? You're in the wrong spot. You were told to go to the tent by the south gate." *Perfectly Pauline* was embroidered on the right breast of his fleece pullover.

Shep blinked fast and wiped the tears away. He cleared his throat and swallowed the sourness in his mouth.

"Last name?" the man said, consulting a clipboard.

"Uh, Shepherd…" He eyed the golf cart and wondered if he could still make a run for it.

"You're not on here."

"It could be under…um, you know what? I am in the wrong place. I mean I misspoke before. I'm crew. I'm a PA."

The man squinted behind black-rimmed glasses.

"I misheard you is all."

"Can I see your visitor pass real quick?"

Shep held out a months-old pass, placing his index finger over the date.

"Let me see that." The man plucked the card out of

Shep's hand. "Wait a second, where'd you get—"

Shep bolted. He ran as fast as his body would let him, while behind him the man spoke urgently into a walkie-talkie. Shep slipped into the first door he came to, feigning nonchalance as he walked quickly down a cavernous white hallway lined with framed, autographed portraits of the studios' stars and bigwigs past and present. Their foot-tall faces beamed down on him as his footsteps clipped and clopped along the marble floor. He ducked into a men's room and shoveled tap water into his mouth. When he looked up into the mirror, he was startled by the face that looked back at him: His lower eyelids drooped, the eyes themselves red and wet. His greasy hair was pasted behind his ears, overgrown and with more gray than he remembered. The salt and pepper was creeping up his sideburns. Worse than that, half-moons of sweat dampened the underarms of his shirt. He dabbed at them ineffectually with paper towels until someone entered the restroom. He pretended to dry his hands.

Back out in the hallway, he lost his way again and found himself going in circles. He kept making turns, but always found his way back to the same faces, bright and backlit, their teeth so white and straight they looked painted. Shep burrowed his tongue deep into the sore in his mouth.

He thought he's found his way back where he started, but when he stepped through the door, he didn't see the trailers or the streetlamp or the fake city street. In fact, he wasn't outside at all, but at the threshold of another white hallway, which he hurried down, his footsteps clip-clopping, clip-clopping in his ears until he reached a bank of elevators.

A bell sounded and one of the elevators opened, releasing a group of people with ID badges clipped to their collars and jacket hems. He slipped in after they'd gone and jabbed at the *Door Close* button. When the door opened again after he'd failed to choose a floor, he pressed 2 at random.

The elevator opened onto another hallway, this one

more beige than white, with warm lighting that fuzzed the building's edges. Then: a shift in the air—a slow hair swoop in the distance, a certain shade of blond—pinged his radar. He was almost certain it was her as he followed her toward the eastern end of the floor, which housed a bustling cafeteria. He crossed an expansive walkway flecked with camel and gold, the sound of his footsteps no longer bothering him as he watched her intently, willing her to turn so he could see her face.

Shep glanced around at the tables. Everyone had a badge; everyone was eating quickly. They were either huddled and laughing with their tablemates or stooped over laptops and phones. He felt exposed again; anyone could look at him and tell he had no business here. He clamped his arms to his sides to camouflage the sweat stains. But when he turned his attention to the long cashier's line, his hunch was confirmed. Lila wore a black velour sweat suit and looked at her phone as she waited to pay for a salad. He watched as she found an empty table and plunked her shoulder bag on the opposite chair. At the other end of the cafeteria, he spied a security guard scanning the room with a walkie-talkie held up to his face, and rushed over to her.

"Hey," he called out too soon, still twenty feet from the table. He caught himself, slowed down, and tried to slow his breath to match.

"Hey, Lila?" he said, feigning casual uncertainty.

"Oh…hey." She looked up from an arugula salad topped with seared Ahi tuna.

"Long time no see…you shooting something?"

"Uh, yeah, you?" She looked tired, her face scrubbed and blotchy. She cut the fish into small pieces and swirled it around in the bed of greens.

"Yeah, yeah, I did, I just got let go from uh…" He saw a framed poster for a medical drama on the cafeteria's wall. "… *Philly MD*."

"Cool."

260   COLDWATER CANYON

He worried she'd hear his heart pounding. He dug his tongue into the sore again.

Why had he lied to her just now? She looked different—tense, bored—with none of the warmth she'd shown him in the past. She seemed a different person every time he got close to her.

"So," he said, "what are you shooting today?" *Keep going,* he repeated in his head like a mantra, *keep going.*

She took a sip of lemon water.

"It's this show, kind of like an updated *Friends* sort of thing? Six friends, big city. One of them's like an interior decorator." She shrugged and looked past him.

"That must be exciting," he said, "like a big break, right?"

She shrugged. She still hadn't taken a bite of her lunch.

"I mean," he continued, "it's not everybody who can score a multi-episode arc out of the clear blue...they must have thought you were pretty special."

She stopped combing her fork through the greens. "Wait, what?"

Shep ran his tongue all along his teeth, searching for a spot that didn't feel hot with disease.

"You know, it's a pretty, uh, plum role," he said, "right?"

She set her fork down.

"How'd you know it was multi-episode?"

"It's, uh, didn't you say..."

"Oh my god," she whispered. She looked closely at his face, then turned her eyes back to her plate and touched her throat.

"It was a lucky guess, I mean, anybody can tell you were gonna be a star, it was only a matter of time, I mean, just *look* at you..."

"I've got to go," she said, pushing her plate away. She picked up her bag and heaved it over her shoulder as she rose from the table.

"Let me walk you," Shep said breathlessly, following close at her heels, but she didn't look back, and when they reached the elevators, she slipped into one that had just opened, and he squeezed his way in after her just before the doors closed.

Neither of them pressed a button, and the elevator ascended to wherever it had been summoned, way up in the sky.

Lila was squeezed into the corner, holding her bag in front of her, eyes fixed on the gold-flecked marble floor.

"Hey, hey," Shep said gently, imagining how he would speak to a scared child. "You okay?"

He saw then that tears were wobbling at the surface of her eyes.

"Hey," he tried again, stepping closer, "what's the matter?"

Shep looked up and saw the number twelve lit up. Only four floors to go till they reached the top. Lila wasn't looking at him, wasn't talking, and if he let her get away this time, she'd never let him get close again. On panicked impulse he reached out and pulled the emergency lever, causing the elevator to rock to a sudden stop, suspended twelve stories above ground.

"What the fuck are you doing?!" Lila cried.

"Hang on, hang on," Shep said. He hadn't known a bell was going to ring. It was so loud it rattled his jaw. He clamped his hands over his ears.

"Just wait!" he yelled. He couldn't think over the ringing.

Lila leapt forward and pushed the lever in again, stopping the ringing and jerking the elevator back into motion.

"Jesus fucking Christ," she said, "who *are* you?"

"We've...I've..." He could still hear the ringing in his ears, swallowing up all the air.

"You're always just *popping up*, I mean...do you like me? Is that what this is?"

"No, no, it's nothing like that—" He rubbed his temples. *Think, think, think!*

"Then what's it like? What is it like? How did you know

I would be here? Just answer a fucking question."

The elevator opened at the top level. Lila shook her head and exited out into a hallway lined with glass-walled conference rooms, vacant while everyone was at lunch.

"Wait," he huffed after her.

"I'm going to the bathroom," she said. "Planning to follow me in there too?"

"Just stop for one second." He eked the words out with the last of his breath and pushed his palms down into his thighs. He didn't have any time left. Lila kept walking. He lunged forward and grabbed her elbow. She wrenched it from his grip and sped up.

What am I doing? What am I doing? The words repeated in his mind, filling in the silence between Lila's footsteps.

"I knew your mom," he croaked.

She was halfway down the hall now. They were alone between glass walls and reflective white floor. There was no place to hide, no darkness, no corners. She turned.

"My mom?"

Shep leaned himself slightly against a window looking out over muggy white sky.

"I loved her. Lila. I loved her, I did, and I told her I was coming back for her. I did, I did, I did."

It didn't matter that he'd never sent those letters. Lorene knew. That's why she came to him in his dreams, in the darkest reaches of his loneliness. She knew. The way he held onto her like she was the edge of a cliff—she knew he would never let go, and he never had.

Lila plunked her bag down on the floor and stared out the window behind him. He saw his hot breath on the windowpane and turned away from it, sunk down to his haunches. The pressure was lifting, but he had to keep going.

"Lila, I never meant to leave her. I got called up, I had to go, and I didn't know she was pregnant; if I'd known I'd have gone AWOL just to stay with her—"

"Slow down," Lila whispered. She was showing her warmth again. He just had to get it all out and she'd understand. That was the kind of person she was.

"And I'm so sorry I wasn't there for you when you were growing up, but I was in a way, because—I always kept up with you, Lila, I always kept an eye out for you because I felt so bad that I couldn't be there, that she wouldn't *let* me be there…"

"You're not making any sense."

Shep took a deep breath and tried to get his thoughts in order. He'd jumped ahead. Of course he wasn't making any sense. He had to speak more plainly.

"Lila," he said, rising up to his knees. "I know this is a shock to you. I wanted to do this differently. But, I'm here now. Lila, I'm here for you. I'm your dad."

As soon as the words left his lips, he felt a lightening in his chest, a tingling in his fingertips. He was weightless, and he couldn't help but grin, even through the pain that held his skull in a vise.

Lila spoke slowly. "No. He died before I was born."

Shep struggled to his feet again. Lila shrank back as he came toward her.

"Is that what she told you? That I died in the war?" Of course. That was why she'd never sought him out. He always thought that maybe someday she'd look for him, meet him halfway. The picture was growing clearer, like a defogged windshield, opening up the view.

"No," she said, taking another small step back. "He died in a tractor accident."

"I never even had a tractor…I can't believe she'd lie to you like that. Oh god, I'm so sorry, honey."

"Stop," she said. Her voice was calm. She took another step back and swallowed. "His name was Martin Cumberland."

They held each other's gazes, the air taut between them as three women filed out of the elevator and clicked their heels along the marble floor carrying takeout boxes and plastic drink cups.

"Marty? No, that's not…no…"

Lila took another small step back.

Shep hadn't even seen Marty in weeks when he was shipped out to the desert. He'd been so consumed by Lorene he'd forgotten about everybody else. How soon after he left had he, had they…?

"How could…" he murmured. There were too many ways to finish the sentence.

Lila looked at her phone.

"Listen, I have to be on set in twenty minutes. I have to go now." She took another hesitant step back.

"Wait," he cried, wiping sweat from his hairline, "forget about your call time—isn't this more important?"

"I'm sorry you're confused about something that really doesn't have anything to do with me, but I've worked my ass off to get this job, so I'm gonna go ahead and do it, thanks." She heaved the bag back over her shoulder and turned to go, but quickly lunged back toward him. "You think every girl who looks like me just gets a career handed to her? There are thousands, *thousands* of pretty girls in this town, so many that looks don't mean anything, so everything I get, I get for myself, okay? Bye."

Shep forged on. He hadn't come here to talk about her acting career. "Just wait, goddamnit, you have to wait." He couldn't let Lorene get away with this. "How do you know Marty was your dad? She could've lied because she didn't think I'd be a good provider, 'cause she thought she could do better…"

Lila turned back to face him, eyes narrowed.

"What are you even talking about?"

"She may have changed, I'll give you that, but I know what she was like then, going after the owner of the D&D—I heard she had a thing with the football coach when we were in school—"

Lila's shoulders tensed.

"—and Marty's family had money. She probably got a nice payout from them after Marty died, with no blood test either—"

"You're making this shit up. You're spinning a fairy tale to make yourself feel better about...*something*, I don't know what, but like I said, it has fuck all to do with me or my mom—"

"No, no," he shook his head. "I'm not explaining it right, I don't mean any disrespect...Lorene and me...we were in love. And even if she didn't know it, I was there, every step, every night I could, before she took you away..." Shep wheezed from the strain of talking through his tears "She must have mentioned me sometime, I know she knew, I know she knew..."

He remembered crouching in the bushes across the road from Lorene's parents' house, catching sight of her silhouette in the window rocking little Lila to sleep in the wee hours, when no one else was around. On those nights, he'd felt a part of something, adding to the love infusion that babies need, that he had to call up from his preconsciousness. He'd longed to hold the girl, to feel her small heart beating against his chest, his love turned to flesh. He'd always imagined Lorene could sense him watching, that she was thinking of him as she looked out her window. Now, Shep had a sobering thought. While he'd assumed Lorene was looking out, bolstered by his love, she may instead have been watching her own shadow on the wall as she rocked and rocked, summoning her strength from within.

How much love had he scattered to the wind all these years?

"Yeah, I'm sure it was really hard for you," Lila said. "Your big sad feelings are *exactly* like being a teen mom scared out of her mind. And for the record, Martin Cumberland isn't my dad either, okay, my stepdad's the one who was *actually* there for me."

Rubber soles squeaked at the end of the hall. "There he is!"

Shep turned to see the two security guards rushing toward him. "Lila," he whimpered, "she lied to you, I swear it, I swear to god."

The men grabbed him roughly by the arms, twisting them behind him so he doubled over. When he was able to look up, Lila had stepped closer. She squeezed her lips shut, and for a second he thought she was about to spit in his face, with the security guards holding him in place to receive it. He cringed and closed his eyes, ready to take it, but it never came. When he opened his eyes again, she was shaking her head at him with a look of bewildered disgust.

"My mom told me to watch out for guys who think I owe them something. Maybe she told me about you after all."

"Are you okay, Miss?"

"I'm fine," she said to the guard, and left without looking back.

Each step she took seemed to both widen and lengthen the hallway—an expanding blank. A flat, white plane extending in all directions. Then Shep felt the pinch of a zip tie binding his wrists and cried out in pain.

***

"Lionel, Lionel, settle down."

By the time he found his way back to the car, it was near dark. He'd been held for hours in a cramped office off the parking garage with only a lukewarm soda. The head of security finally let him off easy with a lifetime ban and a call to Central Casting ensuring he'd be blacklisted.

"Settle down, settle down," he breathed, "I'm here." The dog climbed all over him, pawing and licking.

He climbed over the console and curled up into the backseat with his face buried in the upholstery. It was cool and musty and for a moment transported him to the backseat of his grandmother's station wagon—the smell was the same combination of synthetic fibers and ancient crumbs, the smell of aloneness—and he began to gently rock himself, not to sleep but to a state in between, where reality was held safely at bay.

Soon, behind his closed eyelids, he saw himself running in slow motion down one of the studio's white hallways. But the publicity portraits that had towered over him with their white-toothed smiles and practiced stares were replaced by the missing persons, Eugene Jr.'s neighborhood portraits blown up wall-sized, high-definition sheen replaced by shaky pencil lines and eraser dust, their sightless eyes and boneless limbs in graphite gray.

In his peripheral vision, the lines began to move, the walls crackling like paper, as though the hallway could crumple to a ball at any moment.

He'd still never experienced an earthquake. Was this what it felt like? An assertion of potential energy, a sudden, soft collapse?

A door appeared, white on white, marked only by an asymmetrical rectangular outline, a doorknob that left a dusty black pencil mark on his palm as he gripped it and slipped inside.

The room was dark, filled with rows of mostly empty theater seats. Shep shut the door behind him and sat down in the back row. A screen filled the opposite wall, on which was projected soft flesh and shadow, moving body parts in warm, liquid gold light, in tight close-up so there was no determining context or place. Shep sunk low in his seat and watched, the light flickering across his face.

The camera pulled back to reveal a woman's knees and shins peeking out from underneath white cotton sheets, rough-soled feet rubbing together at the foot of the bed. When the woman sat up, holding the sheet over her breasts, her face remained obscured. Then the camera closed in tight on the woman's eyes squinting at a point offscreen.

Shep sat up tall. *Look down*, he thought, *I'm right here.*

Her gaze stayed fixed above him.

The camera closed in on her lips saying words he couldn't hear. He turned around to see if there was some problem with the speakers that could be fixed.

The woman rose from the bed, wrapped in the sheet, and her hair had a smooth finish, flowing down her back like caramel. The camera pulled back to reveal the room, a million-dollar penthouse with eight-foot-high windows and flooded with the sun of wealth—glittering at a remove, the temperature under seamless, sweatless control. Her face still hadn't been revealed—only parts, no whole.

The woman slunk drowsily toward the light and touched her fingers to the glass, and the sunlight surrounded her before engulfing the whole frame. She was still there behind the light. Shep was certain she was still there. He stood up in the aisle, and a voice hissed at him from behind.

Sit down.

He moved to the aisle and focused, trying to find her shape somewhere in the white glow, but it was no use, like squeezing your eyes shut and focusing on a point of color; it was always just out of reach, always a moving target.

How could he get to her? He tried to reach out toward the screen, but his arms were stapled to his sides. He tried to speak, but he had no voice. Finally, he dropped to his knees on the theater floor and tilted like a falling building until his face met the carpet. He breathed in the buttery popcorn dust and fossilized bubble gum. He couldn't move, couldn't even crawl back to his seat.

Help, he thought but couldn't say.

Shep woke in the backseat to Lionel coating his ear in slobber, filling his head with the sound of lapping and humid doggy breath.

When the dog jumped back into the front seat, Shep's present condition bore down on him like a freight train.

His head felt squeezed between pincers, and the sore in his mouth—it was growing, filling his mouth with blood that flowed down through his body like black tar.

12

It was past dark by the time Shep rounded the corner onto Coldwater. He'd planned on going home when he finally mustered the energy to drive, but was beckoned by a light on inside Parkdale's. Not the main lights, but a glow from the back office. Had he left it on? Only the donut shop was illuminated, though he saw no one inside. The water store was abandoned, the lot empty of cars. He parked and let Lionel hop out of the car behind him.

Shep fished out his keychain to open the door but found it already unlocked. He couldn't have left it this way, he woudn't have. Somebody was trying to make him think he was losing his mind. He stepped inside and ran his hand along a display of bottled water, stepping quietly, his eyes fixed on the light in the back.

Eugene, he thought. Somehow, Eugene. Was this what he'd been building to? All the questions, all the taunts, always waiting for him, acting as if he knew something Shep didn't. Eugene had driven the Phans away, and now it was up to him to defend what was theirs. Though he barely had the strength to remain upright, whatever confrontation was waiting for him, he had to be ready.

There was a crash, a thunk—something fallen, somewhere out of sight.

Shep scooped Lionel up and ducked behind the counter. He tried to think, but couldn't fathom just what might be happening until he thought to check the register. He punched in the four-digit code, and the drawer popped out, empty save for a small pile of rubber bands. A coughing fit overtook him, and he sunk back to the floor. It seemed every ounce of his inflamed innards was being pushed up toward his throat as he spat a string of bile.

Footsteps. On the stairs. Someone had been in the apartment too then. The footsteps were getting louder and sounded like more than one set. If Eugene was here, he wasn't alone. Shep felt he was under siege now. Instinct reared up inside him, the compulsion to defend his ground against the coming assault.

He pushed the rolls of receipt paper out from under the cash register and let them tumble to the floor, patting his hand shakily around the shelf until it landed on the Beretta. He began coughing again, unable to stop or even curb the noise as the footsteps drew closer. Lionel barked.

No, he mouthed in between the hacking, praying for Lionel to be quiet, to let the footsteps pass them by. The gun dangled weakly in his fingers.

But when the coughing stopped, his breath did too, as though it had been knocked out of him. He punched at his chest with the other fist, his vision blurring. He felt himself slipping, with a new, burrowing pain in his chest spreading through to his back and up to his diseased jaw.

He'd been hit? He'd always wondered what it would feel like. When he was a soldier, spending hours in target practice, cleaning guns, carrying and storing them, feeling their constant weight, he'd always wondered. This was it?

Still, the footsteps drew nearer. With a final burst of adrenaline, he braced himself against the counter, aimed in the footsteps' direction and squeezed the trigger, firing off a single blast.

A voice cried out. The footsteps stopped.

Shep fell back to the ground, gasping at the ceiling until his gasps petered out into silence while Lionel cowered, whimpering at his side.

13

The Greyhound pulled up to the Magnolia station at half past three. It was a nice day, depending on one's preferences, with the kind of nonweather Hung imagined was particular to Southern California, though he'd scarcely been anyplace else. The air was still and room-temperature, the sun bright but uninvasive. It was nice enough that he decided to walk home rather than wait around for the sluggish city bus.

He walked slowly, carrying his backpack low like he had in high school and for the semester and a half he'd spent at Cal State Northridge before family obligations buried his academic ambitions. He wasn't eager to return to the store, or to the apartment for that matter. The more slowly he walked, the farther away it all seemed.

After a couple of blocks, he felt a presence behind him and glanced back to see a girl he recognized from the bus. She was around his age, pleasantly chubby in a crocheted white dress. She was dragging a big suitcase, periodically squinting between her phone and the street signs. He'd noticed her across the aisle while he was trying unsuccessfully to get some sleep. He could smell the synthetic vanilla of the lotion she'd bent down to spread up her calves.

Seemingly sensing his attention, the girl called out, "Excuse me?"

Hung stopped.

"I'm looking for an apartment complex that's supposed to be around here. Called the"—she glanced at her phone— "Fine...Gold...Manor?"

Hung knew of the place—the ramshacklest of the ramshackle—with a name that felt like a cruel joke but was likely the result of a thesaurus-happy owner with a tenuous grasp of English. He drew a map for her on the back of a white paper bag.

"Oh my god, thank you so much!"

Hung returned the girl's pen. As she wheeled her suitcase down the street, he wondered if he ought to tell her she was a hell of a long way from Hollywood.

When he reached Coldwater, he dragged his feet through the messy lawns where the sidewalk dropped off, collecting dust and yellow grass over the tops of his white sneakers. He took an alternate route as he got closer to home, through curving residential streets to come up on the strip mall from the back and hopefully escape notice, though El Vaquero was in the alley cleaning his shopping cart with a damp rag. Hung nodded. The guy had to clean it sometime, he supposed. It had to pick up a lot of grime off the street, out of the air, day after day. Everybody's got to look after their things. He unclipped the keychain from his belt loop and let himself in through the back door.

"Come here," Hung's mother said.

"Hang on." His arms were full of groceries.

"You can put them away later. Come here."

Hung set the bag on the counter and sat, though he was anxious about the meat that needed to be refrigerated. He looked at the clock on the stove. Cousin Mai would be home from work soon, and he'd promised to cook, the least he could do in exchange for letting them stay so long.

His mother wrung her hands. She opened her mouth in a false start. Finally, she reached into her purse and pulled out a check. She smoothed it flat on the table and slid it across to him.

He looked at the figure and swallowed. "What is this?"

Hung was annoyed, but not as surprised as he probably should've been, to find the store closed. He'd asked Shep to cover for him because he figured it would be easy enough for him to handle, and because it seemed better that it be an outsider, someone Eugene would have no cause to fuck with.

And, whether it was misguided or not, Hung felt he could trust him.

Jesus Christ, dude, he sighed, checking behind the pizza counter. All the raw pizzas he'd loaded up in the freezer remained as he'd left them. He opened the fridge and found several desiccated pies, congealed together into an ugly stack. He'd told Shep those needed to be cooked and put out the first night. He'd deal with those later.

The register was full of cash. He'd told Shep to always put it in the safe when he closed up. He stacked the bills, counted out the coins, zipped it all into a pouch and locked it in the safe, just until he had time to get to the bank. He'd stayed away too long, had outstayed Shep's competence, it seemed.

It was his own fault for staying out of touch. After his mom told him everything—how the store had been losing money, how Eugene had swooped in, offering a loan at a much lower interest rate than the bank, and how he had later smiled with the kindest of eyes as he explained that the terms of that loan had changed, hadn't she read the fine print?— Hung spent several days closed up in the guest room, mostly face-down on the air mattress. At some point, a microscopic hole formed, so the mattress began to deflate beneath him, its edges rising up on either side of his body.

Hung went up to the apartment. He should have known something was wrong by the way his mom was packing, filling her suitcases with silverware, towels, and food. He had known *something* was wrong, but didn't want to bring it up when she was in such a state, ironing curtains and scrubbing the bathtub in a red-faced frenzy. He threw his backpack on the floor and stood in the empty kitchen. He laid his hands out on the counter and watched the ceiling fan ruffle the faint hairs on his forearms.

The life insurance payout was almost enough, his mother said, to repay the loan, but not enough to pay the steep—and steepening—

interest Eugene now stipulated. He would have to move quickly, to clear out without attracting too much attention.

"Just me?"

His mother wrung her hands again, and Hung fought the impulse to walk out of the room. Next she would start crying, putting a stop to any arguments or simple requests for information. He had to think she knew what she was doing every time she paralyzed herself with emotion, the way she rendered herself petrified in every sense of the word. It was the same thing any time he asked questions as a child, about why they had no photos from their old home in Saigon, why they waited until they were so old to have him, why every plea for a story was met with fraught looks between his parents, then silence. How much silence could a person endure?

Hung pulled the living room curtains and opened the window to clear the stale air. Down in the parking lot, one of Eugene's buddies was washing his car, spraying a hose all over the place, making puddles in the lot's potholes. The spray made little rainbows in the sunlight. The guy sprayed the hose at Eugene's son and a couple of other little kids who were hanging around in front of the water store. They squealed and giggled, pestering him to do it again. Eugene came out of the store and beckoned the man inside with a raised chin. The man handed the hose off to one of the little boys and followed, and the kids started spraying the hose indiscriminately, at the curb, at the dumpster, making a soggy mess, even scattering a group of pigeons who were minding their own business pecking at bread crusts.

Hung poked his head out the window and stared down at the kids laughing and dancing through the puddles.

"Leave the birds alone."

The kids glanced up at him, startled but unaffected, as they continued spraying the hose at cars and at each other.

If he'd known just what Eugene was up to when he

walked in on the little powwow with his mom, he would have put a stop to it. Somehow. But for how long? Hung thought back on that night in Sun Valley when he'd been about to close up with his dad when three men in ski masks walked in and prodded them into the back with the barrels of their shotguns, covering their mouths in duct tape and tying them to opposite legs of the metal desk. His mom had been two doors down, asleep. She found them there in the morning, parched and dry-eyed with their circulation cut off. Hung cried out in pain when she ripped the tape from his mouth, but his father remained silent. Of course the men were never caught.

With the back of his neck pressed to the bottom of the window, Hung envisioned the whole building hanging from his body, the metal frame digging into his flesh with the weight of it. Now he had permission to literally take the money and run. So why did he stare at the blacktop, hatred for Eugene burning through his guts? Freedom isn't freedom if you're chased away.

Hung ducked back inside. He turned on the kitchen faucet, let it run brown until the stream cleared. He filled his hands with cold water and took a drink.

14

Manuelo looked up at the blood-orange moon. He took off his hat and wiped his hairline with a thin white handkerchief, put the hat back on, and stood from his concrete perch to check his blankets: one, two, three, stacked in tight woolen rectangles. He patted them securely into the cart's corner, the silver rings on his fingers sliding from web to knuckle and back again as he ran a hand over his belongings.

"*Shit, shit, shit!*"

Manuelo heard the noise and peeked around the corner. The shopkeeper was backing out of his store, bent over with his shoulders hunched up toward his ears, his small frame swimming in a baggy polo shirt. Manuelo hadn't seen him in some time. He'd seen him return that afternoon, seen him sigh and rub his temples before grabbing at his clatter of keys.

The shopkeeper was dragging something heavy. Manuelo took his hat off again, rubbed his hairline with his white handkerchief, put the hat back on. When the shopkeeper stepped into the streetlight-glow, Manuelo saw that it was a man he was dragging. The man had a hole in the bottom of his boot, holes in his jeans, holes at the elbows of his shirt that were closed up with safety pins. The shopkeeper was holding a blood-soaked towel to his own shoulder, clamping it down with his jaw. He rifled through the man's pockets, barely holding him up with one shaking arm.

"Come on, come on…"

Manuelo stepped back against the building and reached into his cart. He checked his blankets: one, two, three woolen rectangles. When he peeked around the corner again, the shopkeeper was heaving the man into the backseat of a car. He had some trouble folding the man's legs up one-handed to make then fit, using his other hand to press down on the towel.

As the shopkeeper struggled to start the car, slapping the wheel while the engine spit and sputtered, the men across the way emerged from the dark, but the shopkeeper didn't see them. The car finally backed out of the space, rattled down the driveway and made a screeching noise as it sped away with the other man slumped like a pile of rags against the rear window.

The men across the way spread out across the parking lot on invisible strings stemming from their leader, who stepped in front, following the car with his eyes.

Manuelo looked up at the blood-orange moon and heard a whimper.

He peeked around the corner again, and there at the base of the dented old pay phone, a little dog lay on his belly with paws outstretched. The dog was looking up at the blood-orange moon too, his nose quivering and incisors poking up from underneath his bottom lip. Again, the dog whimpered upward toward the sky.

Manuelo slowly crouched, careful not to touch his knees to the dirty sidewalk. He removed his hat and tilted his chin toward the dog, trying to catch his eye without scaring him off.

"*Ven aquí*," he whispered. The words stayed there, hushed, at his lips. The dog stood.

"*Ven aquí, pequeño.*" The dog stepped lightly toward him, his nose vibrating, sniffing wildly. With that show of trust, Manuelo crouched down and let the dog come to him, and gently lifted him to his breast.

"*Sshh, sshh, sshh*," he whispered, laying out a blanket in the cart's top basket. The dog looked at him, expectant but not afraid.

It was time for sleep. Manuelo pushed the cart down the street, the wheels squeaking and wobbling over the sidewalk's bumps and cracks. They came to an embankment, and he maneuvered the cart gingerly down the hill, nestling it against the chain link fence that guarded the shallow river, a few feet from a footbridge, underneath which a narrow futon mattress and pillow were laid out, and beside it, a makeshift table of bricks and boards, topped with candles, books and a small ceramic teapot.

The dog watched as he reached into one of his plastic grocery bags and pulled out a recorder. He wetted his lips and wiped the instrument with his handkerchief. The dog lowered his belly into the wool blanket and rested his chin on the cart's handle while Manuelo played a slow, meandering whistle of a tune.

Birds and squirrels slept in the trees. Ducks were huddled down in the riverbed's hovels and nooks. And scattered in the shadows, people, each of them alone, wrapped themselves in sleeping bags, blankets, towels and newspapers, and rolled over into the earth, waiting for sleep to come.

Manuelo finished his song, cleaned the recorder again, and slipped it back into the cart. He lifted the dog and carried him under his arm, ducking underneath the low bridge, and set him down on the futon, on which he laid out his blankets, reserving one for the dog, bundled at the corner of the bed.

"*Que sueñes con los angelitos,*" he whispered.

The dog was already asleep, snoring softly along with the chirping crickets, the trickling river, the rustling of leaves in the night air.

15

There was a point of purple light burning in the distance, just out of Shep's reach. It flickered, solitary in the blackness. He thought he smelled the smoke of fireworks deployed nearby, and beneath it, closer, the sweet scent of cotton candy, warm and spinning from passing carts.

He didn't have a body, or he had no feeling, no pain. He was tranquil, whether in his body or out of it. After a timeless length of time, a smooth emptiness, the purple light distanced itself further, shrinking to a smaller point, though its shine was undiminished. He watched the light slip away as the dark matter that held him tightened its grip, suspending him, alone, in a womblike darkness.

He blinked. He was *able* to blink, and harsh, bright light flashed in his eyes. He was able to move, too. He lifted himself up an inch and his stomach lurched; he'd been hurtled back into his body without warning. His eyes fluttered again, and he was able to understand that he was in a white room, in a gray bed, with his arms hooked up to various IVs and machinery. Nurses passed his doorway. Voices crackled over the intercom.

Shep rose to his elbows, and his stomach turned over again. He clamped his hand over his mouth; he knew instinctively that if he let it happen, his body would unleash a thick black liquid that would fill the room and rush down the halls, pulling them all under like quicksand.

"Whoa, whoa, whoa, lie down, dude."

Shep obeyed the voice. He lowered himself down to the bed again and opened his eyes. Hung was standing over him, a backpack hanging from his right shoulder. His left shoulder was bulked up with a thick white bandage, with gauze peeking out from the collar of his shirt.

Shep moved his tongue around his mouth, realizing slowly that his mouth was filled with gauze too. He gestured weakly toward Hung's bandage.

"You don't remember, huh?"

Shep squinted. He pulled the sticky ball of gauze out of his mouth and managed to ask in a numb-lipped mumble, "Did I get shot?"

"What?"

He tried to enunciate. "Did...I...get...Shot?"

"Did *you* get shot? Nah, man. Can't say the same for myself."

Shep winced. "Oh no…"

A doctor entered the room then, carrying a clipboard.

"Mr. Shepherd, how are you doing today?"

Today?

Shep stared at the doctor. He searched his memory for some context, some understanding of days and how they might be quantified.

"Okay, you're still a little disoriented—understandable." The doctor nodded. "We'll talk, just the two of us, a little later. When you're feeling more stable." He nodded to Hung. "Visiting hours are up in a few minutes. A nurse'll come get you."

When the doctor was gone, Hung shut the door and approached Shep, pulling his backpack open, and a furry muzzle emerged. Lionel squirmed out of the bag and descended on Shep's neck, licking every inch of his bristly face. Shep let out a hoarse laugh, though the dog's weight was like a pile of bricks on his chest.

"I'm so sorry," he whispered to the room.

"You just grazed me," Hung said. "Kinda expected you to be a better shot, I gotta say."

Shep looked into Lionel's brown eyes. There was so much love in them, such bare, easy love. He'd felt it the first time they sat together in his car, and he felt it now, flooding his diseased body, momentarily soldering the gaps in his heart.

"I'm looking after him. I think El Vaquero wanted to keep him, though. This beast was about to go feral on us."

Lionel settled down, nestling on Shep's chest, their two heartbeats in sync. Shep slowly raised his arms and wrapped them around the dog, squeezing him close.

"I better get this guy outta here before they catch us," Hung said, scratching Lionel's head. Shep nodded and pulled his arms away so Hung could take him. Stashed safely in the backpack, Lionel sniffed wildly, burrowing his nose through a small opening in the zipper.

"You don't have to worry," Hung said in the doorway.

Shep nodded weakly and laid his head back on the pillow. He felt the weight of all the tubes in his arms, the soreness of the many punctures. The weight held him softly down to the bed. Maybe, he hoped, if he went to sleep, he'd see the purple light again, smell those carnival smells and hear that trilling tune. Maybe he'd get close to it again if he sank back down, if he stayed.

Outside, it was one of those windy valley days that felt as though a great fan had been aimed downward from the mountains, setting leaves and scraps of trash skittering down the streets and everyone's hair flying into their mouths.

He pulled Lionel out from the backpack and set him in the passenger seat of Shep's car. He slammed his door shut, but the wind still rattled the windows and whistled against the car's sides as he started it up.

As they turned past the strip mall, Hung gave the shuttered Parkdale's a sidelong glance. Nobody was in the parking lot. Even El Vaquero had seen fit to stay out of the wind. He drove slowly, thinking how easy it would be to imagine that nothing had happened here. To imagine that all his worries had been dreams, and that he was waking up now.

He pulled into Shep's carport. The engine rumbled and sighed as he turned it off. He pulled a duffel bag out from under the front seat and reassessed its contents for the umpteenth time, then zipped it up. He sat still for a moment, clutching it in his lap.

Lionel looked at Hung expectantly.

"What you want, boy?"

Lionel stepped closer to him, panting, his tail wagging, staring up at Hung with bright, open adoration. And in the *huh-huh, huh-huh, huh-huh*, the insistent rhythm of the dog's panting, was a question:

What now? What now? What now?

"Guess we'd best get going," Hung replied.

He set the dog on the pavement. With the leash in his left hand and the bag in his right, Hung squinted against the flying dust. His shirt billowed out from his back like a ship's sail as the two walked in parallel with the shallow, whispering river.

ACKNOWLEDGMENTS

First, thank you to Michael J. Seidlinger for believing in this book, and Janice Lee for making it better than I could have on my own. I also owe a tremendous debt to Judy Heiblum, the book's earliest reader, advisor and champion. I'm thankful for the continuous support of Bruce Bauman, and grateful to Steve Erickson, who published the first excerpt of the book in the dearly departed *Black Clock*. I've learned so much from both of you.

Shep's character was informed by the books *Broken Bodies, Shattered Minds: A Medical Odyssey from Vietnam to Afghanistan* by Ronald J. Glasser M.D. and *Gulf War Syndrome: Legacy of a Perfect War* by Alison Johnson.

In no particular order, I want to thank the following people for various forms of help over the course of this book's writing and publication: J. Ryan Stradal, Steph Cha, Susan Straight, Ben Loory, Sara Finnerty, Katya Apekina, Kim Samek, D. Foy and Lance Cleland. I'm also indebted to Byron Campbell for his sharp eye in the book's final stages.

Endless thanks and love to my husband Abe Kinney, who has read, counseled, and listened to me talk about these characters for years, our daughter Simone, and the best dog in the world, Dee Dee Ramone.

ANNE-MARIE KINNEY is the author of two novels, *Radio Iris* (2012, Two Dollar Radio) and *Coldwater Canyon* (2018, CCM). A *New York Times* Editor's Choice pick, *Radio Iris* was called "a spiky debut" and "*The Office* as scripted by Kafka" by the *Minneapolis Star Tribune*. Her shorter work has been published in journals including *Alaska Quarterly Review, The Rattling Wall, The Collagist, Fanzine* and *Black Clock*, for which she also served as Production Editor from 2011-2016. She lives in Los Angeles, where she co-curates the Griffith Park Storytelling Series.

OFFICIAL

CCM ●

GET OUT OF JAIL
* VOUCHER *

- -

Tear this out.
Skip that social event.
It's okay.
You don't have to go if you don't want to. Pick up
the book you just bought. Open to the first page.
You'll thank us by the third paragraph.

If friends ask why you were a no-show, show them
this voucher.
You'll be fine.

- -

We're coping.

●

CPSIA information can be obtained
at www.ICGtesting.com
Printed in the USA
FFHW021844030519
52235934-57618FF